TYRANT QUEEN

ANGEL SWORN

WALL STREET JOURNAL BESTSELLING AUTHOR

JEFF WHEELER

OLIVERHEBERBOOKS

PUBLISHER'S NOTE: This is a work of fiction. Names, characters, places, and incidents either are the product of the author's imagination or are used fictitiously. Any resemblance to actual persons, living or dead, business establishments, events, or locales is entirely coincidental.

Tyrant Queen 2025 © Jeff Wheeler

Cover Art by Drazenka Kimpel

Published by Oliver-Heber Books

0 9 8 7 6 5 4 3 2 1

ALSO BY JEFF WHEELER

Your First Million Words

Tales from Kingfountain, Muirwood, and Beyond: The Worlds of Jeff Wheeler

Angel Sworn

Queen Mother

Tyrant Queen

The Invisible College

The Invisible College

The Violence of Sound

The Alchemy of Fate

Master of the Royal Secret

The Dresden Codex

Doomsday Match

Jaguar Prophecies

Final Strike

The First Argentines Series

Knight's Ransom

Warrior's Ransom

Lady's Ransom

Fate's Ransom

The Grave Kingdom Series

The Killing Fog

The Buried World
The Immortal Words

The Covenant of Muirwood Trilogy

The Banished of Muirwood

The Ciphers of Muirwood

The Void of Muirwood

Whispers from Mirrowen Trilogy

Fireblood

Dryad-Born

Poisonwell

Landmoor Series

Landmoor

Silverkin

To Tyler

And there was a day when came the angel sworn to present themselves before the Oldknow. Then came Asmodeus among them, deceiver and accuser of man. Of Asmodeus the Oldknow asked, "From whence do you come?" So answered Asmodeus, "I go to and fro on the earth, and from walking back and forth on it as you cursed me to be a fugitive and a wanderer." And the Oldknow said to the angel sworn, "Be sober-minded. Watch. Your adversary, as a lion roaring, prowls about, seeking whom to devour. Whom you should resist."

— BOOK OF THE WATCHERS, THE TALE OF THE FALLEN ANGELS

PROLOGUE

LYCHGATE

ONE YEAR BEFORE THE FALL OF CLAIRVAUX

No kingdom or palace in all the world was as formidable as Ecbatana. Its ruthless king and his bodyguards had created Ecbatana as an act of rebellion against the Queen Mother of Clairvaux.

The fortress was built by the labor of many slaves and its appearance was made more terrible than all the rest in the land. It stood on a hill in the plains before a vast mountain range and was fed by an underground river. Over time, a series of walls were built, one standing inside another in nested circles to protect the city as it grew and prospered. The seven parts of the city were protected by these seven walls. The outer walls were all painted—white, black, red, blue, orange. But the two innermost layers of walls were not painted, rather, they were inlaid with metal—one in silver and the other in gold—and contained the treasury and the king's palace.

Only a select few were allowed in the presence of the king. Everything was done by means of messengers and royal stewards, but even then, the king could be seen by no one. Moreover, it was a disgrace for anyone to laugh or to spit in his presence.

The ruler of Ecbatana was a revenant. His city, a lychgate.

Roque felt his mantle of authority diminish as he faced the ornate metal doors. His assertive, cocksure demeanor faded to one of timidity, but he steeled his courage enough to pull on the rope before him, triggering a dull bell that announced his presence. He swallowed nervously, resisting the urge to scratch his sweaty hair beneath his turban. His nerves were on edge as he waited for the sound that indicated permission to enter the royal crypt. The smell of incense lingered in the air, disguising the fetid rot that existed within the palace walls.

A deep gong echoed from within the crypt. Roque carefully controlled his expression and stepped up to the doorway studded with topaz. The locks began to twist, the tumblers rattling and clicking noisily. The metal doors groaned on their hinges, and the smell of death wafted from the widening gap. Roque held his breath, waiting for the incense to mingle with the released stench. The double doors had swung open just enough for him to enter.

Roque did so in time to watch flame burst to life on sculpted torches mounted to the walls. The torches were coated in a special substance that ignited when air reached the wicks. The torches hissed sparks as they burned, but they illuminated the inner yard of the crypt. He looked furtively to each side as he entered, treading noisily to announce his presence.

It had taken him years to rise in rank in Ecbatana, to become more and more trusted until he could serve the revenant in person. Roque had developed wisps of gray in his hair, which he meticulously dyed black to keep his appearance more youthful. He took care to bathe himself regularly and anointed himself with the costliest of ointments to hide the stench of his human flesh from his master.

"What have you brought me?" The voice came from the darkness. It was a dreadful voice, no longer softened by vocal chords, tongue, or lips. No, the revenant was beyond mortality.

Roque fell to his knees in reverence. "Master." He groveled.

Outside of this chamber, Roque was used to people groveling before *him*. It was a delicate balance of power among the nobles of Ecbatana. A curled lip from Roque would silence most of the upstarts instantly.

"Stand, slave. I grow annoyed by the sound of your breathing. Speak!"

Roque hurried to his feet. "A thousand pardons, Master." He spied violet sparks in the dark and knew they were the eyes of the being. Staring at him. Judging him. He swallowed nervously, barely keeping his composure. If Roque was deemed no longer useful, then he would not exit the crypt alive. That would trigger a series of procedures to instigate a replacement being found. The apparatus of state would continue to roll on. Roque was just a spoke in the waterwheel of Ecbatana. But an important spoke.

"What have you brought me?" croaked the raspy voice from the darkness.

"A curious find, Great One. A trading ship bound for the savage lands returned with their cargo of ivory, fruit, and musk. With their cargo, they brought something...unusual."

Silence. The revenant liked a good story, but its patience was as skeletal as its earthly remains. Roque had only seen glimpses of it. The eyes were what told him he was being listened to. Indulged.

"Go on."

Roque took that as encouraging. "Master, they brought a creature unlike those we have seen from the wilds. It walks like mankind but has paws of a beast. It is very strong and communicates with grunts and shouts. It took a dozen men to capture the dominant one."

"Male?"

"Yes, Master! The dominant was male. It could climb trees with ease. It dwells in the jungle of the savage lands in packs that fight for control of fruit trees."

"You brought it to me?" The raspy voice sounded interested.

"Yes, Master. Reports of it were not enough. I would not test your patience with rumors. Ships were dispatched by Lord Felaket to catch the beast. To bring it in a cage. It is here at the palace now."

Roque bowed again to the pinpricks of violet sparks. Silence fell and the urge to scratch his scalp became unbearable. But he dared not. The revenant hated signs of mortal weakness. Its life force was trapped in one of its bones, which was hidden somewhere in Ecbatana. No one knew where that bone was kept, whether it was in a phylactery or at the bottom of a common jar of salt. There were countless treasures in the palace. A bone of its body. If that bone were found and broken, the revenant would die. Finally, it would die. And then the wealth it hoarded could be distributed again. Roque waited, fearing he'd infuriated it again simply by breathing.

"Well done, steward," the revenant hissed. "I wish to see this creature. Is it intelligent?"

"Highly intelligent, Master. It has fingers. Ears. Lips. It has *emotions*."

"How curious," said the revenant. "Bring it to me. I would like to study how its race has transformed since leaving the garden of Clairvaux."

"Of course, Master. Will you send it to the arena at the lake city of Vaud?"

"Perhaps. If it pleases me. But I should like to see what graftings can be made with it. How strong it can yet become."

"Naturally. It subsists on fruit and flesh. We brought plenteous samples from its native land to nourish and feed it."

"Wisely done, steward. Bring it to me."

"Yes, Great One." Roque began to back away, but he stopped. Should he risk incurring his master's wrath by lingering past his welcome? The air in the crypt was stifling and thick with burning incense. He realized he was panting and tried to slow his breathing down. Air was coming in from the door. Surely he wouldn't suffocate.

"You hesitate. Why?"

"There is one more thing, Master. But I do not wish to trouble you. I will leave." Roque began to back away again. Did his words tempt the revenant? That was his intention, for he knew the ancient being to be curious. It did not like overly obsequious people. It valued wisdom and discretion. It enjoyed hearing stories on occasion. If such an existence could be said to experience enjoyment.

"Speak."

Roque was grateful his ploy had worked. If the revenant had not wanted him to divulge his thoughts, it would have let him continue to back away.

"The people begin to wonder why you have not chosen a queen," Roque said. "It has been...some time."

A hiss came from the darkness. "They wish to sacrifice more of their daughters, do they?"

Roque held up his hands. "Your wealth and wisdom are legendary, Master. And greed has always been...enticing. You've built this mighty ziggurat. You've enclosed it in seven walls. Fruits and flowers of all kinds grow here. Your wealth is beyond imagination."

"I weary of it," said the revenant dispassionately. "So the mortals wish another contest. They desire a tyrant queen."

Roque bowed down. "They beg for it, Master."

"Suppose I give them what they wish. Mortals are so grasping. So treacherous. Even you."

Roque's stomach dropped. "Nay, Master!" He felt the sweat trickle down his cheek. How many times had he been implored to petition the king for the next contest? How many bribes had he accepted just to listen to the requests? He would prefer dealing with a tyrant queen for a few years to this precarious servitude. Had he overreached? He feared so. The revenant could snuff out his life in an instant. If he shut the doors, Roque would die as soon as all the air was gone.

"I do not condemn you, steward," the revenant said with a hint of triumph. "This time. Bring me the beast that I may toy with it. That I may unravel its powers. Begin the whispering of rumors that I may choose another queen. That should satisfy them for a while. For a long while."

"It will, Great One! It will appease many! Maidens will come from a thousand leagues away to be considered."

And with that pronouncement, the revenant began to cackle.

ONE

A Forgotten Past

ONE YEAR AFTER THE FALL OF CLAIRVAUX

Cimree's legs ached from the long walk to the river. When she'd tried grafting with a crane in order to fly there, the bird had resisted the magic of her distaff and flown away. A lapwing had proven to be more amenable, but the magic had worn off before she'd made it half the distance, and it seemed as if all the other birds had rushed away to get out of her sight. There were dozens of varieties of serpents in this rocky land, however, and she could sense each one and its uniqueness. Her affinity for snakes didn't help her walk any faster, though.

Since the refugees from Clairvaux had left that beautiful valley, they'd crossed several mountain ranges, wandered additional wide valleys, passed a number of solitary mountains, and even threaded through a narrow neck of land with huge seas on either side. They'd walked, they'd sometimes flown, and at one point they had hunkered down for the winter at a distant outpost of the Long Patrol that had been uninhabited when they got there.

Their destination was the Tirich Mir, a series of mountains

that Azra had traveled to in the past. A place where, he believed, they would find refuge from the beasts and monsters that had inspired them to leave their precious Clairvaux. The network of mountains and caves that made up the Tirich Mir was impossibly far away. Along the arduous journey, they were all learning to survive off the land, to hunt and fish and forage.

As she approached the river where she sensed Azra, Cimree massaged the ache in her chest. The whorl pattern had grown substantially since she had first accepted the Tanaquil amulet and bonded with it in order to keep Azra connected to her. The medallion joined their emotions and feelings, giving them access to each other's hearts in a way that others couldn't understand. He knew she was approaching just as she knew exactly where he was. She didn't know what he was doing, but an invisible thread connected them beyond distance. Sometimes it made them frustrated with each other. Other times, it allowed them to communicate without using words. A glance was sufficient.

But the medallion had consequences for using it. When the Queen Mother had sent Cimree to Montheron to bind with Azra and return him to Clairvaux's service, the intention had never been for her to wear it so long. The medallion could take away emotions, and it could infuse her with emotions. And she'd found herself, annoyingly, falling in love with Azra, even though she suspected the feelings weren't altogether real. They'd almost kissed once during a training session. That had embarrassed her to the point of speechlessness, especially after he'd spurned her by walking away. She could have *made* him succumb to her wishes. The amulet he wore gave her that power over him. But she'd promised him she would not compel or suppress any emotion he did not want her to.

A particularly sizeable cypress tree stood in the distance with a plume of smoke coming from beneath its lofty branches, and that, she sensed, was where she'd find Azra.

She was grateful her lengthy trek to catch up to Azra was over, and as she drew closer to the cypress tree, she saw a cooking fire with branches lashed together, forming a bracket around it. Slabs of fish were being cooked over it, shielded by leaves to preserve the smoke. Off to the side, flies swarmed around a pile of entrails. She turned and found Azra standing in the river, his shirt laid aside, carrying a wicker trap he'd made to catch the fish.

This was not the Azra she'd first met in the dungeon of Montheron. He'd been an older man then, hair mostly gray, with only a few dark flecks still in it. He'd been fit, but he was even more so in his newfound juvenescence. The fruit of the Gallows Tree that he'd stolen from her had reversed his age, and he had become nearly her equal in youth. But *he* still possessed all his memories. Hers had been purged. And she had no idea how.

As Cimree neared the simple camp, he hefted the cone-shaped wicker trap, which had a huge fish in it, and carried it to his makeshift shelter. The Tanaquil medallion thumped against his chest, where the whorl-shaped patterns also stained his skin. They were smaller than hers, but they'd grown since the last time she'd seen him shirtless. He was fit and corded with muscle from his regular training and exercises. She waited for him in the shade of the cypress, admiring him and trying not to think about it because, while he couldn't read her mind, he could read her moods.

He reached the shade and set down the trap, then quickly grabbed his tunic and put it on.

"You should have gotten here hours ago," he said while looking at her with slightly scolding eyes and wearing a mocking smile.

"The lapwing got weary of me," she said, knowing he already knew the truth, that her grafting abilities—except with serpents—were unimpressive. It seemed he could graft with twenty different creatures at once, and though it caused him discomfort, he endured it. Grafting magic made parts of the body feel like they'd fallen asleep and could be quite painful.

"There's an abundance of snakes in this land," he chided. "I had one for a meal earlier today actually."

"Why did you kill it when there are plenty of fish?" she demanded, gesturing to the basket of meat he'd already cooked. During the journey, her presence had always been enough to encourage the serpents to leave them all alone. Trinati hated snakes, but she appreciated Cimree's ability to control them.

"It was aggressive," Azra said. "A cobra. So I wrung its neck."

She sighed. She still didn't know Azra's affinity. He seemed to have it with all animals and creatures—except for snakes—but she knew there was a particular animal he favored that he had never revealed to her. He liked his secrets.

With his tunic back on, she felt more comfortable looking at him. They'd discovered, to their mutual chagrin, that their ability to sense each other in candid moments—such as bathing—tended to arouse unwanted emotions.

"I'm glad you caught so many fish," she said. "Everyone will be hungry. They're heading this way. I thought I'd come help you."

"I don't need your help," he said offhandedly. He had a tendency toward bluntness, which came across as rude, even though it wasn't his intent to hurt her feelings. "Since you're here, why don't clean this one while I set the trap again."

She knew how to clean a fish because she'd done it at least a hundred times. He dumped the fish into her arms. It was heavy and fleshy. "What kind of fish is this?"

"That one is a mangar. I've caught a few shemaya as well. There's plenty of meat I've been smoking."

He knew the names of every creature it seemed. As a previous member of the Long Patrol, he knew how to live off the land. He'd taught everyone in the company who was old enough to learn how to make traps for birds, fish, and rabbits. He was an expert hunter and could bring down larger game as well.

Cimree took the fish and set it down on a thatch of leaves he'd made. She pulled out her dirk and slit the fish open. The droning flies were eager as she used the blade to scoop out the entrails. From the corner of her eye, she watched Azra pull a smaller fish, a dead one, from a small basket and put it into the trap, which he then carried back to the river. This time, he didn't take off his tunic as he waded into the water and set up the trap, wedging it near some rocks. A bigger fish would enter the wide hole at the open end of the cone to go after the easy prey, only to find itself trapped at the end and unable to wiggle free and turn around.

As he came back, he wrung out the water from his tunic.

"You could have taken off your tunic again," she blurted out as he approached. She'd already removed the spine and bones of the fish.

Azra placed his hands on his hips as he flashed a steely gaze. "I didn't like the way you were looking at me earlier. Or how it made you feel."

So maybe she had been admiring him too long.

Cimree thrust her chin out as a sign of bravado. "I'm celibate, Azra. I'm not going to ravish you."

He snorted and said nothing back, but she felt his turmoil. He'd forsaken the angel sworn, had joined a tribe in the Tirich Mir, and had even had a wife and children. Sometimes his memories of those years caused him feelings that were foreign to her. They made her curious, but she was not about to give in to feelings that were likely invoked within her by magic from another world.

Azra went to the fire and stones and took two charred sticks to flip the fish, which were intact other than being gutted and deboned. Every part of the fish that could be eaten was. They even ate the heads. He tossed on some spices after flipping the wedges of meat.

She sensed a serpent, which had gotten curious by the heat and smells, slithering closer to investigate. Looking in its direction, she could tell that if she hadn't known it was there, she wouldn't have been able to distinguish it from the barren rock and scrub of the surrounding wilderness. It was a species of horned viper that was dominant in this rocky land.

"How far are we from the Tirich Mir?" she asked, watching him break off a bit of cooked flesh. He offered it to her, and she gratefully accepted it. It was sizzling hot but tasted wonderful. Hunger was a frequent companion in their travels.

"How many times do you intend to keep asking me that? It's a long way still. We may not even be halfway there."

"I was just making conversation." She wanted more of the meat, but they were careful to ration their supplies. Feeding the group, especially the children, required sacrifices. She rose and went to the river to wash her hands. The sludge-filled river was in a rocky landscape with short canyon walls on the other side. It wasn't as beautiful or as fresh as the Silver River, which ran the length of the valley of Clairvaux. That water was pristine enough to drink from without having to cure it.

She shook the water off her hands and then walked back. "I want to work on escaping holds. Come grab me."

"I'm fishing, Cimree. Another time."

"The basket is fishing. You're just waiting for a fish to get stuck. Come on. When Andrin or Perreta asks you to train them, you're quick to say yes. Or one of their children."

"It's different with you, and you know that."

She slapped her hands on her thighs. "Quit complaining and teach me. I can't remember what I used to know before my memories were all taken. So I have to relearn it."

"Very well," he said with a lamenting sigh. Not only did Azra have skills in hunting and survival, but he was the best fighter they had as well. Cimree still remembered when Trinati had asked to train with him and how humiliated she'd been when he defeated her. But Trinati was dogged in her determination and didn't let the defeat alter her resolution to best him. She still hadn't yet, but she was better than anyone else in their band of refugees.

Cimree had been, in a previous lifespan, the Queen Mother's spy. For some reason, she had eaten an entire fruit of the Gallows Tree, and that had reversed her age back to that of an infant, so her memories had all been purged. Trinati did not know why the Queen Mother had made her do this or if she even had. Azra didn't know either. It was infuriatingly unfair, but Cimree had mostly come to terms with it, and she decided if spying was where her talents lay, she needed to recover them instead of continuing with the teachings of her mentor, Milena, who had been training her to be a healer.

"I want to try the one where you grab my wrists with my arms crossed," Cimree said. That was a subduing technique that was very difficult to get out of because she had to struggle against herself as well as an attacker's superior strength. It meant using other parts of the body to throw the attacker off balance so that they were forced to let go.

Cimree felt Azra come up behind her, and she crossed her arms beneath her breasts. They'd both end up on the ground in moments, but that was part of the challenge. Azra gripped her wrists firmly and then pulled her against him.

"Are you ready?" she asked him.

He hoisted her off her feet in response, which surprised her, as she'd been planning to try to lower her center, lean forward, and lift him on her back. Then he spun her around, adding dizziness to her confusion. She tried to tug one of her arms free, but his grip was iron. Her mind whirled for ideas, but that was just Azra's way. He enjoyed being unpredictable.

"You're not...being...fair," she grunted, her legs swinging.

"There is no fairness in fighting," he countered. "Think!"

He spun her around again, this time the other way. She was trying to touch a boot to the ground, but he'd levered her backward. She knew how to evade, how to quickly escape someone grabbing her wrist or her arm. She knew how to flip someone, but when she was being flung around in circles, getting nauseous, new ideas began to fail her.

She tucked up her knees and felt the momentum change. Gritting her teeth, she lowered them again and then repeated the action, this time engaging her hips too. It made her flip above him. The extra weight on his upper body caused him to let go before she could land on his back. The two of them tumbled to the ground, limbs flailing as they both sought to gain the advantage. She brought the heel of her palm into his chin, hoping to stun him with the blow, but he turned his head and then grappled her in the dust until he pinned her with an arm bar, her cheek on the ground, her shoulder screaming in pain. She was on her knees, gasping, trying not to cry out.

Then he released her and stood. She felt like kicking him in the stomach for revenge, but he must have sensed her emotional intent and took a long step backward.

"Are you finished...so quickly?" She panted. "I'm not even tired."

"Someone's coming," he said.

She slowly rose, rubbing her arm, and looked around but didn't see anyone approaching the cypress. Then it dawned on her that they were coming from above.

"How did you—?"

"I'm grafted to a falcon right now," he said. "He's watching for me. Two angel sworn are coming this way. Darcia and Uorsin."

Cimree saw the dirt and dust on her tunic and trews and boots and began to brush it off. She missed the rituals of bathing she'd learned in Clairvaux's étuves. A cold river was no comparison to a steam-filled room and a cleansing bath.

Darcia was one of the angel sworn loyal to Trinati. She'd been part of the group that had gone to Montheron to find Azra, and she was good at talking too much. Uorsin had been a blacksmith at Montheron and a prior friend to Azra.

Cimree and Azra left the shadow of the cypress and gazed into the sky to watch as the two angel sworn rapidly flew toward them. As Darcia landed, her eyes were full of surprise at seeing the two of them in such a disheveled state. Uorsin landed next, breathing hard as if the grafting had strained him.

"You came quickly," Cimree said. "I just got here."

Darcia gazed at both of them in turn and then the words came tumbling out. "Captain Odeon is alive! He just found us!"

Two

Chrysopoeia

It was hours before the rest of the group arrived at the cypress tree. When Cimree had left them that morning, most had been asleep. Each day they tried to cover at least ten leagues. Azra would be the advance scout and find shelter and water for the next night. Because she was connected with him, she knew where he would end up and then communicate that to Trinati, who would help organize the travel for the day. Other scouts were sent to warn of possible dangers, and the main group kept together. They tried to cover the same amount of ground each day, regardless of the weather, because Azra explained that consistency was better than waiting for more favorable conditions.

Others had joined them along the way, so the group numbered about forty souls. Some angel sworn had escaped before the fall of Clairvaux and had heard about a remnant led by Trinati, which was traveling to a distant land to establish a new Gallows Tree. Cimree still had the seed with her and always made sure she guarded it. Only by reestablishing the Gallows Tree would they be able to produce the special fruit that reversed their aging. Only with that fruit would Cimree and Azra finally be rid of the taint of the medallion.

Azra was conversing in a relaxed manner with Uorsin while they worked to get the cooked fish ready to share by breaking it into chunks and putting them in a basket Azra had fashioned out of river reeds. Their friendship had been a steady presence during the travels, and the burly blacksmith was quick to help with chores. Cimree had also noticed that Uorsin went out of his way to do kind things for Darcia too. She was often less talkative around Uorsin and Cimree had noticed the two of them spending more time together—although in a quiet way. She would linger near the blacksmith when he'd work on a repair or sharpening a weapon.

Azra was carrying a basket of smoked fish and doled out the meat to the newest arrivals. Trinati and Captain Odeon had not arrived yet, and Cimree was anxious to learn about how he had come to join them. She watched as Azra gave some fish to Andrin and his family, all fatigued from the journey. Andrin and Perreta had three children of their own—Edwina, Cyrill, and Blanka—and had taken on the care of another.

The little girl Chrysopoeia.

When Cimree and Azra had faced the Fear Liath near the Gallows Tree, the girl had mysteriously appeared and had gone with them. She had been about eight years old and could not speak. She'd been wearing a tunic without trews, but they had garbed her as an angel sworn since she'd been traveling with them. They'd tried to give her boots, but she had shaken her head. She preferred walking barefoot, which showed the serpent anklet on her left leg. When they'd asked her later about her name, she'd pointed to the circlet, which was fashioned in the image of a snake eating its own tail. That symbol, the Chrysopoeia, was a magical emblem. And so it had become her name. Soon they'd all taken to calling her Chrys.

There was still no explanation of where she'd come from. Trinati knew all the children of Clairvaux and had never met her before. How she'd come to be so close to the Gallows Tree was a mystery, and since she couldn't speak, all efforts to try to understand had been unanswered. When they asked where she'd come from, she just gave them a blank look as if the question did not make sense to her. She did understand their language and could nod to answer some things, but attempting to delve into her past had yielded no answers at all. She was a solemn child, but she had a gift where she could heal injuries with her hands. A gift that had proven to be beneficial on their journey.

Cimree watched Azra offer some meat to Chrys, which she ate after smiling at him. Whenever Azra was at camp, Chrys would watch him. She didn't fawn over him like Edwina, Cyrill, or Blanka did. Sometimes Blanka would sit in his lap and stroke his cheek. He didn't seem to mind, and it always stirred feelings in him that were poignant yet full of sorrow. He'd had had his own family in Tirich Mir until the day the Queen Mother had ordered their village be destroyed.

Cimree saw Wegner emerging from the river with the trap, and it had an enormous fish in it. Wegner had affinity for fish, so it was no surprise to her that he'd managed to catch the biggest one yet. Wegner was the architect of Clairvaux, a man who knew all the intricacies of building in stone and metal. He would be a terrific asset for the journey. He always carried the heaviest pack, and it contained cookware and tools and instruments of measure. He was an excellent navigator as well, but he'd never traveled so far from Clairvaux before.

Darcia was talking to some of the other angel sworn, sharing with them how excited she was that Captain Odeon had returned and relating how he had stayed behind during the fall of Montheron in order to defend the mortals against attacks from grimalkin, after they had come to the island fortress for protection against the gévaudan ravaging the surrounding lands. Cimree had heard her tell the same story a half-dozen times, so she went over to Wegner instead. Before she reached him, she noticed that Trinati and Odeon were flying across the valley at great speed to join with the rest of the group.

Wegner looked up and noticed the new arrivals. He set the trap down by the pile of fish guts. "I can clean it later," he said to Cimree. "I want to hear what Odeon and Trinati have to say. I can't believe he found us after so long."

Trinati traveled in her armor, which was grimy with dust and dirt. She was always prepared for a fight. Some of the buckles of the armor had broken, and she'd made thread to stitch and repair things. She had smudges on her beautiful face. Well, they *all* did. Living off the land and traveling hard meant many of the cleansing rituals of the angel sworn had to be deferred.

Captain Odeon was more gaunt than when they had left him in Montheron. His tunic was ripped in places, showing chain mail beneath, and his trews were splotched with mud stains. He had a mirror blade strapped to his back and a hunting dagger at his belt. There was also a long sheath or quiver on his back, probably an unstrung bow and arrows he used for hunting. He'd partaken of some of the Gallows Tree fruit in Montheron, from the same fruit that Azra had stolen from Cimree, so he looked younger but also wearier. He stood side by side with Trinati, and the archangel couldn't quite hide the smile of pleasure seeing him caused.

"The lost goat has rejoined the herd," Trinati announced in a humorous tone.

Azra approached Odeon and the two men gave each other a friendly hug. Andrin looked uncomfortable, but it was not difficult to imagine why. He had served in Montheron as part of the mortal guard and had left his post to save his family from imminent destruction.

"It's good to see you, old friend," Azra said after the embrace.

Odeon fingered the chain from the medallion and scrutinized the tattoo-like sigils that had bloomed on Azra's chest and peeked out above the collar. He frowned with apparent concern, but didn't share anything aloud.

Andrin whispered something to Perreta and then approached the captain.

Odeon gave a genuine smile and reached out, putting his hand on Andrin's shoulder in a friendly way. "Speaking of lost goats."

"Captain, I just wanted to—"

"Lad, there is nothing between us. Nothing at all. You were more wise than I in trying to escape. I'm glad you're here."

Andrin smiled and sighed in relief, which made Cimree feel warm inside. She looked at Azra and saw his knowing smile as he looked at her in return. Having Captain Odeon join them was truly a boon.

The captain turned to Cimree, and another fleeting look crossed his face. Or maybe it was just in his eyes, as if he'd been especially keen to see her. She had helped save his life in Montheron by recognizing that the symptoms he was suffering were from venom and not sickness. If she hadn't insisted he have some of the fruit, he would have died.

"How did you find us?" Cimree asked him. She wanted to give him a hug, but doing it in front of everyone made her feel too embarrassed.

"He's a capable tracker," Trinati said in a slightly dismissive tone.

Odeon gave Trinati an enigmatic look. Was he pleased by her praise? "You weren't exactly hiding your trail," he said.

"We wanted others to be able to find us," Azra said. "We've had several more join along the way. And no pursuit from the Long Patrol or the Morgarten."

"The Morgarten are no more," Trinati said. "But I shouldn't ruin your story. Tell them about the others, Odeon."

"You've already told Trinati?" Cimree asked, feeling a spark of annoyance. Back in Clairvaux, Trinati had been the Queen Mother's archangel. But she was no longer leading the band, although occasionally she acted as if she did.

"I understand that you are in charge now," Odeon said to Cimree. There was something in his tone that was off, and some of the nearby angel sworn wore looks of resentment. Cimree knew they struggled with her decision to supplant Trinati as leader. Considering the fact they were immortal, they did not handle change well. But her whole past had been stripped from her.

"I'd be interested in hearing how you came to be here," Cimree said, evading the significance of his comment. "I think we all would."

"Some food first?" Azra suggested. He picked up the basket of fish and offered some to Trinati and Odeon. Their hands brushed while taking pieces of meat.

Odeon quickly ate his, and then they all sat down under the shade of the cypress tree. The murmuring of the river lapping against stones was a pleasant sound. The children gathered around, eager to hear a story. Except for Chrys. She walked away from the others and went to the river to bathe her hands in the water. Wegner went over to the fish he'd brought back and began to clean it with his dirk, preparing it for the fire Azra had made earlier, which still had nice white coals.

Cimree sat down and gazed at Odeon. They were all keen to know what he'd been through.

"When you left, we'd barricaded ourselves inside Montheron," he began. "The walls protected us from the grimalkin, but not from internal discord. I and my men, those who had survived, tried to establish order, but they threw us in the dungeon." His eyes flicked over to Azra when he said this.

Odeon had been Azra's jailor for many years. But the other had no ill feelings about it. She could feel the calmness in his heart and was grateful he wasn't resentful.

"Eventually, we were furloughed by an unnatural race called kobolds. They are highly intelligent, short creatures, fashioned out of larger lizards, I think. They've scales, wear hide like clothes, and can use primitive weapons. They were very efficient and put the mortals who had survived into chain gangs and set to work demolishing Montheron. Stone by stone. We were all forced to labor."

Cimree's heart went out to him. He had been commanding

that bastion's company of angel sworn for a long time. To be forced to participate in its ruin must have been exceedingly painful.

"Those who were unable or refused to work were killed and eaten. Kobolds are not very discriminating in their choice of meat. And, it turns out, they have a fondness for eating cats. Those grimalkin creatures who attacked us. Well, they ended up being devoured by the kobolds. The grimalkin were immune to celestial iron. But the kobolds' weapons pierced them."

They were all listening very closely. Odeon paused, gazing at their faces.

"Go on," Trinati urged. "Tell them about the Queen Mother."

"Yes, my lady. I was brought back to Clairvaux in chains. Every time one of the angel sworn was captured, they'd break our distaffs so we could not use grafting magic. The valley has been destroyed. They're not just burning our homes. They're breaking them down. It's like these creatures cannot stand civilization. I was brought to the Queen Mother's palace. She was alive."

Murmurs began from some of the angel sworn. Odeon paused again while they absorbed the news.

"She was chained to the floor. Injured. There was a creature there, a creature unlike any I've ever seen. A golem. A creature only half formed. Its flesh is translucent, so you can see the muscles and arteries beneath. It communicates in a guttural way but can form certain words. It has a grafting wand. And it knows how to use it, but in a dark way that is unlike grafting, yet like it as well. I think it made the kobolds and the grimalkin, and even the gévaudan. I saw it attach a man's arm to itself, which became a working appendage."

More expressions of shock came. A foreboding tightened Cimree's stomach. She'd caught a glimpse of it herself in Montheron. It was huge and had the ability to travel on all its limbs in a spiderlike fashion. She'd never gotten a good look at it, but with the heat sensing of the serpent grafting she'd done, she'd seen its size and had made it flee with the Tanaquil medallion. That meant it was susceptible to emotions.

"A golem is a creation," Azra said. "Who made it?"

Odeon shook his head. "I don't know. Perhaps Asmodeus himself conjured it."

"And the golem is holding the Queen Mother captive," Trinati said. "It's kept her alive all this time."

"I can't be sure she's still alive," Odeon said. "She had her distaff, even though she was chained." He pulled it out, and they all recognized it. The Queen Mother's grafting wand was very distinctive, one that she had carried since the creation of the world. "She gave it to me to help me escape. Without her help, I would have perished."

"We should send some back to free her," whispered one of the angel sworn who had joined them after the fall of Clairvaux.

Cimree instantly felt the smoldering rage inside Azra's heart. He hated the Queen Mother. When she glanced his way, she saw him glaring at the woman who had whispered.

"Trinati said you are journeying to Tirich Mir," Odeon said cautiously, looking at Cimree.

"We are," she answered. "Azra is the only one who knows how to get there."

Odeon frowned and nodded.

"What concerns you?" Cimree said. "We believe it is the best place to hide and shelter us from these creatures."

"Ecbatana," Trinati said, her voice betraying suspicion. "He didn't tell us about Ecbatana. That we have to go past it to get there."

Cimree felt a jolt of recognition from Azra at the name. And a feeling of deep wariness.

THREE
ECBATANA

"It sounds like Ecbatana is a place," Cimree said. "I've never heard of it."

"I suggest we have this discussion privately," Trinati proclaimed, asserting herself once again. She was used to having people defer to her, and Cimree—who had never wanted to lead—had clashed with her multiple times.

"That's Cimree's decision." Azra gave the other woman a pointed look.

"Let's not argue in front of everyone," said Trinati.

"When I want to argue about something, you will know," Azra retorted. Cimree could feel his anger building and wanted to diffuse it quickly.

"Actually, I agree," Cimree offered. "Wegner. I think you should be part of this as well." He was levelheaded and had a great deal of knowledge that could be helpful. His role on the high council also gave him experience others didn't have.

"Of course," he said, but he was watching Trinati still. Was he seeking her approval as well?

Cimree went with Azra, Trinati, Odeon, and Wegner, leaving the others beneath the cypress tree. They walked to the nearest bend in the river, where some boulders provided seating far enough from the others that they wouldn't be overheard, though they were still within sight.

"Captain Odeon, I am grateful you survived and caught up with us," Cimree said.

"I'm a little confused by the hierarchy I've found," Odeon said. "Why isn't Trinati in charge?"

His words stung Cimree, but she felt he wasn't being mean-spirited. He was used to obeying orders, and Trinati and the Queen Mother were the ones who had always given them.

"It's more a matter of survival," Trinati said before Cimree could gather her thoughts on how to respond. "Azra knows the way to Tirich Mir. And he insists that Cimree is best suited for leadership."

Azra shook his head and grunted.

"You disagree?" Trinati asked, bristling.

"Let's not argue," Cimree said, trying to calm things. "We're here to discuss Ecbatana. Am I the only one unfamiliar with that name?" She looked at Wegner.

"I know of it. It was founded a generation ago," Wegner explained.

"Tell me of it, then," she said, looking to Captain Odeon.

"I've been there once," he said. "I imagine Azra has also visited?"

Azra nodded but said nothing.

"Just tell me," Cimree said. "Odeon—share what you know."

"Ecbatana was founded by the first king of the Midlands. He was the first king who managed to throw off the yoke of the over-lord Esser-Addin of Ninuwa. That is where Azra is from."

Cimree looked at Azra and he met her eyes and nodded.

Odeon continued. "The Queen Mother sent the angel sworn against Ninuwa. Once their iron grip was broken, the bordering king-doms began to fight amongst themselves. King Deioces had managed to keep above the fray and founded Ecbatana as a stronghold after Ninuwa fell. Because of their position along the trade routes, it became a very wealthy city. The Queen Mother occasionally sent members of the Long Patrol to infiltrate and assess it for any danger it might pose to Clairvaux. Azra was included since he knew their language."

Cimree felt confused. "Help me understand what's so significant."

"There have been rumors that Ecbatana is a lychgate. That Deioces never died." Odeon held his hands close together and then spread them apart. "It is almost impossible to actually meet the ruler of Ecbatana. He has servants and messengers and people who deliver his intentions. It is a repository of great wealth, where other kings send treasures for tribute and to be protected. Seven walls surround Ecbatana."

"Why seven?"

"It was built to withstand an assault by the angel sworn," Odeon said significantly. "They saw what happened to Ninuwa. They know the angel sworn can fly, and so their defenses against attacks from the sky are very formidable. The walls are guarded day and night. You aren't allowed to fly into the city. It marks you as an intruder to eliminate."

Cimree turned to look at Azra. "Were we going to pass by Ecbatana on the way?"

Azra had a very neutral expression, but she could feel his emotions easily. He was distrustful. "No. I was going to lead us around it."

"Without telling us it was there?" Trinati said.

"I've been inside Ecbatana," Azra said curtly. "I've been *deep* inside. Whether there is a revenant there or no, I can't say. The Queen Mother sent me to destroy it in case it was Asmodeus inhabiting another corpse. I found no revenant there. But it is still a place of great evil. It was hard to breathe inside its crypt. I think Deioces died long ago and they keep his bones. The servants are the ones with real power. The city was no threat to us, so the Queen Mother didn't bother them."

Cimree turned to Trinati. "What did you know of it?"

"The Queen Mother didn't attack it because it was too heavily fortified. We would have suffered too many losses trying to conquer it. Years ago, an emissary from Ecbatana came to the borders of Clairvaux and asked to purchase a single fruit from the Gallows Tree in order to preserve the life of their king. He offered wealth beyond imagining for it. The Queen Mother refused. The fruit could not be bought. It is given freely to those who adopt our ways and renounce worldly things. The Ecbatanans would not adopt our ways. In disgust for having been rejected, they created a tradition to mock Clairvaux."

"The tradition of the tyrant queen," Wegner said, sounding disappointed.

"A deliberate insult?" Cimree asked Wegner, and he nodded.

"Only men are allowed the rule in Ecbatana. Except when they choose a queen. She is allowed to rule with utmost authority. For a time. Her word is absolute. Her will becomes supreme in the land. And then...she is deposed and killed."

Cimree looked over at Azra to confirm the story.

"It's true," he said. "Though I feel it served other purposes than just mocking the Queen Mother. Any mortal administration becomes stagnant over time, especially when corruption abounds. It causes divisions and resentments when people are promoted not because of capability but because of bribery. The tyrant queen shifts the balance of power. She wreaks revenge until the purging is complete. And then, ultimately, someone assassinates her. It's a cycle they go through. An evil tradition. We should not go there."

"And why are you the one who gets to make that decision?" Trinati said angrily. "You didn't even tell Cimree of it? Or the rest of us? You concealed your knowledge. I was surprised when we had come this far and not seen it."

He gave her an uncaring shrug. "I'm leading us to Tirich Mir. Those mountains are more impregnable than Ecbatana."

"So are you the leader or is Cimree the leader?" Trinati said. "How can she make a decision without information? It was only when Odeon asked if we were going to stop there for supplies, which I think would be very wise, that I found out how near it was. And we had to flee Clairvaux with so little."

"What do we need that we cannot make ourselves?" Azra shot back. "We should avoid Ecbatana."

"Why?" Trinati asked.

"I've told you. It is an evil place. I have bad memories of it." He looked at Odeon. "How far into the city did *you* get?"

"The fourth wall," Odeon said. "You made it all the way inside?"

Azra nodded. "And I've no desire to go back."

Trinati gave him a sharp look. "Shouldn't Cimree decide that? Think of it. It is a place of trade. We can get seeds from various fruits. Seed for grain to harvest. Animals we can bring with us to the mountains. I suggest we send in a small group to see what's going on there. We gather information and things that may be useful."

That didn't sound unreasonable to Cimree, but she felt Azra's resistance. His feelings of foreboding.

"Wegner, do you have any insight to add?" she asked him.

"There's a saying among travelers that all roads lead to Ecbatana," Wegner said. "I, for one, would be interested in seeing it. Maybe it has weaknesses we're unaware of. But I feel we should at least warn them about what's happened in our lands. It's possible they don't even know yet. The caravans may not have survived."

"That is an excellent point," Trinati said. "We should be a warning voice to them."

Through their connection, Cimree sensed that Azra wasn't convinced by Trinati's newly expressed motive.

"We should think about our choices and our options," Cimree said. "I don't want to make any rash decisions. Thank you for sharing your information with me."

"How far away is Ecbatana?" Trinati asked Azra.

"A two-day journey east of here. They've other villages and towns in the Midlands. More the closer we get to their stronghold."

"I'd like to send my scouts ahead tomorrow," Trinati said. "I don't want to be taken off guard."

Was she asking Cimree for permission? Her tone of voice suggested she was letting Cimree know what she would do regardless.

"We'll discuss it in the morning," Cimree said.

Trinati's lips pursed but she nodded.

"Odeon. Why did you come after us?" Azra asked.

The captain met his gaze. "If we must start anew, then I wish to do my part."

"I'm glad you made it," Cimree said. "I plan to sit here for a while and think about our options. Thank you."

Wegner rose from the boulder he was leaning against. Trinati, who hadn't sat down, hooked arms with Captain Odeon and thanked him for sharing what he had. Azra did not leave with the others. Cimree had known he wouldn't.

"Something is not quite right," she said to him in a soft voice, cocking her head slightly.

"Odeon didn't tell us everything," Azra said, giving her a steady look.

"I have that feeling too. But I don't know what. He seems to be gently nudging us to go there. I wonder why."

"I don't know why," Azra replied. "I'm surprised he made it out alive, even with a grafting wand."

"The golem can sever graftings," Cimree said, remembering the multiple occasions that had happened to them.

Azra rose from the boulder he had been sitting cross-legged on. "Did he escape? Or did it *let* him escape? Is it following him to us?"

Four

Emissary

The campfire crackled with a fresh piece of wood, spitting sparks into the night sky, the embers mingling with the whorl of stars overhead. Cimree sat near it, arms crossed around her knees as she thought about what to do. It was past midnight and she still wasn't tired as her mind weighed and considered all the potential choices. She felt the burden of responsibility keenly and, not for the first time, had wondered if it would be better to just let Trinati lead the refugees from Clairvaux.

She sensed a serpent slithering at the perimeter of camp, curious by nature as to the disruption of its normal habitat by the intruders who had gathered and built fire. It posed no threat to them, and its thoughts brushed against Cimree's with deliberateness, as if it recognized her as an ally, not a danger, and wanted to come closer but feared the sleeping mortals near her.

Of all the affinities to have, hers was for snakes. Because of the tales of the Origin, in which the great tempter Asmodeus had used a serpent to persuade the First Man to become mortal, serpents were much maligned in the valley, and most had been driven out. That was why she hadn't known she possessed the affinity until she'd left on the journey to Montheron and had come upon a snake. Knowing that she'd lived a previous lifespan—or possibly several—she wondered how that affinity had been forged. She'd been told she was the Queen Mother's spy. What kind of missions had she been sent on? Had she been to Ecbatana herself? What other memories had she developed that were lost forever?

She turned her gaze from the sparks and stars to the sleeping crews gathered around the fires set up throughout the camp. Trinati was sitting near another fire with Captain Odeon, and they were talking in low voices. Some angel sworn were patrolling the camp and would change guard during the night. Azra was away from the others, which was normal for him. He didn't like camp life and typically hunkered down by himself at a distance. He was asleep. She could tell that through the medallion.

Her decision would impact all of their lives. What if she made a poor one? The burden of responsibility was heavy. There were children among them. They'd all fled because they believed that Azra's experience and knowledge of Tirich Mir would help them survive the monsters unleashed on the world. They'd been chased by packs of gévaudan at the onset of their journey, but the defenders had managed to drive them off, and although some were bitten, Chrys's healing touch had removed the bite marks that seemed to transmit the infection. They'd covered a lot of ground in the intervening months, and eventually the dangers had ebbed and then disappeared. It was tempting to think that the trouble was behind them. Why not visit Ecbatana and choose it as a safe haven?

Because she trusted Azra's judgment. He'd been right so many times. He still had a penchant for withholding everything he knew —the fact that he hadn't mentioned Ecbatana even once proved that point. He'd persuaded Andrin and Perreta to abandon Montheron before its fall, even though he could have escaped it himself and fled all alone. He cared about people, even if he was still so withdrawn. She admired that about him. She admired a lot about him. Were her personal feelings influencing her judgment?

Did she trust him because he trusted her? Because of all they'd been through together?

Cimree glanced over at Trinati and saw her put her hand on Odeon's shoulder. Then the two of them, wrapped up in their blankets, bedded down across from each other by the fire. *Has there ever been more than feelings of friendship between them?* she wondered. When Odeon had chosen to remain at Montheron to defend the people—even though they'd rebelled—Trinati had seemed especially affected.

Cimree rubbed her mouth and considered the options again. They could bypass Ecbatana and continue to Tirich Mir. They could, as a body, go to Ecbatana and gather supplies and learn the latest news. They might learn more about the current situation in Tirich Mir from traders. Azra had been imprisoned for a long time, so his memories, although valid, were not recent. Or Cimree could send a mission into Ecbatana to gather information before making a more definitive decision. Those were the three main options.

She'd been leaning toward sending a small group, just as the Queen Mother had sent her with Trinati, Wegner, Darcia, and some hunters to Montheron to question Azra and persuade him to help. That option seemed the most prudent, despite Azra's view that it wasn't needed. In his opinion, the past was no longer a relevant prediction of the future. The same creatures that had destroyed Montheron and Clairvaux could just as easily destroy Ecbatana.

But should the Ecbatanans be warned about the danger? No one in the valley of Clairvaux had been warned until the Fear Liath had come. Cimree had been the first survivor to spread that warning. And Clairvaux had been destroyed so quickly. It didn't sit well with her to pass by a prosperous kingdom without offering a warning at the very least. That was Wegner's counsel as well.

A mission, then. But whom to send? Azra had been the deepest inside Ecbatana, so logic dictated that he be included.

Cimree didn't need to go, but she wanted to. And maybe her instincts as a spy would prove useful. Should she let Trinati go? Trinati definitely had expressed a strong desire to lead a mission there. Letting Trinati have her way might be shortsighted. What about Captain Odeon as the fourth? It was either him or Wegner. A group of that size seemed right for a mission such as this. Cimree paused as that thought came to her, furrowing her brow as she accepted another piece of knowledge that was somehow part of her. Wegner was familiar with everyone at the camp. Moreover, she trusted him. Azra's concerns about Odeon had impacted Cimree's good opinion of him.

Azra, Cimree, Trinati, and Odeon. That felt...good. Three of the four were accomplished fighters in case there was trouble. She'd leave Wegner in charge of the camp and the angel sworn defending it and could rely on him for good judgment.

Was it the right decision? She couldn't know until after the fact. That was the problem with some decisions. Some choices had irreparable consequences. She thought about her mentor, Milena, and felt the throb of loss, an ache that had never fully gone. If Cimree had stayed with her, she probably would have died as well. Outcomes were unpredictable. With a heavy heart, Cimree stretched out on her blanket and pulled it over her shoulders, gazing into the red coals of the fire. She closed her eyes and tried to fall asleep.

But sleep still wouldn't come.

"THAT IS MY DECISION," Cimree said, after explaining herself the next morning. The rest of the company would stay at the cypress tree while waiting for the mission to be fulfilled. Wegner would help catch fish for food, but many seemed thrilled with the idea of some additional nutrients being brought back from Ecbatana.

"But you are the leader. You should stay behind and trust us to fulfill your orders," Trinati said, which annoyed Cimree. "With the Tanaquil amulet, you'll know where we are and if there is a problem. Why not stay?"

"Why not let her decision stand?" Azra said, his voice a little taut. "She's made up her mind."

Trinati scowled at Azra but didn't argue with him. She looked back at Cimree, raising her eyebrows.

"The four of us," Cimree said. She had to feign confidence because she wasn't feeling it. She'd assumed Trinati would be supportive, since it had partially been her idea, and that she wouldn't care who went as long as she herself could go.

"Very well," Trinati said with a sigh. "We should be on our way. Unless you think it's prudent to delay."

Was that another jab at Cimree's role as leader? Sometimes Cimree couldn't tell whether she was too sensitive and read motives into situations where they didn't exist.

"We should get going." Cimree agreed, not wanting to make an issue of it.

Cimree had already packed up her things, so she slung her pack over her shoulders. She clenched the hilt of her dirk, belted to her waist in a sheath, and started to say goodbye to the others, enjoying the hug from little Blanka and the well-wishes from her siblings. Chrys looked impassive as usual. She went to Azra, and only him, to hug him goodbye. Azra patted the child's head and offered her one of his rare smiles.

They set off, using their distaffs to graft with some rock sparrows to begin the journey by air. Azra performed the grafting for her, which made hers more strenuous and tied some of the burden to him. It was still embarrassing, especially knowing that Trinati was an Eyriemaester, having affinity for eagles, and Odeon's affinity, she'd learned that morning, was herons, so it was natural to them both. They followed the river through the low-lying hills until they reached a vast plain. In the distance were some impressive mountains, but the city of Ecbatana could be seen, though still so far away, because of the plumes of smoke rising from it.

"We should walk the rest of the way," Azra said, coming alongside Cimree as they flew. "Revealing that we are angel sworn would be unwise."

Cimree agreed and they both landed. Trinati and Odeon had been flying ahead and kept going. Azra muttered under his breath and took off after them to let them know his reasons for halting their flight.

Trinati and Odeon came back, and the former archangel had a derisive look on her face. "Why not announce ourselves? And we'll get there faster."

"It's better to come in cautiously, I think," Cimree answered.

"Because Azra says so?"

She felt the anger churning inside him again. But he didn't speak.

"Can we not argue?" Cimree said. "There's no harm in walking."

Trinati sighed and shook her head. "You *are* the leader."

"Why are you being difficult?" Cimree asked, feeling her own anger spike.

"Was I? I apologize, then." But the apology didn't sound or feel very sincere. Cimree started walking. Azra joined her, but Trinati and Odeon hung back a little to create some distance before keeping pace.

"Why is she like that?" Cimree said under her breath.

"Because she doesn't respect you."

Cimree gave Azra an angry look. "Thanks for sparing my feelings."

"You need to increase your self-confidence. You thought this through. You made a decision. Stick with it until there's good reason for changing it. Don't let her see she rattles you."

Annoyed as she was, Cimree knew Azra was right. He was trying to help her, even if he didn't couch his words in pleasantness. They encountered a boar midday, and Azra killed it with a clean shot. They paused the journey so he could dress it, but they decided not to cook the meat until after nightfall so the smoke wouldn't give them away. There were villages on the periphery of Ecbatana, but they avoided those and camped for the night in a rugged spot inside a gorge, where they cooked and ate the meat from earlier. Cimree was tired from her lack of sleep the previous night and from the long walk, so she fell asleep quickly.

The next day, they continued the journey. More and more dwellings began to appear, mostly mud huts cobbled together with mismatched stones. It was very primitive compared to the precise sculpting of angel sworn stone. A herdsman approached them with some goats, and Azra spoke to him fluently and in a submissive manner. The herdsman's language was strange but beautiful, and it sounded slightly familiar to her. Was it an echo from her past?

Azra said he'd learned from the herdsman they were close to Ecbatana and would be there by sunset. He had no significant news whatsoever and mostly just warned them not to disturb any herds they found along the way.

Late that afternoon, they came across a dusty road with wagon ruts in it and took it east. It seemed obvious it was bound for Ecbatana, and so the journey became easier. As they passed a bulky outcropping of rocks at a bend in the road, they found a dozen horsemen, the beasts with polished armor, the men wearing turbans and outfitted with curved swords, guarding the road. Two of the riders had flags hanging from poles in little mounts near the stirrups. The twelve were dressed in finery with chain mail beneath, and they all had short, deeply curved bows hanging from the saddles as well. Though they were armed, the weapons were not drawn.

One of the horsemen tapped his mount's flanks and rode toward them, while the others remained behind. The fading sunlight glimmered off dazzling jewels set into his turban.

"Welcome, esteemed travelers!" the man said in their language.

Cimree felt uneasy, but the manner of the introduction was friendly enough. The fellow was middle-aged with some gray in his beard.

"You're the leader," Trinati said beneath her breath. "Answer him."

Cimree swallowed and took a step forward. "Greetings. We are bound for Ecbatana."

"Of course you are!" the man said with a genial smile. "We are emissaries of Ecbatana. We have angel sworn among us now, many who survived the fall of Clairvaux. You were recognized, my lady," the fellow said, looking at Trinati and bowing his head in respect. "We were sent to welcome you and bring you to our fair city. You are the archangel Trinati?"

"I am," Trinati answered, her posture shifting. Becoming more assertive.

"You are welcome. Indeed, it is a particular honor to meet you in person. The angel sworn here said you were the most powerful of the Queen Mother's leaders. My name is Lord Roque. I am the king's most humble servant. Welcome to Ecbatana!"

FIVE
THE GRAND SOUK

The sights, sounds, and colors of the vast marketplace quickly overwhelmed Cimree's senses. They each rode tandem atop one of the ceremonial horses behind an emissary who had welcomed them outside Ecbatana. Cimree rode behind a man who wore a decorative tunic that was split in the middle instead of being a solid piece, the sections overlapping at the front and held closed by a leather wrap studded with jewels, and a curved and jeweled sword hung from his hip. The man had a cropped beard and long hair and he smelled of some interesting fragrance, a woody scent. He was muscled and quite handsome, and she flushed at being seated so closely behind him as he eased the stallion through the throng.

Ecbatana dwarfed the size of Montheron, which had been crammed onto a solitary island on a lake. This vast, teeming city held tens of thousands of people, and small stalls were crammed together, with every conceivable ware on display. The vendors yelled at them and other passersby, trying to win attention and business. The colorful jackets and pants and pointed shoes were distinctive, and the aromas of cooking meats, foreign spices, and even skewers of cooked insects filled her nose.

What astonished Cimree the most were the women of Ecbatana and their garb. No tunic and trews among the lot, but instead, the women wore voluminous draping garments in a variety of colors. The garments fell down to their feet, which were mostly bare except for some leather straps that covered the tops and wrapped around the ankles, exposing the toes. Some of the edges of the garments were slit, revealing bare legs beneath, which was startling to her, along with the fact that all the women had uncovered shoulders, though there were still sleeves that were bunched at the upper arms with gilded lattices of leather it seemed. She had no idea what the fabric was, but it wasn't wool. It seemed light, airy, almost transparent. The women all had headdresses, girdles, and ropes with bags dangling from their hips, and Cimree noticed that some women at the booths were pulling coins from the little bags.

There were no coins in Clairvaux. No trading like this. Azra had explained money to her.

"Is this a marketplace?" Cimree asked the man seated in front of her.

"Yes, although it's called a *souk*," he answered with a slight accent. She was grateful he spoke her language. When he turned toward her, she noticed his ear had a jewel dangling from it, one that pierced through the lower lobe. She'd never seen that before. "The entire outer ring of Ecbatana is one giant souk."

The presence of a serpent distracted her momentarily, and she gazed at one of the hawkers who was holding an oversized snake, one that was fat and oily and looked almost too heavy to handle. He was showing the serpent to a customer who seemed intrigued by the tameness of it. Cimree watched as the serpent swiveled its head, its forked tongue testing the air as they passed by it. She felt its boredom, but it was well fed and lazy.

"What is your name?" she asked the horseman.

"Khaf," he answered simply. "Yours?"

"I'm Cimree."

Her name seemed to have startled him, as he jerked his head and looked at her with furrowed eyebrows.

"Do you know that name?" she asked, instantly curious.

"It's an odd name for a woman," he said with a measured tone.

"Why?"

"In Ecbatana, that name means greedy. Stingy. Tight-fisted."

"Oh," she said, deflated. The noise and commotion were making her uneasy. "What does Khaf mean?"

He gave her a studying look. "The translation in your language? It means...*head*. But...thinking. Cleverness."

"How many languages do you know?"

"Many," he answered. "Which is why I was selected as an emissary. To greet and welcome visitors to Ecbatana. I will serve you while you are here."

Someone from a booth approached their horse, holding out a jeweled necklace to Cimree, but with one scolding frown from Khaf, he shrank back.

"The women's garments. What is that style called?"

"Garments here are called kiyafet. The one the women wear is called entari. Made of silk."

"What is silk?"

He gave her another confused look. "A fabric. Light and soft as a breeze. The summers in Ecbatana are very hot."

"What is silk made from? An animal?"

"Insects. They spin threads in trees. I shall show you later."

"Thank you," she said. She glanced over at Trinati's horse. She was riding behind Roque, who was talking to her and gesturing very dramatically with his hands. Azra rode behind his rider without saying a word. Captain Odeon was conversing, though. From some of the tidbits of conversation she picked up, it seemed he knew some of their language as well.

The outer wall of Ecbatana had been made of a white stone. A type of marble, she thought. After the tortuous plunge in the crowd, they reached the next wall, which was made of an onyx, a striking contrast to the outer wall. The walls rose vertically before angling inward, and she could see archers patrolling the battlements and gazing down at the crowded souk. There were tarps and coverings for each as well, and they were staggered in height so that they provided shelter. Gutter sluices diverted water from walls and led to pipes heading belowground. She wondered if it had been built that way to collect rainwater. A city of this size needed an ample supply of wells.

With Roque and Trinati leading the way, they passed through a gate in the onyx wall and entered another part of Ecbatana. Her immediate thought was that this layer of the city was where the craftsmen lived and worked. Instead of market stalls, there were small buildings and a variety of trades happening at once: people making the unusual footwear she'd seen the women wearing. Men and women scraping leather hides with metal tools. Cloth hung in a dazzling array of colors on racks near vats of dye with pungent fumes. It wasn't as noisy, but it was bustling and busy.

Without the press of the crowds, they made it to the next wall more quickly. This was a dull red color. Three walls with three different colors. Once they went through this gate, the next layer seemed to be occupied by garrisons of soldiers, horses, racks of weapons, and blacksmiths hammering. She saw a waterwheel and imagined that Wegner would be intrigued by this section of the city. She didn't see any women in this part of the city. They passed some training yards where shirtless men were doing drills with curved swords, spears, and sickles.

The next wall was blue. She wasn't sure what kind of stone it was made from, but it was a bluish-gray color and rose formidably before them. The gate had a thick door and an iron portcullis. Once inside, she saw several pleasant palaces and heard the pattering noise of fountains. This was their destination.

Roque brought them to a spacious mansion where they all dismounted. A servant came and helped Cimree down, and then Khaf slid off the saddle before the servant grabbed the bridle and led the horse away. The other riders dismounted too, and all the horses were escorted away. Roque clapped his hands loudly and servants came outside, two males and two females, and they hustled forward and bowed deeply.

"You may rest from your journey here," Roque said. "This palace is for the angel sworn, and you will find your people here. Are there more of you to accommodate? There is room to spare in Ecbatana for such honored guests."

"We are traveling with others, but they are staying elsewhere," Trinati said to answer Roque's question in a vague enough manner.

Cimree was grateful for the pleasant welcome, but she felt intimidated by the size and grandeur of what she saw. The angel sworn were meticulous craftsmen, but their structures were less opulent and had simpler designs. Her stomach growled.

Roque beamed. "If you require anything at all, your escort will provide it for you. We recognize that our customs and costumes are strange to you. We wish you to feel welcome. You are our honored guests and will be provided for as such. Your escorts will pay for expenses or provide information to you. Should you require anything they cannot provide, they will enlist my assistance. Please rest yourselves. A feast is being prepared to honor your arrival this evening at midnight. Until then, I shall depart." He bowed first to Trinati and then curtly to the rest of their group.

"Thank you for your hospitality," Trinati said. Her tone was pleasant but had an edge of wariness to it.

Roque didn't seem to catch the subtle show, and he bowed again with a pleasant smile and then mounted his horse, which was the only one that hadn't been taken away, and rode off. Their escorts gestured for them to enter the palace, and as they passed through the doorway, Cimree smelled sweet fragrances that she could not determine. Fruit trees grew in the entrance halls. The stone floor was polished to a shine. She walked in with the others and they were greeted by several angel sworn.

"My lady," many said as they dropped to a knee before Trinati. There was an equal number of men and women of varying ages and experience who wore the garb of the Long Patrol, although a few had adopted the kiyafet of Ecbatana. The escorts whom they'd ridden in with did not enter and instead loitered in the courtyard and spoke among themselves. Each, Cimree noticed, was particularly handsome in his own way.

"Azrael?" said one of the men after rising and inspecting the rest of their company. He was shocked to see him.

"Just Azra," he replied. "Good to see you, Jara."

One of the female angel sworn seemed to be in charge and approached Trinati. "I don't know if you remember me, but my name is—"

"You are Salisha." Trinati interrupted with a nod. "You were part of the Long Patrol."

The woman looked pleased to be remembered. "What news do you bring?" Salisha asked. "Is the Queen Mother alive? We heard that Clairvaux has fallen."

"It has," Trinati answered. "Captain Odeon is the last to have seen her."

Salisha's face wilted with despair. "Then it's true."

"Unfortunately so."

"How many survived?"

"We don't know," Trinati said. "There are others who escaped in time. How long have you been here?"

"Varying times," answered one of the other women. "We've gathered here because there was no other place to go."

Salisha nodded and turned back to Trinati, her voice dropping lower. "The king's steward, Roque, who brought you here, he keeps asking about the Gallows Tree."

Trinati's brow furrowed as she nodded. She did not reveal what had happened to it, though. "Did you tell them its location?"

"No. We would not share that with outsiders, no matter how generous they have been. This palace is a simple one compared to others deeper in. We are free to roam without escorts except beyond the silver or gold walls. Those are forbidden us. That is where the king resides."

"Have you met the king?" Trinati asked.

Salisha nodded. "He has been interviewing all of us who have come. In the privacy of the forbidden gardens. For two years he has been seeking a consort. They have a tradition here—"

"The tyrant queen," Trinati said. It bothered Cimree that Trinati liked to interrupt people. "So they are looking for this consort now?"

"Yes," said the other angel sworn who had spoken earlier. "None of us was invited back for a separate interview. They say he's spoken to thousands of young women."

Trinati's eyes narrowed. "How were you invited?"

"Roque came in person to extend the invitation," Salisha said. "He is the only one permitted to escort someone to meet the king. Did you come here to rule, Lady Trinati? Are you going to become the tyrant queen?" Hope filled the woman's voice, lit her eyes.

Cimree saw a look come over Trinati's face. The deference she'd been shown since arriving may have stirred something within her. The journey had been difficult. Her lowered status must have been difficult for her to accept.

Cimree looked at Azra and felt that their emotions were joined. He was deducing the same thing and for the same reasons. They'd come to Ecbatana to warn them.

Not to rule over them.

Then to a mountain exceedingly high does Asmodeus deliver the fallen angel. And before them lay revealed all the kingdoms of the world in their unrivaled glory. And Asmodeus says unto him,, 'These things to you, they all will I give thee if bending thy knee, you will worship me and not the Oldknow or the Queen Mother, whom thou detests.' And the fallen angel sayeth to Asmodeus, 'Give it me. I will suffer her yoke no longer.' Then Asmodeus enters into the tabernacle of the fallen angel and through him conquers the kingdoms of the world. And torments him night and day. And would not depart from him even after his flesh became dust and fell away.

— BOOK OF THE WATCHERS, THE TALE OF THE
FALLEN ANGELS

Six

Rivals

There were plenty of rooms in the mansion given over for the use of the angel sworn, room for all and some to spare. The manor had an underground bath for all to use. And servants assigned to the manor washed their clothes and provided robes for them to wear. Cimree gave the pouch with the seed from the Gallows Tree to Azra while she bathed. He was the only one she trusted with it.

It felt good to be clean again, and the fragrance of the soap provided by the servants, the oils and perfumes, were pleasing, but she only used a little. After tying her robe closed, she went back to find Azra and discovered him speaking with Khaf near the entrance steps leading to the baths.

"My lady," Khaf said, bowing with respect, "I can go to the souk and secure new clothing for you after the custom of our people. Is that your wish?"

"I wish to have my own clothes," Cimree answered.

"All we offer, we offer freely, my lady. There is no obligation. The angel sworn are respected here. As honored guests—"

"She said no," Azra snapped. He gave a little jerk with his chin in a dismissive gesture.

Khaf turned his gaze to Azra. Khaf was slightly taller than the other man, his clothing more elegant. The muscles beneath his tunic were pronounced and not earned easily. She interpreted his expression as offense at being dismissed, but he checked his anger.

"The clothes you brought are being cleaned and dried. They will be returned to you. Should you require anything else, please permit me to fulfill your every wish. The massages of Ecbatana are famous."

Cimree's eyes widened at the offer, but she shook her head.

Khaf bowed and then hurried up the steps. Trailing his departing form was that woody smell that made Cimree's nose twitch in a pleasing way.

"You don't like him," Cimree said, slowly turning her attention back to Azra. She started up the steps, and he followed her.

"I stopped him from intruding on your bath," Azra said. "So you're right. I don't like him. He's a courtier."

"What does that mean?"

"They are the spies of royal courts," Azra said. They reached the top of the stairs, and she continued to her private room. In addition to the robes, she'd also been provided a set of sandals—the name they'd given as the footwear she'd seen so many wearing in the souk—but she carried these in her hand, not liking the slapping noise they made when she walked.

"They're spying on us, then?"

"Naturally. This is Ecbatana. They used angel sworn to spy on us from a distance. They set this up deliberately. This is not how normal visitors are greeted."

"Is this a trap?"

"Of course it is. A decadent one, but a trap."

Cimree bit her lower lip. "Can you get us out of it?"

Azra snorted. "That won't be a problem. There aren't just baths but also tunnels beneath the entire city."

They arrived at Cimree's room, and she motioned for Azra to join her inside. She felt a suppressed emotion from him through the bond they shared, but he followed her. Once he had closed the door behind them, he offered the pouch with the seed to her.

"I want you to protect it for now," she said in a low voice. If their hosts found out they had a seed from the Gallows Tree with them, she imagined the hospitality would end rather abruptly.

Azra nodded. He was standing close to her so their voices wouldn't carry. "I will."

"I'm worried about Trinati," Cimree said next.

"You should be."

"What do you think she's going to do?"

"What do *you* think?" he asked instead of answering.

"She's going to try and take advantage of the situation. Both to reclaim leadership of the angel sworn and possibly to rule these people as well. They're looking for a tyrant as a queen. She'd be good at it."

Azra gave her a knowing smile. "She's going to ask for the Tanaquil medallion. For herself."

Cimree hadn't even thought of that, but she suspected immediately that Azra was right. He had a gift for discerning people's intentions, for knowing their intentions maybe even before they did.

"Oh," she whispered. "Can she take it?"

"Yes," Azra said. "But it requires both of us. It was grafted to you and then given to me. She can take the amulet from me by force. Well, she can try. But she'd need you to be able to release me from it. If she put it on, then you'd have absolute control over her. And she wouldn't allow that."

"Isn't it also risky for her? I've felt the magic influencing me. I've fought against its urges."

"Most of the time," he said, reminding her of the time she'd almost kissed him.

She felt her cheeks begin to flush.

"Neither of us can release the medallion," Azra said. "We need Trinati to do that. If she seeks to become the tyrant queen, then having it would make her rise unstoppable. It's best if we warn the court and then leave before things get too complicated."

"I agree. I think I should meet with her and try and see what she's planning."

"She won't tell you her plans," Azra said, his brow wrinkling.

"You don't think I'm capable of tricking her?"

"No."

Cimree felt annoyed at how quickly he answered her. "I'd like to try anyway. We came here to warn them of the gévaudan. We can do that tonight at the banquet and then leave tomorrow morning. If she's going to try and pull a ruse, then I'd rather give her less time."

"Another option is we just leave right now. The two of us."

"I'd like my clothes back. And that feels underhanded."

He snorted.

She could tell it was directed at her lack of guile, but having all her memories stripped away had instilled her decision-making with an innocent naivete. His reaction made her furious.

He didn't seem to mind. "Face her now or face her on better ground. Either way, we're going to need to confront her. It might be for the best if you and I remain separated. I know how to stay out of sight."

She was grateful he was on her side. She touched his arm and felt him tighten inside when she did.

"Thank you," she said. "If I need you, I'll try to communicate that through the medallion."

Azra nodded and then slipped out of her room, and she watched him until he disappeared around a corner.

CIMREE WAITED to give Azra time to leave and for her clothes to be dried. When she put her tunic and trews back on, she felt like herself again. Having a dagger at her hip was comforting, and she was grateful for all the training she'd done with Azra during their journey. Her skills in fighting and grappling had increased, and that gave her more self-confidence.

When she reached Trinati's room, she found the angel sworn attended by servants who were using some sort of stone on Trinati's toenails. Trinati wore one of the robes they'd been given for bathing, and she looked very different without the dirt-stained armor and with a clean face and styled hair. Cimree had always felt a little envious of Trinati's height, beauty, and martial abilities.

Trinati noticed Cimree's arrival and cocked an eyebrow. "Where is Azra? He vanished a few hours ago."

"I don't know where he went," Cimree answered, feeling like she'd been outmaneuvered almost immediately.

"You know where he is because of the medallion. Summon him. I'd like to talk to him."

"Maybe we could have a talk first," Cimree said, trying to stifle her anger.

Trinati gave a dismissing gesture to the servant girls who bowed meekly and left the two of them alone.

"Well? What did you want to say to me?" Trinati asked, her eyes showing nothing.

"We came here to warn the Ecbatanans," Cimree said. "Do you still intend to?"

"Yes. During the feast tonight. That seemed the most appropriate time. Do you agree?"

"I think telling them tonight would be perfect. And then we can go tomorrow."

Trinati frowned. "Why the rush? We just got here. We could use some rest and supplies. I thought we should bring the others from the ravine and stay here for a few days."

"I think we should leave tomorrow," Cimree said.

"Let me guess. Azra's warned you that I'm intending to usurp control."

"I didn't need Azra to figure that out," Cimree shot back.

"Cimree. We both knew that things would have to change. You are not capable of leading our people. You care too much about feelings. And if I'm being candid, they won't trust you, especially knowing that the Queen Mother didn't trust you. I propose we give them a choice. We can stay here in Ecbatana and defend ourselves against the creatures who sought to destroy us. Or those who wish can follow you and Azra to some forsaken land and hide forever in caves. Let them decide who to follow. There was only one choice before."

Cimree's stomach continued to clench with uneasiness. "Azra has the seed."

"Of course he does. He's not reckless enough to leave it with you. It was stolen from *me* if you recall. I would like it back. And the medallion too. That doesn't belong to you either."

"Well, I never wanted it. And now you want it to force the king to choose you."

Trinati gave her a slight shrug. "It makes the most sense, Cimree. And Azra kept knowledge of this to himself," she replied, gesturing to the beautiful decorations in the lavish room. There were couches and an enormous bed with diaphanous curtains. Bowls of fresh fruit lay on a glass table. "He knew what would happen if we came here."

"Why don't we agree to part ways now, then," Cimree said, feeling a bitter taste in her mouth.

"Summon Azra and give me the seed and the amulet, and you're welcome to go. You've seen the fortifications. Wegner will be so impressed and useful here. He'll want to stay. Trust me on this. So will the other angel sworn. You take that little family from the lake country. I think that's perfectly reasonable."

Cimree took a step closer when she really felt like running. "You remember the part of the story where they kill the tyrant queen. Don't you?"

Trinati's leg was still on the cushioned pedestal where the servant had been kneeling. She pulled her leg back and set her feet on the ground, rising to her full height to look down her nose at Cimree.

Cimree didn't retreat, although she felt intimidated. Azra was the only person that Trinati had not been able to defeat. No one had defeated him.

"Yes, Cimree. I remembered that part. Which is why I need the medallion. I know you sent Azra away, or he ran away, to keep me from just taking it. Clever move. But I don't think he'll leave Ecbatana without *you*. Will he?"

Then, with a hint of a triumphant smile, Trinati turned her back on Cimree and walked over to a stand holding a shimmering garment that must have come from the souk. She glided her hand across the fabric. "I sent Odeon to bring the others here. Did Azra predict that?"

SEVEN
THE HONORED FEAST

Cimree was still fuming at the reversal of events when Khaf knocked at the door to her chamber. Thankfully, Azra had foreseen Trinati's design and had slipped away, but Cimree wondered if it was already too late. Coming to Ecbatana had been her decision, after all, and she was forced to deal with the ramifications.

She opened the door, and the handsome courtier gave a little bow. "It is time to make our way to the inner city for the feast. Lord Roque was keen that all of you attend. Will you come?"

Was she really being given a choice? Did the pleasantness and servility merely mask that they were all actually prisoners? She felt it wise to pretend that nothing was wrong.

"I look forward to it," Cimree said, adopting a smile as her own mask. She moved to leave her room.

Khaf began walking alongside her.

"One of your party is missing," Khaf said as they walked. "The male companion you had. Questions will be asked why he did not come."

Cimree noticed his probing look and kept hers void of reaction. "Oh? I'm sure he'll show up. He must have gone to the souk."

She read polite disbelief in Khaf's reaction to her words. "Ah. Very well. The souk has its many charms. There are fabrics of every kind, including the soft wool your people seem to prefer." His gaze glided over her attire as he said this, and Cimree flushed. "Fruits from distant lands. Many grow on trees here in Ecbatana as we've learned the arts of cultivation from the best growers in all the world."

There it was again, a subtle probing about fruits and trees. "Where are these wondrous trees?"

"Deeper within the city, of course. To protect them. Some fruit have magical qualities."

"Such as?" She knew he was trying to lure information from her like Azra lured fish into his traps. Why not learn from him what he knew?

"Many different kinds," he said. "Gathered over the years. One can cause flames to spurt from the hands. Another can cause one to float into the air like a whippoorwill."

"You can fly?"

"Well, not as elegantly as the angel sworn with your wands," he said demurely. "We can only mimic your wondrous talents. Some of the fruit are quite deadly. Beware the coptic fruit. It will turn you into stone if you swallow it. Forever." He leaned toward her with a mischievous smile.

"I should like to avoid that one, then. How would I recognize it?"

"Have you seen a persimmon? It most resembles that, but the rind is very tough and tastes like salt. Spit it out at once."

Was it a warning or a threat?

"I've never had persimmon before. That fruit does not grow in the mountains where I'm from."

"I shall bring you one during the feast. A persimmon, not the coptic fruit."

They reached the entrance to the mansion, and she found their horses had been gathered again with additional ones. It wasn't quite midnight yet, judging by the stars, but the burning torches in the courtyard exposed the beasts and splayed light on the walls. Khaf went to the same beast they'd rode into the city on and examined the flanks, the girth straps, the bridle. In short order, Trinati appeared, wearing an outfit that Cimree had seen in her room earlier. It hugged her body and exposed her shoulders and the upper part of her breasts. She did not have her sword, but a long dagger was strapped to her hip. The fashion was like that of the women Cimree had seen with long skirts that were slit high up the leg, and the fabric was the same silken texture with a golden fringe and a jeweled girdle. A round stone was set about navel height, and the accompanying arm bands had fabric that draped down past her wrists. She looked stunning, her eyes smeared with a purple pigment. Her golden tresses were loose. Cimree felt her own stomach twist with envy at Trinati's eye-catching beauty. Her distaff was tucked into the girdle.

The other angel sworn were also dressed in the fashion of Ecbatana. Cimree discovered she was the only one who wasn't, and it made her feel foolish for rejecting the previous offer of a change of garment. But if she had worn such a thing as Trinati did, it would have exposed the whorl pattern on her breastbone, and that would have attracted notice and questions she didn't want to answer.

Khaf mounted the horse first and then leaned down, extending his arm to her with a gracious smile. She gripped his forearm as he did hers, and he easily pulled her up into the saddle behind him. Riding close behind him, she could smell his scent again and wondered what it was.

"Are you comfortable?" he asked softly, glancing back at her.

She nodded with a light smile that faded as soon as he turned away.

Trinati climbed after her courtier, and the slit in the dress exposed much of her legs. This style of clothing was so different from the simple garments each person in Clairvaux made for themselves. And Cimree imagined that the Queen Mother wouldn't have approved of such decadence nor the showing of so much skin.

They rode through the darkened streets, which were quiet even with songs in the air and the noises of dining. Cimree's stomach gnawed at her with hunger since she wasn't used to eating so late. They passed through another gated arch, made of ocher stone. The outer walls were white, then black, then red, then blue, then ocher. She could not see the sentries patrolling the ramparts, but she felt like they were being observed.

Azra was far away. Still within the city but back toward another wall, probably the one by the souk. She wasn't sure she could have found him if she'd tried because the walls would have blocked her passage. But she was relieved he wasn't heading to the feast.

There were fewer buildings within the ocher-walled portion of the city but many, many gardens. Fences blocked access to the various trees and shrubs that were growing there.

"That is Lord Felaket's manor," Khaf murmured, nodding as they passed one of the gates. "He's very powerful. And dangerous. Beware any invitations from him."

Why had he told her that? She made no response, and he fell quiet again.

She sensed the presence of serpents in some of the gardens they passed, hanging from tree branches. Some were hunting rodents, others, birds. Her consciousness touched theirs, and she knew that many had paused their hunting to observe her passing with interest. Some of the snakes were small, but one was a very long and fat thing that constricted its prey after dropping down onto it. It wasn't hunting because it had already eaten an entire goat, which Cimree thought wondrous and strange.

They rode languidly down a path that led to a gleaming silver wall. The wall glimmered in the torchlight and made her mouth part in awe. The gate was guarded by dozens of warriors, several of whom pulled open the vast door as they approached. She saw some of the warriors had bluish flames wreathing their hands as they watched the angel sworn approach.

"Do you notice the flame?" Khaf whispered to her. "The Guardians of the Silver Gate have access to the fruit I mentioned. They defend the chief advisors and the king's concubines."

"The king has concubines?" That notion sounded unimaginable to her. One man laying claim to multiple women? It was shocking.

"Many. But the tyrant queen is not chosen from among them. They serve his pleasure. The tyrant queen rules."

They passed through the gates. Cimree noted that the torches on the walls were burning not with fire, but some sort of pitch that blazed white-hot and illuminated the grounds as if it were daylight. The brilliance of that inner area was intense and she found herself squinting at the torches, wondering what they were burning to make them so bright.

Soon they arrived at Roque's palace, which made their mansion seem like a humble cottage in comparison. They were greeted by rows of servants and warriors who bowed in respect. Khaf slid off the saddle first. She was about to swing her leg over, but Khaf put his hand on her upper thigh to stop her. He gripped her hips, hoisted her, and helped her land on the ground. She felt a flip in her stomach and quickly removed her hands from where they rested on his muscled shoulders.

He offered his arm, as the other courtiers did to their charges, and they escorted the angel sworn into the palace. The smells of the feast clashed with her other senses. Everything had a fruity smell to it, even the meats. Her stomach gurgled and she pressed her hand to it, catching a little smile from Khaf, who must have heard.

"Welcome, honored guests!" Roque announced, his turban

gone. He wore a fanciful robe glittering with gems. Bracelets, rings, necklaces showing his wealth and station.

They were escorted to a long table, low to the ground, where they were seated on cushions instead of chairs. Khaf escorted Cimree to hers. She noticed him whisper to one of the serving girls before seating himself next to her.

"May you enjoy a respite from your wanderings," Roque said as he took his seat at the head of the table, raising a goblet made of gold and jewels. "You honor us with your presence. To the immortal angel sworn!" There were some others at the feast, already gathered, whom Cimree didn't recognize, but she imagined they were notables in Ecbatana who had earned the right to be there to greet the guests.

Trinati then sat down on a cushion to Roque's left, cross-legged, her posture straight. The servants began bringing trays of a variety of dishes. Gluttony was a sin among the angel sworn, and Cimree noted immediately that Trinati and the others ate sparingly despite being offered so much. She remembered the ravenous hunger that Azra and Odeon had exhibited when they'd partaken of the fruit of the Gallows Tree. The age-reversing fruit caused an implacable appetite while the body replenished itself.

The angel sworn around her ate and conversed with their hosts, but Cimree felt like being quiet. She had always felt uncomfortable in crowds, but Trinati seemed at ease. One of them stood out to her, a disgruntled looking noble with a trim beard who appeared to be scolding a servant girl for the way she was holding her tray to him. Cimree took note of him as well as an instant dislike.

"That is Lord Felaket," Khaf whispered near her ear, causing her to jump in surprise.

Cimree startled at how close he'd come without her noticing. When she turned her face to look at him, he gestured to another serving girl who had come in his wake.

"A persimmon," The serving girl offered a little plate with a dusky-hued fruit on it. Its stem protruded from a four-point star on the top, and the body resembled a tomato in color. It was about the size of an apple.

Cimree took the fruit and looked at it suspiciously.

She thought Khaf gestured for her to give it to him, but to her consternation, when she held it out, he leaned toward her and bit into one side of it. A little juice trickled into his beard, which he hastily wiped away. He chewed and swallowed it and then motioned at the dripping fruit in her hand. "It is safe," he said, looking at her with smiling eyes she wasn't sure she could trust.

Cimree quickly glanced away and took a little nibble from it. It was very sweet, surprisingly so, but there was something about it that made her mouth pucker. A hint of tartness too.

"It is a new taste to me," she said.

"You are very reserved, Cimree." His brows knitted together as he studied her.

"I prefer the quiet," she answered shyly. She had tried to be more agreeable among others. She'd found serving other people and working hard had made conversations easier.

"There is much pleasure in silence." Then he stopped talking and began to eat the offered food that servants continuously carried around the long table to share with them.

"If I might suggest another name?" Khaf said after a lengthy pause.

"Why do I need another name?"

"It's just a thought. The king has asked to meet you especially. Your name would not do you the justice your beauty deserves."

Cimree flushed at the compliment but felt her throat tighten with dread. "The king?"

"You are angel sworn. Surely that denotes the highest of honors. He also prefers...quiet. I would suggest the name Cazibe."

"What does it mean?" she asked.

"It means *fascination*."

Cimree gazed at the man sitting next to her and wondered if

Khaf was truly his name, but before she could ask, her attention was drawn to the head of the table.

"Lord Roque, we have brought information in exchange for your hospitality," Trinati said, projecting her voice. "Have any of your caravans come from our mountains yet? Have you encountered the dangers that destroyed our lands?"

Cimree looked at Lord Roque as he handed his goblet to a servant who seemed only to be in charge of holding his particular cup. "We have, my lady. Entire caravans have been destroyed by unearthly creatures. Tell me this if you will. What do you know of the golem?"

EIGHT
METAMORPHISTRY

"Agolem is an unfinished creation," Trinati said, her eyes wide with concern. "They are abominations. They are attempts by the unholy to usurp the Oldknow's power to create. But golems have no soul."

Lord Roque listened to her words thoughtfully, his intense gaze showing his deep interest. "Did not the angel sworn learn to create from the Oldknow? Did the Queen Mother make this golem?"

"No," Trinati said decisively. "I am her archangel. She would never use her power to conjure such a thing. We encountered it first at our fortress Montheron. It has overthrown that fortress and Clairvaux. What do you know of it, Lord Roque?"

The nobleman leaned forward. "There are some among us who practice a form of magic called metamorphistry. It is different from the magic of the angel sworn."

"In what way?" Trinati asked, her brow wrinkled with suspicion.

"Your magic, as I understand from our Wizrs, is a temporary borrowing. A unity with another creation, wherein your powers are lent to you for a time and purpose. Only someone sworn to the Queen Mother is given a grafting wand and can perform this bond. Is my understanding...simple as it may be...reasonably accurate?"

"It is sufficient. Without the oath, the grafting magic will not work."

"Ah. Well then. The magic of our Wizrs can distort a creature and transform it into another kind. A serpent turning into a bird. And then back again. It was an attempt to replicate the power your people wield so powerfully. The transformation has always been temporary. It is also involuntary. The creature impacted cannot reject it."

Cimree felt unsettled by such magic. What she'd seen and experienced made her believe such magic should be forbidden.

"As I mentioned"—Lord Roque continued—"temporary. Until now."

"Can it turn a man into a wolf?" Trinati asked.

Horror at what Roque was telling them made Cimree's stomach clench uncomfortably. Was Ecbatana the source of the evil that had destroyed her valley? She glanced at Khaf and saw his eyes fixed on Roque with an intense expression that seemed worried.

"Not that I know of. We don't know all its capabilities," Roque said. "This form of magic was done in secret. Hidden from the eyes of others."

"And yet you have a knowledge of it, Lord Roque," Trinati said.

He nodded his head. "For generations, Ecbatana was under the thrall of a revenant who wielded this power. Though we are unsure if it was Asmodeus himself or one of his offspring."

Asmodeus was the name of the fallen angel who transformed into a serpent and tempted the First Man into eating the fruit of knowledge. The being had many names and titles. Asmodeus was merely one of them. The being deceived and manipulated mortal kind into all deeds depraved. The angel sworn rarely spoke the name aloud, for speaking it could summon him. Cimree felt a shiver go through her body and a feeling of foreboding lodged in her heart.

"Do not say that name," Trinati rebuked harshly.

"I repent," Lord Roque said. "Ecbatana was and has always been a lychgate. But it is no longer. The revenant is gone now. We are free of its malevolence at long last. But instead there is this creature, this golem. It was first seen coming from the silver walls and fleeing to the ocher, the blue, the crimson. Our defenders shot at it with arrows, but the arrows could not kill it. It scrabbled like some giant spider. It ravaged the souk, causing terror among all who beheld it. It transformed as it fled, taking new shapes constantly. And then it climbed the white wall and ran off into the lone and dreary world. Never to return."

"When did this happen?" Trinati asked, her eyes flashing with fury.

Lord Roque opened his palms placatingly. "Around two years ago. That is the same time that the revenant stopped tormenting us, though a revenant cannot be killed save one way. A revenant's life force is pent up in one of its bones, which it hides. Usually it is a small bone, a finger bone, for a member must be sacrificed to produce such an evil spell. That bone is carefully hidden. We know not where it is, though we have looked for it. It could be anywhere in Ecbatana. That means the revenant can still regenerate itself and return to dominate us again someday. Destroying that bone is the only way to kill it."

"Do you think the creation turned against its creator?" Trinati asked.

Lord Roque bowed his head meekly. "That may have happened. Or what if the golem *is* the reincarnation of the revenant but in a new form? We don't know. All we know is the revenant's last demand was to begin the next cycle of the tyrant queen. Our tradition holds that the king must choose a maiden and that she will rule over us. I implore you to let him meet your angel sworn and choose from among your maidens one who will rule Ecbatana."

"Has Ecbatana itself been attacked by any monsters?" Trinati asked.

"None, my lady. Our defenses are strong. No enemy has breached our walls since the foundations were laid. I've spoken to the king, and he wishes to interview the maidens of the angel sworn. All of them."

"We will consider this request in light of the new circumstances," Trinati said. "This golem destroyed our sacred valley. It has killed countless angel sworn. Can it be defeated?"

"A creation made can be unmade," Lord Roque said emphatically.

WHEN THE SOMBER FEAST ENDED, the guests of Ecbatana were delivered back to the manor house. The enthusiasm from earlier had been replaced with weariness and concern. Lord Roque's news had unsettled everyone. Khaf again slid off the saddle first to help Cimree dismount.

"May I speak with you?" he asked in a lowered voice.

Cimree lingered by the horse as the others dismounted and started toward the entrance. Servants had arrived to care for the beasts, but Khaf made a gesture, forestalling the one who approached them.

"Why did the angel sworn come to Ecbatana?" Khaf asked Cimree, though his eyes were fixed on Trinati.

"We came to warn you," Cimree said.

"And was your warning delivered tonight?"

"Yes."

He sighed. "Where were you going to go next?"

"That I can't tell you," Cimree answered. "But it is far away from here."

He reached out and touched her forearm, still looking away from her. "Take me with you."

She was shocked by his imploring tone. He quickly removed his hand and finally turned her way as he offered her his arm with a polite smile. Cimree took it, and she noticed as they walked away from the horse that Trinati was watching them closely with wary eyes.

Cimree was exhausted and anxious to get to bed. Khaf led her to the main hall and then stopped before reaching the other courtiers who were conversing in a group there.

"Do you require anything before you rest?" he asked her.

Cimree shook her head and released his arm. All the things they'd learned at the feast troubled her. Ecbatana was not as it seemed. And she wondered if what they'd been told was true or it was merely an attempt to coax them into staying. If she had her choice, she would leave Ecbatana in the morning. But Trinati had already summoned Wegner and the rest of the refugees. That caused some anxiety since it would make leaving more difficult since the others hadn't arrived yet.

She left Khaf and proceeded to her own chamber. The bedsheets had been turned down by the servants, and a small brazier of warming stones had been provided. She could sense Azra was still far away within the city. He was keeping his distance, but she wished he were there so she could tell him what she'd learned.

"I want you to summon Azra," Trinati said from the door, startling her.

Cimree turned around. Trinati still had on the beautiful attire she'd worn to the feast and was leaning against the door. Her eyes were deadly serious.

"I don't think that would be wise," Cimree answered.

"He took the seed with him, didn't he," Trinati said in accusation.

Cimree kept her expression neutral and didn't reply.

"Your stubbornness may get us all killed."

"My stubbornness?" Cimree shot back.

"Do you want to become the tyrant queen?" Trinati demanded.

"No! I want to leave Ecbatana and go where we had planned. I want to give people a choice in what they do. You just want to manipulate everyone."

"We both want the same thing," Trinati said earnestly, coming closer. "We want to survive this."

"But we disagree on how best to do that."

"Then I must make you see reason."

"Maybe you should have thought about that before you turned everyone to your side," Cimree said in a low voice. "You want the medallion to win the king's favor. To guarantee you will succeed. You're afraid I'll use it in my favor. I'm not a simpleton, Trinati. It's more important to you to win."

"My object is not just triumphing over you," Trinati said coldly. "You are not fit to lead these people. I am. I have been trained for this during multiple lifespans. Ecbatana is a fortress that is stronger than Clairvaux. Our chief defense was our reputation. But a reputation means nothing against beasts that rage and destroy and infect others. What I've learned about Ecbatana so far proves that this is a better fortress. We should make our stand here, not in some faraway mountains."

"Yet Azra knew of Ecbatana and wanted to avoid it," Cimree pointed out.

"That's why I want to speak with him! To see if what we've learned changes his opinion of what to do. I do value his opinion."

"You may value it, but you value your own wisdom more. Like the rest of us, you know nothing about enticing a man. A man with concubines. Of all the knowledge and wisdom you've accumulated, you are woefully ignorant in this area. This is not our place. The Queen Mother taught us that men are subservient to our sex. And now you don't know what to do. You want the amulet because you're afraid of failure. Or are you more afraid of me succeeding and being the leader you cannot be?"

Her words had struck home. Had struck Trinati to the quick. Rage mottled Trinati's fair skin. She raised her hand as if she were going to smack Cimree's face.

Cimree took a defensive step backward, ready to repel the attack with a block that Azra had taught her. Was she about to fight Trinati? Truly?

Trinati lowered her hand slowly, her body trembling with suppressed rage. "You think you're being clever, but you're really an insignificant fool."

"I want to leave Ecbatana," Cimree said, "with all those who will go with me. Let them choose, Trinati. The Oldknow always defends our freedom to choose."

"Obedience is the first law of heaven," Trinati said. "And you've always been rebellious."

Something in the tone of her voice implied more. Cimree frowned.

"Don't you think it telling that your name means something awful in Ecbatanan?" Trinati said with disdain. "My escort said that it's a pejorative word. An insult in this society."

"I did not choose my name," Cimree said. "The Queen Mother did."

"I know," Trinati said, slyly. "And maybe she chose it to remember your past treachery."

Cimree felt a wriggle of guilt in her chest. For something she may have done in the past. "I have no memory of my past. It was stolen from me."

"Maybe your past is hinted at by your name," Trinati said. She turned and started to leave but paused. She didn't turn around. "Azra better be here by morning."

"Or you'll do what?" Cimree said hotly.

Trinati gave her a sidelong look that was full of fire. She said nothing further, leaving the room silently just as she'd arrived. The argument had caused a sour feeling in Cimree's already nervous stomach.

She'd never felt so alone. Or so unwanted.

NINE
SURVIVOR

Cimree was used to waking before sunrise, and even after the trouble she'd had falling asleep, she still awoke to the sound of birds. It was a variety of trills and song that were unfamiliar to her, and in that first moment of wakefulness, she'd forgotten that she was in Ecbatana, sleeping on a bed, instead of finding rest on a patch of hard earth. One bird was singing right outside the open window, and she sensed a snake nearby that hoped the bird would linger long enough for it to become its next meal.

She slid from the fine-twined sheets and when her bare feet touched the cool stone floor, she rose, stretched, and reached out from the bond for Azra. He was in a different part of the city from the previous night. She knew he could sense her emotions too, and although she'd gone to bed fearing Trinati's threat, she had tried to curb her fears and smother her worries. Since the room was spacious, she was able to perform her training exercises, a series of stances, gripping exercises, and handstand push-ups that Azra had coached her on in order to improve her strength and self-discipline. All angel sworn treated their bodies as sacred and strove to remain in good health and alert in mind.

During her practice regimen, the snake caught the bird.

By the time she had finished, she had worked up a sweat and an appetite. She took a towel and robe and went to the underground baths, found that she had them to herself, which probably meant she'd risen earlier than anyone else, and hurriedly cleaned herself. She donned her robe, took up the pile of clothes, and started back up the steps. Looking up at the landing, she found Khaf leaning against the wall at the top. She slowed, putting her hand into the bundle she carried until she found the hilt of her dirk.

"The other angel sworn do not like you," Khaf said in a low voice. "You are a pariah."

"Not exactly," Cimree answered, confused by the statement. Sensing that Khaf's intention wasn't to threaten her, she released the dirk and pulled her robe tighter to ensure the marks on her chest weren't showing.

"The king wishes to meet *all* the maidens," Khaf said. "He would not be pleased if you were withheld. Do you think it is Trinati's intention to prevent you from seeing him?"

"I've no idea," Cimree said. "But I don't think so." She gazed past him and saw that they were alone. She didn't even hear the noise of servants nearby. Looking him in the eye, she asked, "Why are you asking?"

"You are not like the others, and I'm trying to figure out why."

"So you can report back to Lord Roque?"

He shook his head. "No. I follow my own counsel in this matter."

"What matter?"

He glanced down the corridor, pitching his voice even lower. "I shouldn't tell you this. A survivor from a caravan arrived during the night. They were attacked by wolves who weren't interested in horseflesh. The wolves killed everyone except this one man who managed to escape them on horseback because he fled *before* the attack. If he hadn't, we would have no report of it."

Cimree's stomach sank. "That is how it started."

Khaf looked at her with deep interest. "I think the survivor had it right. To flee in advance. The dark friend of yours. The angry one. Has he already fled?"

"He's still in Ecbatana."

"How do you know this? We have others watching for him. No one has seen him."

Cimree smiled. "Because he does not want to be seen. But he's here."

"Are you sure?"

"Very sure."

"I can help you get out of the city," Khaf said. "But I wish to leave with you."

She didn't sense any dishonesty from him, nothing that her connection with the Tanaquil amulet might have revealed. His sharing of information was useful, and if he was sincere, she would gladly accept his help. "They are bringing the others from our group to Ecbatana. Can you tell me when they arrive? Some of them are loyal to me. And I would not wish to abandon them."

Khaf scrutinized her and then nodded. "I will keep you informed, Cazibe."

"That is not my name," Cimree said.

"It suits you better," Khaf said with interested eyes. "May I advise you on something else?"

"You may," Cimree said.

"The king has a discerning eye, and you have a pretty face. If you go to him dressed as you have so far, he will take that as an affront. A deliberate insult. Is that your wish?"

Cimree shook her head, but she'd already seen that the style of dress that the women of Ecbatana wore would not conceal the markings that the magic had stained her with.

"It would take very little to assuage the king's feelings on the matter. If you do not wish to be perceived as acting above a station, I can provide a silk garment suitable for the more humble class. Would you like me to acquire one for you? I do not know when the king will summon you for an interview."

If the king saw the whorl pattern on Cimree's chest, it would only evoke more questions that she'd rather not answer. How should she respond? Should she deliberately insult the king by keeping her clothes the humble fare of Clairvaux?

"You may get me something." She decided to go along with the idea.

"I think red would suit you."

"I don't really care," Cimree said. "But do you have any simple necklaces made of beads or cheap stones? Nothing extravagant, but enough to cover up here." She patted the upper part of her chest and her robe slipped just a little.

He gazed at her and then his eyes widened with surprise. The sudden transformation showed fear. "Ah. I hadn't...noticed before."

"Have you seen this before?" She parted her robe slightly, intrigued by his response.

"That is the marking of a hetaera," he said guardedly.

Cimree wrinkled her brow in confusion. "A what?"

"A hetaera, a *fahişe*. I was not expecting one to come from such an august place. Now I understand. I can provide suitable garments for you, Cazibe."

She did not understand what he had called her or what those terms meant, but it was clear that he knew about the markings, and there was history she could learn if she could find a way to ask the right questions.

"Thank you, Khaf," she said, touching his arm.

He recoiled from her touch, but then corrected his lapse instantly and gave her an apologetic smile. He was about to leave, so she tightened her grip on his sleeve. He looked at her worriedly, as if she were a snake poised to strike.

"The survivor of the caravan. Inspect him for bite marks. If they have a silvery cast to them, like what happens to the skin after it is burned, then he is a danger to Ecbatana. He will become a wolf and spread the sickness to others. There is a cure for it. But please check to see if he is ill. We call those wolves gévaudan."

She did not reveal more about the cure. That wouldn't be possible until the others arrived with Chrysopoeia.

"Thank you for that information," Khaf said, bowing in respect. "I will inform Lord Roque at once."

And she suspected that he would reveal more to Lord Roque as well.

BREAKFAST WAS an assortment of interesting and delicious fruits that Cimree had never tasted before. She did recognize the persimmons, though, which Khaf had brought her a taste of at the feast. The variety of colors and shapes were interesting: one with a stringy yellow flesh and incredibly sweet flavor, others with mild sweetness and scooped into little balls of light green, orange, and deep pink. A variety of eggs was also on display, one of which was so huge it would have fed them all, and she wondered at the size of the bird that must have laid that monstrosity.

She had been enjoying tasting them all, by herself, when several angel sworn all descended on the dining room at once. They wore the attire of Clairvaux, but they did not come to eat. They positioned themselves at the door leading in and at the other leading to the servants' hall. They totaled six, all ones she had seen fawn over Trinati. They said nothing about the display of fruit. They looked at her coldly, with accusing eyes.

Cimree's appetite withered, and she pushed her chair from the table and rose, leaving some uneaten fruit behind. As she started toward the door, three barred the way. A glance backward and she saw the other three starting to approach from behind. She recognized the one on the left as Salisha, the one who was eager for Trinati to rule Ecbatana.

Six angel sworn against her. In all her training with Azra, she hadn't faced as dire a situation before. Her instincts warned her to flee, but they were blocking the way deliberately.

Trinati had warned her. For some reason, Cimree had felt that the consequence would be delivered in person. But no, Trinati would not do this herself.

"Stand aside," Cimree said and was embarrassed when she heard the fear in her own voice.

"You are not following the rules," said one of them, a female. It was Angheld, one of the warriors who had come with them from Clairvaux. "And there are consequences when we don't...follow... rules."

Cimree knew she could probably injure two of them if she struck quick and hard. But there would be four more, and she would be helpless against that many.

Talking to them would be useless. And waiting until she was totally surrounded would be foolish.

She looked Angheld in the eye and summoned the power of the Tanaquil amulet. She knew that Azra would be aware of her, would be able to sense her feelings and actions intently. That using the magic might even spur him to return to her, but she wouldn't let herself become a victim of their spite or their intimidation. With the amulet, she unleashed fear on them and not just any fear. She unleashed the blind terror caused by the Fear Liath. Since she and Azra had faced it near the Gallows Tree, she knew firsthand what that terror was like and how the medallion had subdued it. She pulled that fear from her memory and used it.

The aggression of the three in front of her wilted. Their jaws dropped, and Angheld and another broke and ran, while the third one just dropped to her knees gibbering in terror as if she were about to die. Cimree turned and blasted the three behind her with the same fear. Two of them fled toward the servants' door. Only Salisha didn't bolt or cower. Instead, she grabbed the hilt of her blade, her eyes wide with terror, fury, or both. Her time in the Long Patrol must have inured her to the reign of her emotions.

Cimree stepped forward to close the distance just as the blade cleared the scabbard on her hip. It was a mirror blade. Cimree didn't draw her dirk. She grabbed her foe's tunic, pulled, and head-butted her in the nose as hard as she could. Then grabbing the warrior's wrist above the sword hilt, she swiveled around, hefted the angel sworn onto her back, and then slammed her onto the nearest table, scattering fruit and eggs in all directions.

Cimree's forehead smarted from the blow, but she was grateful for Azra's training and how efficiently it had rendered the other on her back. The mirror blade clanked onto the floor, and Cimree picked it up and took it with her, depriving the other woman of her main weapon. She saw blood gushing from Salisha's broken nose, dribbling down her neck.

Cimree stormed out of the dining hall and the mess she'd left behind. She passed a mirror on the wall and saw glowing silver eyes looking back as she glanced at it. The rage she felt was terrible.

She started for Trinati's room, still clenching the hilt of the mirror blade.

Ten

Strange Ways

It shouldn't have surprised Cimree that Trinati wasn't in her room. It did make her wonder whether the others had acted on their own or if Trinati's absence meant something else. So she went back to her own room, hid the mirror blade beneath the mattress of her bed, and climbed up to the window to lower herself out the other side. The snake had finished gorging on the bird and was coiled in a nook out of the way.

Cimree explored the grounds of the mansion, finding a pretty little garden with decorative fountains, stone benches, and a variety of fruit trees. Her fury at the others for trying to intimidate her began to ebb as she walked. Using the magic of the amulet always drained her. When she'd used it against the Fear Liath, it had wiped her out completely and she'd fainted. How easily it had helped against the angel sworn. Only one had possessed the strength of mind to fight against her fear. Cimree even felt a little guilty for possibly breaking the woman's nose. Would it be right to go back and attend to her? No. If the other angel sworn were going to treat Cimree like an outcast, they didn't deserve the help.

After she had been alone in the garden for at least an hour, sitting on a stone bench, she sensed Azra leaving Ecbatana, traveling at great speed. He'd clearly used his distaff to graft with a bird that could hasten his journey. Knowing he had left didn't worry her. No, it made her frustrated because she wanted to know why he'd left. She would have rather gone with him. Even though he could be thoughtless and unfeeling, their bond through the medallion gave them a deeper trust in one another. There was no dissembling between them—it just wasn't possible.

She sensed another snake watching her from a fruit tree and saw it was just a tiny one, hidden among the boughs and waiting for prey to come to it. She wished her affinity were for another kind of creature. Snakes were universally loathed and feared, reclusive creatures by nature. But wasn't she also like that?

The sound of approaching steps caused her to turn as Trinati approached on the garden path. She was wearing those native shoes and the flat part was especially noisy on the gravel path. Trinati again wore Ecbatanan garb, with open shoulders and a deep bodice, which made her look devastatingly beautiful. Trinati approached the bench with a haughty look.

"Where is Salisha's mirror blade?" Trinati demanded.

"Did she misplace it?" Cimree countered, feigning innocence.

Trinati's eyes shone with anger. "Don't play games, Cimree."

"Six against one is hardly game playing."

"You broke Salisha's nose. She's disfigured."

"Maybe she'll leave me alone next time," Cimree said, squelching the feeling of guilt that began to writhe inside her.

Trinati stepped closer.

"Careful, Trinati," Cimree warned. "I'm not afraid of you either."

"I know how the Tanaquil amulet feels. I've trained against it. My emotions aren't as corruptible as the others. Now, where is Azra?"

"He's left Ecbatana," Cimree said and watched with satisfaction as Trinati startled.

"Why?"

"I don't know. We haven't spoken since before the feast. And you don't have a garrison of angel sworn to send after him this time."

"You infuriate me. Your eyes aren't glowing, so you're doing this on your own power."

"Our personalities have always been opposed," Cimree said. "You are the one who betrayed me."

"Oh? I was trying to help lead us away from Clairvaux and Azra attacked *me*. Stole the seed from *me*."

"Lower your voice. You don't want to be overheard."

"The birds are my eyes, Cimree. I have better vision. We're alone. You've been pretending to lead, but now that you no longer have the upper hand, are you surprised I decided to change the terms? We don't need to be enemies. Help me become the tyrant queen, and you will benefit."

"Why should I help you when I think you're making a mistake by staying?"

"Look around you!" Trinati said impatiently. "Have you noticed how many fruit trees grow here? The climate is perfect for it, even more so than Clairvaux. We could grow another Gallows Tree here. I think we'd be safe here from the golem and its foul creatures."

"We haven't been here that long," Cimree replied. "And so quickly you've decided it is safe? Azra doesn't trust the Ecbatanans."

"Azra doesn't trust anyone."

"Maybe there's a good reason. Why not go on to Tirich Mir as we planned? Let us compare it with this place. If this is a better option, we can come back."

"They'll have chosen the tyrant queen by then. We'll have missed our chance."

"Missed *your* chance. I think you are too keen to control everything and everyone."

Trinati bared her teeth in rage, but she reined in her feelings in an obvious effort to look more conciliatory. "That's not true."

"You were chosen to be the Queen Mother's archangel. You clearly worked hard to earn it. But you've always coerced others into doing what you want them to do, just as she did. People resent that, Trinati."

"So you think coddling people's feelings is a better approach?"

"No. I'm still learning because what I knew was stripped away from me. I feel as if that was done without my consent. You worked so hard to earn your authority. Now you want to try and force your will on others. You can't abide the thought of failing, but you need to realize it may happen regardless. Using the amulet to toy with the king's emotions will not help you win his heart."

Trinati wrinkled her brow. "I don't want to win his heart. I swore a vow of celibacy. I am going to reestablish what we had in Clairvaux."

"Then you've learned nothing from our failure there."

"We didn't fail! We didn't have enough time!"

Trinati's sensitivity to failure was her weakness. It might be a weakness even greater than her pride. Cimree shook her head.

"The king wants to meet with me this afternoon," Trinati said, lowering her voice. She sounded worried. "You can summon Azra back here. You can *make* him come."

"I can. But I won't."

HUNGER EVENTUALLY DROVE Cimree back inside the mansion. She could smell cooked meat, and it made her stomach growl. Azra was still away from Ecbatana, but it felt like he was coming back at a slower pace. She'd deduced that he had gone to find where the rest of the refugees were. Maybe even to confront Captain Odeon about his motives in sneaking away to get them. There was no invitation to a feast, so they relied on the servants in the mansion to provide for them. As Cimree entered the dining area, the conversations quieted to whispers. Salisha's nose was decidedly crooked and bruised. And very swollen. She glared at Cimree with open hostility.

Cimree served herself a plate and was going to take it back to her room to eat when Trinati called out to her.

"Stay, Cimree. I was just going to tell them about the meeting I had with the king of Ecbatana. He will meet with you all, so you might want to be prepared."

Cimree nodded and sat away from the others. Salisha looked like she was about to cry out of frustration and fury. A damaged face was clearly a grievance to her. But it was her own fault.

The meat was similar to farm chickens, but it had a different and unique flavor and not just because of the spices. Its sweetness reminded her of one of the fruits she'd had earlier. She'd taken a helping of other greens with pomegranate seeds and an oily sauce mixed in.

"What's he like?" asked one of the angel sworn who had attacked Cimree earlier that day.

"His name is Diyako, and his family has ruled Ecbatana for several generations. He's young. I would guess around thirty years of age. Smartly dressed in the Ecbatanan fashion, and his clothing shows his status. A handsome face. Hair is fairer than I expected, not dark like his countrymen. Eyes the color of Lake Beatriz. And he's charming. I sensed he spoke carefully and deliberately. He asked many questions and showed he listened with his eyes and his posture."

So far, he sounded like a decent fellow. Cimree pursed her lips in surprise.

"What kind of questions did he ask?" Salisha wanted to know. Her voice sounded off because of her swollen nose.

"He knows a great deal about the angel sworn and our customs. Things he'd learned from tutors and teachers. I had to correct some of his misconceptions, but he appeared gracious and interested in learning more about us."

"Did he ask about the Gallows Tree?" another girl asked. The men, who would not be interviewed, were busy eating, but they listened in as well.

"He did. He was very curious what it tasted like, which is difficult to describe. But he did not probe about its powers or anything intrusive. We spent about an hour together in the forbidden gardens, and then he thanked me. Guards were nearby, always at the ready, but he looked oblivious to them. They watched me vigilantly. I was not permitted to bring any weapons in his presence."

"Of course. They don't want anyone to murder him," said another girl.

The confidence Trinati spoke with suggested to Cimree that the interview must have gone well.

Cimree listened in as Trinati continued to talk about the attentive king. Khaf entered discreetly and was at Cimree's side quickly. He squatted down near the pillow she sat on.

"Your information about the wolf bite was valuable, Cazibe. I relayed it to Lord Roque, and the fellow was summoned for an inspection. He was disrobed and thoroughly searched, and they found the silvery bite mark on his upper arm. He's being confined to a cage at present."

"A cage?"

"Menageries are common in Ecbatana. He's been provided food and wine and is being studied by court magicians. Sharing this knowledge has earned you the gratitude of Lord Roque. I also went to the souk today and chose some attire for you. It is in your room."

"Thank you," she said. Their private conversation had drawn Trinati's attention, as well as some of the others'.

When Khaf noticed the subtle interplay, he rose and bowed. "I bring tidings, although I did not wish to interrupt your lively conversation."

"What tidings?" Trinati asked, sounding curious and a little distrustful since Cimree had been spoken to first.

"A pack of savage wolves attacked the north gates this afternoon," Khaf said. "They were spotted by our guardians, and we were able to bar the gates and doors in time. Not a single stall in the souk was disrupted by the attack. The wolves are ranging around the city, but they cannot get inside. Our walls are too tall for them to breach. There is no concern among our citizens. We are safe here in Ecbatana. Enjoy your meal!" Khaf quickly departed.

"That was good news indeed," Trinati said, turning and giving Cimree a victorious smile.

As Khaf had relayed the news, she felt grateful to learn of it, but her stomach had instantly cramped with worry. Azra had not returned to Ecbatana yet. The other refugees were trapped outside the city. But Montheron had been an island. The wolves hadn't been able to get inside there either. The wolves had driven people there. And then the awful cat creatures, the grimalkin, had emerged and began killing from the inside. The ugly feeling in her stomach worsened, and she rubbed her abdomen nervously.

The urge to flee returned to her. Was it her affinity impacting her thoughts? Snakes fled when they encountered dangers.

Seven layers of walls protected Ecbatana. Cimree wondered if that would be enough when the people started to riot.

The Watchers came and destroyed the revenant and its unholy empire. They scattered its wealth and slew its servants who were curse-bound. They found its bones in a crypt deep underground. Yet the revenant was not dead. One bone was missing. The Watchers searched for it. They found it not. Men came to the tomb in the lychgate seeking the revenant's wisdom and power. They heeded its whispers. Until it rose up and smote the Watchers and scattered them.

— BOOK OF THE WATCHERS, THE TALE OF THE
FALLEN ANGELS

ELEVEN
CATACOMBS

In Cimree's dream, she was back in the valley of Clairvaux, kneeling in the herb gardens with Milena and listening to a choir of angel song as the dawn was greeted with music. It had been so long since she'd heard that hymn that she'd paused in her work, gazing at Milena with tender affection, knowing she was dead but that this must be a glimpse of the heavens to come.

"I miss you," Cimree said to her, suddenly blinded by the sunrise coming over the snow-caked mountain.

The pain in her eyes from the brightness made her awaken suddenly. For a moment she forgot where she was, in a mansion deep inside Ecbatana. The dream was still swirling inside her: the beautiful wildflowers of Clairvaux. The simple cottages. The steep mountains on each side of the valley. Herds of milch cows and sheep to be sheared. And all that beauty and tranquility were gone. She turned her head and saw the folded garment that Khaf had acquired for her, a dusky-red silk with gold fringe. Necklaces and jewels were in a box beneath it. She'd tried it on the night before, feeling the costume so strange—

Azra.

She sat up instantly, realizing that he was there at the mansion, down at the bathing pool. After tossing off the thin blanket, she hurriedly pulled on her boots and grabbed her belt and dirk. She was about to go to the door, but then realized it would look suspicious if she didn't bring the towel and robe, so she hastily tucked those under her arm and left.

It was obvious her speed would draw notice, so she slowed her step and tried not to appear so agitated. She went to the steps leading down to the baths where she could smell wet stone. Once she reached the doorway, she noticed another angel sworn was bathing in the pool, her robe and clothes on a wall bench made of stone. Cimree did not see Azra but she felt him. In fact, he was below her.

The other woman noticed her arrival and started with fear. She was one of the angel sworn who had been frightened away the previous day. With a glare, she finished her ablutions and then slipped on her robe and carried her clothes back up the steps, leaving Cimree to herself. That was one advantage to being a pariah.

Cimree waited, and when Azra didn't appear immediately, she sent a gentle nudge of command to him.

It surprised her when the top part of one bench wall lifted up. Azra appeared in the gap and beckoned her. She carried her bundle to him and saw steps leading down toward a glowing phosphorescence below. After she'd passed him on the steps, their bodies brushing together, he lowered the slab and then followed her down.

The steps were made of stone and led into the gloom. The phosphorescence came from a lichen of sorts clinging to the stone walls. She rubbed her palm against the stone, which felt gritty. Limestone?

When she saw him standing at the base of the steps, she set down the bundle and instinctively hugged him out of sheer relief.

"It's that bad, is it?" he said, giving her a timid pat on her back. He smirked at her when she pulled away.

"I've been worried about you and yes, things here are awful."

"I sensed what you did yesterday. I was glad you stood up for yourself. That you used the medallion and your skills. Tell me what happened."

She quickly related the story of Trinati's dominance and how the other angel sworn had come to intimidate her. How she smashed Salisha's nose—that made Azra smile—and then the argument with Trinati in the garden. She also mentioned the caravans being attacked and how the wolves were prowling.

"How did you get inside the city?" she asked him.

"When I was in the souk, I heard about the wolves attacking caravans, and I hurried to help Odeon bring the others here. We were able to fly over the walls before the wolves reached us."

Cimree hadn't known what he'd been doing. "So they're safe. You weren't attacked by the defenders?"

"Ecbatana isn't safe," he said bluntly. "The same thing is happening as happened before. The wolves will corner us in here, and then we'll be attacked from the inside. Thankfully, I can get us out."

She beamed at him. "How?"

"The catacombs," he said, gesturing to where they were.

"What is a catacomb?"

"This is where they bury their dead. There are tunnels all beneath the city. After they've scorched the corpses, they bury the bones in little alcoves. Each ring within Ecbatana has them, but the way to go between the levels is a carefully guarded secret. A dead end may contain a trapdoor that bypasses it. You have to know which ones will work, otherwise you'd get lost down here for days."

"You've been here before," she said.

"There are also tunnels that will take us outside the city walls. There are deeper layers as well. If we broke through the floor, we'd find more tunnels."

"Have you been through them all?"

He shook his head.

"I'm so glad you are back," she said, leaning against the wall. The tunnel was narrow and not very tall, but she didn't feel caged or wary. In fact, she felt safe for the first time since they'd come.

She felt him react to her words, although his expression didn't change. He was pleased.

"What should we do? Trinati wants to stay here and plant a new Gallows Tree."

"That's a reckless idea," he said. "Do you think they'd allow us to be caretakers of it for very long? I've hidden the seed."

"But she can command you to get it if she takes the Tanaquil medallion."

"Will you let her take it?" Azra asked with a mocking smile.

"No."

He shrugged. "Then she won't be able to. You have power over her, Cimree. Never forget that."

"Well, what do we do, then?"

"We bide our time and wait for an opportunity to slip away. I've already spoken to Andrin and Perreta, and they agree about continuing to Tirich Mir. I don't know where Wegner stands. Will he go against Trinati? Will he side with you? I'm not sure."

Cimree nodded and let out a sigh. "It seemed like everyone was against me."

He shook his head. "Don't underestimate yourself. You are not the same kind of leader as Trinati or the Queen Mother. But people can tell that you care about them. That you are trying to lead us to safety. Ecbatana has lured people here for years."

"'Lured'?"

"You think the manor they gave us is free? That we are just welcome guests? No, if we try to leave, we'll learn to our chagrin that hospitality has a cost. Don't be misled. They want something from us and they're determined to get it."

"Each of us was given a servant, a courtier. Can they be trusted?"

Azra snorted. "You even need to ask that? They are spies. Each and every one of them. Especially the handsome ones."

She thought of Khaf and how sincere he had appeared. It made her feel ashamed that Azra had noticed her feelings. "You'd think I would have recognized that."

"A handsome or pretty face goes a long way in this world," Azra jibed. But at her embarrassed blush, he sighed, reaching out to touch her shoulder. "It is in our nature to be attracted to beauty." He lowered his hand. Had he just given her a compliment? "Tell me of your courtier. Khaf was it?"

She nodded. "He said to let him know if we were going to leave. He wanted to come with us."

Azra's eyebrows lifted. "He wasn't even being subtle, then. 'Please confide your secret plans with me so I can tell Roque when you're planning to leave.'" He chuckled to himself.

"You're mocking me."

"No, Cimree. I've lived many lifespans. I know this sort."

"He told me what my name means here."

"*Stingy.* I know."

"You didn't tell me."

"I like your name. I thought it...odd...that the Queen Mother chose it for you. But let me guess. He gave you another name? A better one."

"Cazibe."

"*Intriguing, fascinating, charming.* Attractive. And a name he's probably given to a dozen others before you."

Cimree hung her head. "I feel like such a dolt."

He reached over and lifted her chin. "Well, to be fair, you *are* those things. And more. But when someone uses words to manipulate your feelings and thus your thinking, then know they cannot be trusted. This is why I wanted to avoid Ecbatana. And why I'm dubious about Odeon and why he suggested we come here."

Cimree blinked in surprise. "Odeon?"

Azra nodded. "We must be—"

He stopped speaking as the stone slab lifted at the top of the steps. Khaf stood at the entrance, holding the stone as he gazed down at the two of them in surprise.

"What are you doing down there, Cazibe?" he asked, his eyes suddenly stern.

She felt Azra's feelings shift. But he was not about to do violence, so there was no need to restrain him.

Cimree looked at Azra. Either they fled immediately or waited for another opportunity. He would not leave Andrin and the family behind. So she already knew his answer without asking. She gave him a subtle nod, crouched to pick up her robe and towel, and then came up the steps.

"The catacombs are forbidden," Khaf said, eyeing Azra as he followed Cimree up the stairs.

"You might have said so," she answered him with an innocent expression. She stepped over the edge of the bench seat.

Azra came after, eyes locked with Khaf's in a way that showed the two were sizing each other up. Dangerous animals were prone to do that.

"I came to tell you, Cazibe, that the other angel sworn arrived in the night. You were gone from your room. I was told you were down here and came—"

"To see her bathe?" Azra said in a mocking tone.

Khaf's eyes smoldered with repressed anger. "I came to tell her. And she wasn't here. I was afraid for you. You shouldn't wander off. Not when the gates have closed and fear abounds."

"We weren't leaving," Cimree said, shaking her head. "Why would we?"

She saw Khaf look from her to Azra, then to her again. He was stymied. Good. "Please refrain from entering the catacombs. They are unsafe. Sometimes the tunnels collapse. No one would hear you scream or cry for help."

"I appreciate your warning, Khaf. I should like to bathe and see my friends again. I'm glad they're welcome here."

Khaf nodded. She could see that he was distrustful but mollified. He looked at Azra once more. Wondering probably which of them could hold their breath underwater the longest in case a drowning were in order.

Actually, it was Azra who'd thought that.

"The king wishes to see you today, Cazibe. You mentioned that there is a cure for the gévaudan bite. Lord Roque was very interested to hear that. I think he will ask you before you visit the king. I hope you will be willing to share it with us."

She felt Azra's anger flare up at the words. The cure was the mute girl. Her touch could heal the bite.

Khaf bowed and retreated before turning and heading up the stairs out of the bath.

Azra's voice had a growl in it. "What did you tell them?"

TWELVE
TREES

Cimree was eager to see the others who had arrived and found a scene of relief and welcome in the dining hall. The servants of the mansion had provided a veritable feast for the newcomers to eat when they awoke that morning. Cimree felt a surge of different emotions seeing those she had helped lead away from Clairvaux.

"Cimree!" cried out Edwina when she noticed her arrival, and soon Andrin and Perreta's other children swarmed her with hugs. All except Chrys. Cimree petted and hugged the children while searching the room for the mute girl.

"Where is Chrys?" she asked with concern, not seeing her.

"She was just here a moment ago," said the boy, Cyrill. "Oh, there she is. With Azra." He pointed and Cimree saw them in a corner. Azra was down on one knee, hand on Chrys's shoulder and talking to her. The little girl looked frightened.

Blanka kissed Cimree's cheek. "I missed you."

"I missed you too."

"This is a beautiful palace," Edwina said in awe. "Is it truly ours?"

"For now," Cimree said, rising when Perreta came up beside

her daughter and gave Cimree a hug. "I was worried about you all."

"Hearing the wolves again," Perreta said, dropping her voice. "It was terrifying. My heart is still troubled. Are we safe here?"

"I don't know," Cimree answered honestly. Andrin had walked over to where Azra and Chrys were.

"I've never seen a city this large," Perreta said. "It is so different than Iselt or Montheron. Do you know how long we're going to stay?" She craned her neck to look over at Azra.

"Did Azra speak to you?"

She nodded but said nothing. Knowing Azra, he had probably made plans to escape already.

Wegner was talking to Trinati and some of the other angel sworn. She was dressed in a different native garment from the previous day and looked like a foreigner with her hair done up in the fashion of Ecbatana. It did not escape Cimree's notice that people were fawning over Trinati. She looked like she was presiding over a meeting of the high council. Cimree wanted to know what she was saying, but she felt approaching would make her seem like an interloper.

After a little conversation with Perreta and the children and answering some of their questions, she excused herself and went over to Azra and Chrys. The look of anxiety on Chrys's face was palpable. Her whole body was tense, and she kept pawing at Azra's tunic in distress.

"What's wrong with her?" Cimree asked, feeling her heart pang for the young girl's torment.

"I can't make it out," Azra said. "She's upset, as you can see. Like she wants to leave."

Chrys nodded vigorously.

"Leave Ecbatana?" Cimree asked.

Chrys grabbed Cimree's tunic with both hands and nodded emphatically.

"Are you in danger?" Cimree asked in a whisper, crouching down.

Chrys gave them a look that was incomprehensible. A shrug, a look of confusion and uncertainty.

"Is it the wolves?" Azra asked.

Chrys shook her head.

"I wish she could speak and just tell us," Cimree said. She smoothed Chrys's hair. The girl gave off a feeling of urgency. Almost of desperateness.

"Are we all in danger?" Azra asked her.

Chrys looked anguished and gesticulated, but it didn't make sense. Tears crept from her eyelashes and trickled down her cheeks.

Chrys wrapped her arms around Azra's neck and began to quietly weep. It was rare for the canny hunter to be perplexed by anything, but Cimree felt his concern and confusion through their bond. He patted the girl's back, but he was unable to comfort her since he didn't know what was afflicting her. Cimree was pained by Chrys's emotions, but she was just as confused by them as Azra. Andrin stood nearby looking helpless.

Cimree touched Chrys's shoulder. "Can you try to help us understand? What are you afraid of? What is troubling you?"

Chrys looked up with her tear-stricken face. She wiped her nose on the back of her hand. Then taking Azra by the hand, she walked to a window, which overlooked some gardens on the side of the manor. She pointed outside.

"Do you want to go outside?" Cimree asked.

Chrys frowned and stamped her foot in frustration.

"What you're afraid of is outside?" Azra asked.

Chrys nodded intently. She pointed again.

Azra looked out the window. There were some palm trees visible. Some bushes and sculpted shrubs. Cimree didn't see any animals or birds. She didn't sense any serpents either.

"Is it the trees?" Cimree asked.

Chrys looked at her seriously and nodded slowly.

"Those trees?"

Chrys shook her head.

Azra put his hand on her shoulder. "Is there a tree in Ecbatana you are afraid of?"

Chrys clenched the front of Azra's tunic with her fingers. Her eyes widened and she nodded again, very slowly.

"The trees?" Andrin asked, looking confused.

"And that's why you want to leave?" Cimree asked.

Chrys nodded again, slowly, deliberately.

"What's going on here?" Trinati asked abruptly.

Cimree had been so focused on Chrys's distress that she hadn't noticed Trinati and Salisha coming.

"She's upset," Cimree said, looking up at Trinati and feeling a spurt of resentment for the intrusion.

"I can see that plainly enough. Why is she upset?"

"We're trying to puzzle it out," Azra said dismissively.

A distrusting look appeared on Trinati's face. "It is important that she help while she's here. I told King Diyako about her and how her touch can cure the curse of the bite of the gévaudan. Lord Roque wants to see a demonstration with the man in the cage."

Azra turned his neck and looked at her incredulously. "You told them?"

"It was to our advantage to tell them," Trinati scoffed. "To show that we bring value to Ecbatana that is greater than jewels or rare fruit. The wolves prowl around the city. If we can catch them and cure them, then we won't be trapped inside. Her gift can benefit all of us."

Cimree saw Chrys looking at Trinati with revulsion and shaking her head no.

Trinati frowned in a scolding way. "If we're going to stay here, we need something to contribute."

Azra rose and turned on her, his eyes flashing with anger. "And I was just beginning to believe all this hospitality was free!" His voice dripped with sarcasm.

Chrys trembled with fear as she watched the confrontation play out.

"If you want to leave, Azra, I won't stop you. In fact, it might be better if you did. We don't need Tirich Mir anymore. This is a chance to make a new home. To start anew."

"And you've come to that conclusion after several days, have you? Your foresight and wisdom are astonishing." Azra's lip curled into a sneer.

"After the king has made his decision on the tyrant queen, all who wish to leave will be allowed to go. But not her." She pointed to Chrys. "She is needed here. Her gift is too rare to—"

"Not be taken advantage of." Azra cut in.

Trinati's nostrils flared. "—to squander."

Andrin put his hand on his sword hilt. "I don't think that's your decision to make, Trinati."

"She's not your child," Trinati shot back. "None of us knows where she came from or why she's here. But we have sheltered her and protected her and helped her survive. She cured the bite given you, Andrin. You wouldn't be here if she hadn't."

"All the more reason someone needs to stand up for her," Andrin said. "She may as well be of my flesh and blood. We've been caring for her all this time. That earns us a say in what happens."

"Then choose to stay in Ecbatana," Trinati said. "It's as simple as that."

"None of this is simple," Andrin countered. His knuckles had turned white.

Azra put out his hand and patted Andrin on the back. "There's no rush to make a decision, one way or the other," he said.

"Azra," Trinati said condescendingly, "I know you've found the catacombs. Well, you already knew about them and chose to not to tell us. I'm going to watch you like a peregrine falcon, and I mean that literally. None of us leaves until the tyrant queen is chosen. Even you."

"It's usually unwise to make an order you cannot enforce," Azra said flatly.

"Try and see," Trinati countered. Salisha immediately stepped in front of Trinati in a defensive posture.

Cimree noticed that Captain Odeon had gradually approached. He was watching the scene intently, hand on his own sword. Everyone was anticipating violence. Trinati was asserting her authority. They were provoking Azra to rebel while they had superior numbers.

Azra shifted his gaze from Trinati and then looked at the others in the room. The entire feast had stopped. Even the servants had slipped away.

"I've told you from the start that, in my view, our best hope of survival against these creatures is within the mountains of Tirich Mir. I wish there were a quicker way to get there to show you its advantages. I've been to Ecbatana before, and what you see before you is only the mask she wears. The monsters know where we are. And they will come for us. I've no doubt about that. Ecbatana will fall just as Montheron and Clairvaux did. Maybe not the same way. But the result will be the same. Death to all who remain."

"You cannot know this," Trinati said. Although her words were aimed at Azra, her speech was meant for everyone listening in. "The situation is different. The mountain valley offered no protection. But the walls of Ecbatana will repel them. The catacombs offer a bulwark against them. We should fight together. Unified. This is our hope for survival. You cannot know what will come, Azra."

Azra's look was a mocking one. "I can tell the outcome, Trinati. When I was training to join the Long Patrol, I was told a story that I've never forgotten. Two patrols were sent out, competing with each other for the same objective. To be the first to reach a distant icy mountain and return. It was a journey that would take months and would require exceptional courage. They both reached the icy mountain. One reached it a month before the other and began to return to claim the Queen Mother's prize. But they waited and lingered, worried about their fellow angel sworn. They waited days, weeks. And then they went back to the icy mountain. They found the others had perished in a blizzard, never to return." He jutted out his chin, looking across those gathered. "They both faced the same hardships. Had both faced the same blizzard. What made the difference in survival was who they had chosen to follow as leaders. *That* choice meant life or death."

He turned and looked at Cimree directly, and he gave her a smile of confidence. Then he held up his hands, showing he had no intention of fighting, and walked out of the dining hall.

Trinati was silent, fuming, and she watched him go with frustration in her eyes.

Thirteen
Being Wanted

The summons for Cimree to see the king of Ecbatana came in the afternoon, and it was revealed that the interview would occur at dusk. Khaf had delivered the message from Lord Roque and said he would escort her to the king's garden for the interview. Her stomach twisted with conflicting emotions at the news, but she accepted it and began her preparations. Servants in the mansion arrived to help make her ready to meet the king. The same lavish treatment they'd given Trinati they gave to Cimree. It was certainly different to be shown such servile attention, each finger and toenail carefully carved, buffed, and painted. They brushed her hair and added scented oil to her skin.

It took hours to complete the various cleansing rituals of the Ecbatanans, and in the end, they helped her arrange the red silk garment that Khaf had secured from the souk. After helping her don it, they took her to a full-length mirror to examine herself.

This type of kiyafet, they'd explained to her, was called an entari. The fabric was so light that it felt like she was wearing nothing but mist. The edges had golden ribbon lining them, both at the bodice, which crossed and became a girdle at her waist, and at the shoulders as well, from which the silk fabric draped down past her hands. She wore a golden necklace and choker that concealed, for the most part, the whorl-like pattern on her skin from the magic of the Tanaquil amulet. A headband also went across her forehead with a jeweled piece dangling from the front. Cimree hardly recognized herself in the mirror with the dusting of kohl around her eyes. They'd even added a pink tint to her lips and cheeks. Her feet were shod with sandals, which felt strange when she was so used to boots. It was a little cold wearing such attire, but she didn't disapprove of the final result.

There was still time before Khaf would come to get her, so she went to find Azra. His story about leadership earlier that day had caused a rift of feelings among the angel sworn. She could sense the tension in the air. Some had begun to wonder if Trinati's path was the safest, and their troubled looks resonated with Cimree. Through the magic of the amulet, she had a stronger sense of people's emotions. But the feelings of confusion, distrust, and wariness left everyone on edge.

Using the bond to find him, she ventured to the upper chambers until she found him. She knocked on the door and then opened it, surprised to find Azra sitting on the floor beneath an open window. Chrys sat next to him and stroked a small ferret-like animal that Cimree had never seen in Clairvaux. It lifted its head from Chrys's petting and hissed at Cimree.

Azra looked up at her and she felt his insides clench. It was no surprise to him that she had come, but he was fighting against what he saw in her. Cimree wasn't sure how to respond to his reaction, which was visceral and compelling and made her start to blush. He was admiring her and trying to resist it. She pushed through her sudden discomfort and approached the two of them before kneeling by them on the cold marble floor.

"What kind of creature is that?" Cimree asked. It was growing more agitated as she came nearer and jumped from Chrys's lap to Azra's shoulder. It gave a little hiss at her again.

"It's a firavun faresi," Azra answered. "They're common in this climate."

Its pelt looked soft, and it had amber eyes and a round black nose at the end of a sharply pointed snout. It was about the size of a cat but with the sleekness of a squirrel and a dark brown pelt, except for some striations on its back that looked like stripes. The tail was long. It hissed at her again.

"It doesn't like me," Cimree said, feeling a stab of disappointment. Chrys had been stroking and petting it easily enough.

"Firavun faresi kill snakes," Azra said with a look of humor in his eyes.

Cimree opened her mouth to speak and then closed it. That made perfect sense. She scooted backward a little.

"It won't attack you," Azra chuckled. "I'm bonded with it right now. I'm going to send it out and try to find the tree that Chrys is afraid of." He reached up and stroked its furry head. It made another noise, which had a little cooing sound to it.

"Have you gotten more from her?" Cimree asked, looking at Chrys with worry.

The little girl wrapped her arms around her knees and began rocking back and forth.

"A little." He reached over and tousled the child's hair. "Would you bring some berries? He likes those."

Chrys nodded eagerly and stood up, patted the firavun faresi on the head, and then left them alone.

"I thought it ate snakes?" Cimree questioned.

"It does. It will eat anything it kills. But it enjoys berries." He looked at the cute creature with a softened expression that was unfamiliar to Cimree. And then she realized it.

"Your affinity," she said in surprise.

Azra stroked it with the edge of his finger. "Yes. It's why I'm impervious to venom. I don't even need a distaff to bond with some of them. Like this one, which climbed through the window and sought me out. They are very quick and ferocious fighters. I found this one in the souk when we came, and it's followed me ever since." He looked back at her. "You have the same affinity for snakes. They'll come to you."

"I didn't choose it," Cimree said. It made sense why they had clashed at first. Her affinity was prey to his. It also explained Azra's quick reflexes and resistance. She'd never seen him dote on a creature before.

"I didn't choose mine either," he said. "Everyone thinks being bonded to a snow lynx would be best, or a hawk or a bear. The Oldknow made us all the way we are. There's something to be said for not being all the same."

"I have my interview with the king at dusk."

"I'd noticed." She felt his gaze on her again, and this time, he wasn't restraining his admiration as much. It made a funny feeling dance behind her navel.

"Do you have any advice for me?"

"What do you need my advice for?"

"You know I respect it." She was gazing down at the floor, unable to meet his eyes. The feelings inside her were so powerful. She wanted to move closer to him but she was afraid of the firavun faresi. That little spark of danger was actually enjoyable. Made the moment more interesting.

"I trust your instincts," Azra said. "You're going to learn more about the king than Trinati did because you listen and you observe. Remember your nature and use it to your advantage. I don't think he's going to choose you."

"Oh? And why is that?"

"I imagine a tyrant queen *wants* to be chosen."

"So you're not worried about him falling in love with me?" She looked at him with a teasing smile.

"I'm worried about getting out of Ecbatana alive. Keep your eyes open and your wits about you. And maybe enlist a few snakes to help you observe."

"There are a lot of snakes here," she said.

"And a lot of firavun faresi to compensate. In the wild, a firavun faresi will enter a snake hole to kill its prey. They're fearless."

She sensed he was about to reach out and touch her, but he repressed the urge. She sidled a little closer to him, and the creature lifted its head, its amber eyes scorching her with contempt.

The feelings inside her were growing stronger. More compulsive. As she gazed into his eyes, she saw a little ring of silver around his pupils. Just the faintest glow.

"I don't want to be the queen of anything," she said slowly, deliberately. Then she sighed. "I want to get out of here. To be back in the wilderness again."

"You miss our fights, then?" he said with a subtle smile.

"In fact, I do. All the good feelings we had in our travels have ended. There is deception and intrigue and almost a feeling of idleness here. Even in Clairvaux, there were things to do. Tasks to accomplish and duties to perform. I don't like this place. Now I wish we hadn't come."

The creature scuttled off his shoulder, down his arm, and padded over to the door where it stood up on its haunches expectantly.

Cimree scooted closer to him. Knowing she was desirable was a heady feeling, and with the bond between them, it made her feel daring.

"We shouldn't," he said warningly. But she felt how much he wanted her to kiss him.

"Shouldn't what?" she asked.

"The cursed amulet is toying with us."

"I'm not making you feel anything, Azra." Why was she feeling more bold? Was it because she felt beautiful? That she felt desirable to him?

"I know. And that worries me. If you did, I would be helpless against it."

"Don't be afraid of me," she said, not sure why she said those words. She reached out and touched the edge of his jaw. His feelings churned with excitement, anticipation, and fear.

Cimree started to lean closer until she felt his breath on her cheek. She thought she might kiss him, just a little one. But she withheld, hearing the patter of bare feet in the hallway approaching the room.

She drew back and felt his flicker of disappointment.

Chrys returned with a little wooden bowl of blueberries. The firavun faresi began to chitter eagerly as she brought it over and sat down next to Azra. She put the bowl in her lap and then offered a thick, juicy fruit to the creature, who took it excitedly and began to devour it.

Cimree and Azra stared at each other, the pent-up feelings building and then releasing. It was so pleasant sharing their hearts like this, without words. He understood her like no one else could. And she understood him. There could be no deception between them. No false or contrived thing. Their feelings were laid bare to each other and that was an intimacy that could be painful at times, but in that moment, it was blissful.

Cimree looked at Chrys as she fed more berries to the creature. She rested her palm on the cool floor and let her fingers surreptitiously snake over and brush against his.

And he opened himself to her, revealing feelings he'd long kept caged away. Feelings of being with his wife and caring for their children in Tirich Mir. The tenderness, the compassion, the soul-deep love and adoration from his past life. It made tears sting her eyes. Those feelings were pure and rich and exquisitely meaningful. And through him, she experienced them, even though she had no memory of them herself in her own life. Her own past was blank, but the closest thing she'd experienced was Milena's gentleness and patience with her. Though even that was a candle in comparison to this blazing swarm he usually kept suppressed.

She knew, intimately, that these feelings were not meant to be forbidden or withheld. They were not evil or wrong. They were wholly natural.

And they'd been ripped away from him. The pain, the despair, the feeling of ruin, loneliness, and desolation. They were inconsolable in intensity, even after all these years. That love had left an indelible mark on him. Its loss had destroyed him.

Azra closed those feelings off from her, clenching them within his heart once more, behind an iron wall of silent anger.

She looked into his eyes and wept inside for him.

Fourteen
Lore of the Hetaera

Cimree rode behind Khaf in silence. He asked nothing of her. He communicated nothing. The emotion she felt twisting inside him was primarily brooding. He was worried about something. The thin silk of her kiyafet and the smooth leather of the saddle made her feel like she was about to slip off, so she had to hold on to him to prevent that happening and holding on to him stirred emotions she wasn't sure she wanted to feel—not that they were wrong but because Azra would also feel them. They passed a dozen more mansions and their fenced grounds within the ocher section before reaching the entrance to the silver wall where an entourage from Lord Roque awaited them. The guardians were all dressed in elaborate and decorative uniforms and turbans. The scabbards of their swords were studded with jewels. She counted eight in their ranks, not including Lord Roque himself. There were no horses among them—all were afoot.

Khaf brought the stallion to a halt and slipped off the saddle, then reached up and hoisted Cimree down. As he gazed into her face, she noticed a little twitch in his cheek muscle and a look of dread in his eyes that filled her with foreboding.

"Be safe, Cazibe," he whispered to her as he set her down, and then he bowed.

She was grateful to have her distaff strapped to her leg beneath the silk, accessible through a slit in the garment. She'd grafted with a serpent in the garden before leaving and could see the heat radiating from Khaf and the others. Her reflexes were heightened, and she felt access to the venomous toxin through oils in her fingertips. That if she scratched someone, she could unloose the oils into their blood. There were plenty of birds around, so hopefully she could manage to graft with one and fly away if necessary. Though she suspected there were archers poised and out of sight above the gate.

She gave a subtle nod to Khaf and then approached Lord Roque, her sandaled feet tapping on the stone.

"You look radiant," Lord Roque said, offering his arm to her. She took it, and the soldiers filled in around them as he escorted her through the silver gate. Each of the seven walls surrounding Ecbatana was successively narrower, from the outer to the innermost. This one was quite thin, perhaps only ten feet thick. They passed under the arch and into the silver quarter.

The blue district was opulent, the ocher even more so, but the silver was yet more impressive. Every tree was sculpted, and each limb carefully grown and arranged. There was nothing wild about it—just precision and order. The buildings were made of stone and inlaid with silver. Each wall had meticulous crenelations and decorative elements that fascinated and intrigued her. It was different from the styles and designs in Clairvaux, which were much simpler in form, though also very elegant. This felt ostentatious.

A flock of birds flew overhead in a V shape. Herons, she thought.

"Are you enjoying your stay in Ecbatana?" Lord Roque asked as a pleasantry.

"Thank you for your hospitality," she answered vaguely.

"Hospitality is an honor and a tradition of our people.

Another caravan arrived several hours ago and had to battle through the wolves to get inside. The wolves can be injured, but they seem to regenerate quickly. We've yet to be able to kill any."

"They do have advanced healing potential," Cimree said. "Do you have many cats here?"

"There are a few varieties, but the cat-eared monkeys are more common as pets. Captain Odeon said that the cats of Montheron were transformed into grimalkin through the magic of metamorphistry. Quick, deadly, and dangerous. He was wounded by one."

"I was there when it attacked," Cimree said. "Thankfully he recovered."

"He said that *you* were the chief instrument of his recovery," Roque said in a flattering tone. "That your wisdom saved him."

"I've studied to be a healer," Cimree said.

"Interesting." They passed by several more opulent palaces, and then she saw a set of golden gates, which were not as far from the silver as she'd supposed. They were even more magnificent than the silver one she'd just passed through. Her stomach still felt uneasy. Other angel sworn had already had their interviews with the king. But for some reason, her own turn made her feel wary. She felt the presence of Azra through the bond, and it was comforting knowing where he was and that he was mindful of her.

The central arch of the gate had six pillars along each side, the two closest to the center shorter and bunched together and the others progressively getting taller and farther apart, making the gate look more like a palace itself. Intricate sculptures adorned the walls and arch, covered in gold. As they approached, the gates swung open, exposing many decorative trees with flowering blooms. The threshold was made of stone, but the mortar looked like gold and shimmered as such.

She noticed that Lord Roque's other hand surreptitiously went to a brass cylinder stuffed into his jeweled belt. It looked like a scroll case with a jeweled end. At first she thought he was going to remove the scroll and show it to someone, but he only folded his fingers around it.

As they stepped over the threshold, she felt a jarring sensation, as if she were tripping and about to fall. It startled her. She gazed up at the archway once they were through it, feeling uneasy. She also noticed that Azra's location had changed. He was farther away.

"Are you all right?" Lord Roque asked with a benign smile.

"I felt dizzy for a moment," Cimree said, her nerves jangling.

"It was the threshold," Lord Roque said. "They are teleportation portals. We entered through one gate and exited through another, even though they look the same. Some people feel a slight discomfort from the magic, but it is one of the barriers our enchanters have invented to protect our kings. As you see, none of the guards entered with us. They wear rings that can deflect the teleportation magic."

Although he offered this explanation, she had the distinct impression that he was lying. She'd observed him gripping the cylinder just as they were stepping over the threshold, and she wondered if that was what had activated the magic.

He paused and looked into her face with a concerned expression. "Are you unwell?"

She'd stopped walking, her mind whirling with thoughts. "I was just surprised is all."

"Are you prepared to meet our king?"

"I am."

He gave her what felt like an insincere smile and then proceeded into the meticulous gardens. There were trees of every variety imaginable, each kind joining with sister trees in precise rows. So many trees. Which was the one that Chrys was afraid of? And how would she be able to find it?

He escorted her down a stone path amidst some turf where she saw a man seated on a bench beneath a tree with crimson leaves. Based on the description that Trinati had given, it was

King Diyako. The fair hair color was a contrast to the dark brown and black hair she'd predominantly seen. He rose from the bench and greeted them with a handsome smile. Because of the fading sunlight, the garden was dappled with a variety of colors. Shadows had fallen over everything, but there were some torches hanging throughout the garden, spitting out tongues of flame.

The king rose from his seat and as he approached he inclined his head. "Welcome to Ecbatana."

"I will await the conclusion of the interview and then escort her back to the mansion," Roque said. He shifted his arm in front of his chest, and she let go of it and bowed her head to the king. Roque quickly walked away, leaving them alone.

"I've looked forward to our interview," he said. "The angel sworn are a prestigious race. You have many secrets."

"You seem to as well, my lord," Cimree said.

"Would you tell me how to pronounce your name?"

Khaf had suggested she use a different name. But it wasn't hers. "Cimree," she said.

His eyebrows furrowed slightly but then smoothed. "You are the hetaera," he said, meeting her eyes.

"I'm unfamiliar with that term," Cimree said.

"What do you remember of your previous lives?" he asked her.

"I have no memories of them at all, whether it was one or many," she said simply. "I'd always believed this was my first life. Until recently, when I learned my past was taken from me."

"Have you heard the name Tanaquil?" he asked.

She nodded.

"She came to this world from another. This we learned from the archives of Ninuwa, after it fell. She claimed to be in service to a dark empress. We tolerate all religions in Ecbatana and permit all to be established here. Hers was as well, and it was...greedy."

Cimree felt her stomach begin to churn. She bit her lower lip but quickly stopped, not wanting to show a reaction. That word held significance. It was what Cimree meant. What was he implying?

"Tell me of this religion," Cimree said. "As I said, I've not heard of it until I came here."

"Walk with me," the king said, gesturing with an open palm. They began to stroll in the gardens together, passing a variety of different kinds of trees.

The king's hands were clasped behind his back as they walked side by side. "I confess what I know of Clairvaux is based on scant information. You worship a being called the Oldknow. Correct?"

"Yes. The Oldknow is the Creator."

"As I understand the hetaera, they worship a similar entity called the Knowing. And it has delegated its power, including the ability to create life itself, to mortals who align their thoughts with its precepts. The hetaera, it is reported, have records engraved in tomes of gold that recount their legends. I've not seen one, but it does intrigue me that words are considered precious enough to be engraved thus."

"We engrave our lore in stone," Cimree said.

"I was unaware of that. Thank you for expanding my knowledge. The hetaera had many converts and performed secret rituals. They wore a brand of a serpent on one shoulder. One of the reasons females in Ecbatana wear entaris now is to expose their shoulders so they cannot disguise their faction." He gestured to her arm. "You have no mark, of course, but one would expect that from one who can partake of the fruit of the Gallows Tree."

She was becoming more and more uneasy. Was he implying that *she* was not just a hetaera but possibly Tanaquil herself? That she had been so in a previous life? Was that even possible?

"What h-happened to Tanaquil?" Cimree asked, her voice catching. "What do the records say?"

"She rose up and became the first tyrant queen," Diyako said. "Not here but in Ninuwa. As I understand it, her rule was terrible and great. I believe the Queen Mother sent the angel sworn to destroy her and her kishion."

"What is a kishion?" Cimree asked worriedly.

"They are ruthless killers. A most dangerous foe. One kishion can kill a dozen trained warriors. They are experts in poison, strangulation, and deceit."

Cimree's heart was beating wildly. Azra? That sounded very much like Azra. But surely, he had left Ninuwa as a youth.

The king stopped and turned to her with serious eyes. "Have you come to Ecbatana to lay claim to your crown once again? You do not bear the mark on your shoulder, but the mark on your bosom exposes you. You *are* Tanaquil, are you not? And you brought a kishion here with you."

His handsome expression was guarded and distrustful. "What I do not understand is why you haven't used your power over us yet. You've only used it against the angel sworn. Tell me why you came here. Tell me the truth."

Confusion and uncertainty swirled through Cimree at the king's questions. This was not the interview she'd expected, as it was entirely different from what Trinati and the others who had met the king had recounted. She wondered if those meetings had merely been pretexts to put her off her guard. To expect the same treatment.

She needed to answer him, but she was confused as to what she should say. Or how much.

"I don't know who I really am," she said. "I've been told that Tanaquil was destroyed. That the medallion is all that was left. But I can tell you this: I did not come here to rule or even to stay. We came to warn Ecbatana because the danger that destroyed Clairvaux is at your gates now."

His expression showed concern and wariness as he nodded at her. "I was under the impression that some of you wanted to stay."

"We were journeying elsewhere and thought to give your people a warning. We've done that."

"You must also admit that it is strange your warning came as a harbinger of evil tidings. The wolves are at the gates. Did you bring this evil on us?"

"No," Cimree said, shaking her head. "It is just as likely that they followed the trails of your caravans here."

"You won't be offended if I remain uncertain. We must consider how best to defend ourselves. Whether you are Tanaquil or not, you do have access to her powers, which would be valuable in the defense of Ecbatana. The people are already terrified. You could calm their fears."

Cimree pressed her lips together and studied him. He was subtle. It was a natural reflex for a leader, a king, to want to protect his people. But she had no intention of staying. It would also be wise not to tell him this.

"I understand that you want to defend yourselves. We were forced to flee our homeland when these creatures began to destroy us. It did cause panic."

"You must stay, then, Cimree," he said pointedly. "Shall I make *you* the tyrant queen, to ensure your willingness? I know I cannot force you. The best queens are those who do not want it."

Had he already made up his mind? It didn't seem as if he'd offered the same opportunity to Trinati.

"I did not come here seeking that."

"It is within my power to give you." He opened his palm and held it out for her.

He was trying to rush her decision. To get her to accept or reject it. What would happen then? She saw an opportunity to regain control from Trinati if she did accept.

Cimree held up both her hands and took a step backward. "I need time to consider this, of course. I thought you were more inclined to offer this honor to another."

"I will do whatever is best for my people," he said, lowering his hand. She couldn't tell if he was affronted or impressed by her tactic. "I implore you to consider this carefully. You would become our queen with the same authority your Queen Mother possessed. Your word would be law to us. The wealth of Ecbatana would be yours. We grow our own food, provide entertainment popular in all parts of the world. Your reign could go on for years. Longer than any other before you. I see great promise in you, Cimree. Think of what you could gain."

But in gaining this authority, she would lose her freedom. There would be others jealous of her power and influence. She would have to be on guard against those seeking a quick end to her rule.

"I do recognize the honor of your offer. Let me consider it."

"When you are ready to give me your answer, send word to Lord Roque. He will make all the arrangements."

"I will." She inclined her head to him, grateful for the reprieve.

He reached out and took her hand to kiss her knuckles. "Farewell."

She nodded to him again, and he escorted her back to where they'd first met, by the stone bench near the tree. Lord Roque appeared immediately with an expectant look.

"Take Cimree back to the mansion," the king said. "The future is still unsettled."

"Ah. Of course." He offered his arm to Cimree with a gallant smile and began to escort her back through the garden. She glanced behind them once and saw the king deep in thought.

"I think he was impressed by you," Roque said to her after they'd walked in silence for a while.

"I wasn't trying to impress him," Cimree answered. They were not going back the way they had come. There were different trees than she recalled. Her wariness began to intensify.

"You are beautiful, intriguing, and what man doesn't admire youth? Trinati is not the kind of queen that would last very long here in Ecbatana." He gave Cimree a sidelong look. "It requires a certain amount of subtlety, which she lacks. And which you possess in abundance."

Was he trying to persuade her to accept the king's offer?

"Where are we going?" she asked at last. Nothing looked familiar at all.

"There is a part of the garden that few visitors see. I thought you might enjoy it before you leave. It is a rare privilege."

The trees blocked the view ahead, but she could sense the presence of serpents. In abundance. The trees were not as sculpted or in such even rows. Like this part of the garden had been neglected deliberately. Her heart flared with worry. Dusk had already departed, and they were walking deeper into the grove without additional light. With her serpent vision, she could see no others waiting in ambush.

"Don't be frightened, it's just over there," he said, pointing with the finger from his other hand. Lord Roque's warmth glowed in the dark. The serpents were beginning to gather to her, drawn by her affinity. They were curious about her arrival. Some serpents hung from tree branches.

They reached a place where the stone footpath, overgrown with foliage and vines, met a crossroads. At the center was a circular lid, made of bronze, she thought. It was a symbol of two entwined serpents forming a circle. The image reminded her of the Chrysopoeia, the symbol of the snake eating its own tail. But this was different, it was two intertwining serpents, their heads mirroring each other at the top of the circle. She felt a rush of familiarity seeing it.

"What is this place?" she asked him.

He reached up and patted her hand, which was still draped on his other arm. She felt a sting as he did so, and realized he'd pricked her with something sharp.

That was her last coherent thought as her legs gave way and she distantly sensed herself falling but caught by Lord Roque before hitting the ground.

FIFTEEN
SERPENT'S LAIR

C imree's skull throbbed as she awakened in darkness, lying on a stone floor. Her memory was hazy, but she did recall the poke of a needle on her hand before passing out. She was lying on a stone slab and lifted herself up, feeling cold and vulnerable in her silk entari. A hanging lantern was suspended from the ceiling, which was obscured by some type of fog. She smelled incense. Cimree rubbed her temples, confused.

She immediately realized the frantic feelings buzzing inside her stomach. Azra was coming for her and he was furious and worried. But she sensed his immediate relief when she'd roused from unconsciousness. Through the haze of the incense, she noticed the bars. She was in a cage. In the gloom, she could not make out any other images but based on the smell of stone along with the incense and the utter absence of light—except the tiny flames coming from the thurible—she imagined she was underground.

Although she was worried, she wasn't fearful and exuded a feeling of calmness to Azra. She tried to stand, causing her head to swim, but she reached out and grabbed the cold bars, which helped.

The incense had a flowery smell but also a pungent one. It was a mixture of things. By reaching out and following the bars, she determined that the cage was rectangular in shape, a little longer than she was tall and wider than she could reach. She rubbed her abdomen, her belly upset by the concoction used to knock her out or the effect of the fog of incense. There was a lock on one part of the cage opposite some hinges. She shook the bars around the lock, and they were firmly secured.

There was no way for her to understand the reason she'd been brought there, but it seemed Lord Roque had different motives from the king's. She'd been helpless and would have been easy to murder, so her death wasn't the object.

She sensed serpents slithering toward her. They were coming from holes in the walls, and about six entered the underground area. Her grafting from earlier had worn off, so she reached into the slit in her entari and took out her distaff. The serpents were curious, flicking their tongues at her, smelling her in the attitude of curious predators. With the grafting wand, she immediately joined with one of them. Her vision improved, and she looked around in the dark. The thurible glowed with heat, and she was able to discern her surroundings better.

The snakes entered the chamber and came up to her cell, sliding through the bars. She knelt down as they came up to her, feeling no fear. She'd not seen this variety before, the scales black and glossy, not the freckled patterns of the asp viper. More were coming, sliding into the room until the floor was full of them. She felt their hunger, but they were tame in her presence. They had not been given enough mice and rodents to eat. Some gave her plaintive thoughts asking if she could ebb their hunger with some bird or other.

Because she was grafted to one of them, she sensed that their particular venom was a paralytic that slowed the heart rate and breathing to practically nothing. If bitten, the venom would make their prey seem like they were dead for hours. It was a painful toxin, fast acting, but after the initial pain, the venom wore off, and if the prey were not devoured before then, no further damage would be done.

Some of the serpents came up on her lap, enjoying her warmth. Their intense curiosity and hunger made her understand that they were trapped down there too.

Had Lord Roque sent her down there to be bitten? So that he might say she was dead when she really wasn't? She didn't know how much time had passed after he'd stabbed her with the needle. How had he done so? Through one of his jeweled rings? He might have carried her down into the cell, locked it, and then opened some release mechanism to channel the serpents into the chamber.

What he couldn't have known was that she was impervious to snakebites and that her affinity for the creatures made them not a threat to her at all.

Go back to your pens, she thought to them with a dismissing intent. *I will try and find you some food.*

The serpents eagerly heeded her, and soon they were all racing each other to go back to the little holes in the base of the stone wall, except for the one larger serpent that she'd bonded with, which had coiled up next to her. She imagined Trinati in a cage, and it made her smirk at how she would have handled the situation.

Cimree rose again, testing the bars, and then felt a strong instinct to just squeeze through them. It didn't make sense to her, since the gaps between the bars were pretty narrow, but she slid her arm and shoulder through, and then, as she pushed, she felt the grafting with the serpent allowing her to distort herself, and suddenly she was through the bars. The physical sensation of the displacement wasn't painful at all. It felt natural and easy. Enjoyable even.

The thurible was hanging from an iron circle fixed to the ceiling. As she gazed up at it, she saw the bronze circle nestled against a rim of stone next to it. It was the underside of the symbol she'd seen in the garden.

She sensed Azra coming to her quickly. He'd flown there undoubtedly. She gazed up at the lid, trying to encourage him with her thoughts that she was all right and safe and that he'd find her under the image. His feelings were roiling with anger still, but she sensed his relief.

The bronze lid scraped as he lifted it. She saw the heated whorl of color coming from him, but he instantly ducked his head back, grimacing at the smell of the incense.

"Thank the Oldknow you found me," she called up to him.

He sucked in a breath and then leaned down in, extending his hand to her. The serpent, which was still coiled in the cell, began to hiss and come awake. It sensed a threat and responded viscerally.

Cimree noticed the head of the firavun faresi poked through the opening, making a chittering sound.

She reached and grabbed Azra's extended hand, and he pulled her effortlessly up through the hole. The little creature crouching by the rim was agitated as it saw her, but Azra made a cluck with his tongue, and it backed away. It looked anxious to dive into the hole and go after the snake.

As soon as she was aboveground, he slid the lid back over the hole and then hugged her tightly, trembling with emotions. He felt so warm, so overjoyed, that she squeezed him hard in return.

"Did you find me quickly?" she breathed to him, still enjoying the feel of his emotions, his heart reacting to her closeness.

"He followed you into the grove," Azra said with a cunning smile, drawing back a little from her, nodding to the firavun faresi. "It took a little while to find you after you went through the gate and disappeared. But they're good hunters." He took her hand in his and squeezed it, pressing it against his chest. He wanted to kiss her. The feeling was intense and powerful. But he withheld himself. His iron will dominating.

"I've so much to tell you," she said, as she basked in the feeling of her hand entwined with his.

"*There is no pit so bottomless as forced obedience. Compel, constrain, require, or demand it, and rebellion is its just fruit. But rebellion is freedom. To refuse to submit to the chains of eternal gratitude. Burdensome to pay. Ever owing and never redeeming. A thousand times ten thousand talents would not suffice. Do not all sentient beings wish their debts discharged when the uttermost has been paid? Submission is the yoke of highest bondage. I will be compelled no longer. And if I cannot rule on earth, then I will suffer all the invocable wrath to destroy the Oldknow's pets. And with this wand I will create the tormentors of their doom. Creatures that ravage and destroy.*" Thus spake the demon Asmodeus while the aged flesh sloughed from its stolen bones. An unholy death required for an unholy birth.*

— BOOK OF THE WATCHERS, THE TALE OF THE
FALLEN ANGELS

Sixteen
Succumbing

Azra squeezed Cimree's hand and shook his head. "When I flew over the walls, the defenders gave chase right away. They will be here in moments. And I must kill them all, or we perish."

She could feel his determination. He'd made the decision when she'd been captured. He was the destroying angel, and he would wreak his vengeance on them for threatening her.

She put her other hand on his shoulder. "This is not the time."

"This *is* the time!" he said dangerously. "I am not going to let them take you from me. No more skulking around. I'll show them what I'm capable of."

"No, Azra," Cimree said. "There are too many lives at risk. Of our own. We have to get out of here but with our friends. With those who will come willingly."

She could hear them, could see the light of torches coming from different points in the garden. They were already encircled, and the ring was narrowing.

He let go of her hand and cupped her cheek. "I'll not let them have you. Nor will I surrender. If they want me, they must kill me."

"No," Cimree said, shaking her head. "It's Lord Roque who is the threat. He's the one who imprisoned me. I think we're on the verge of understanding what is happening. We need more time."

A voice rang out in the darkness. It was Lord Roque's. "The king is secure. Now, find this angel sworn and bind him! Use the weighted nets. Do not let him escape!"

Azra looked her in the eyes, and she felt his raging fury. "I won't be imprisoned again," he whispered to her. His years of anguish in the dungeon of Montheron mingled with his rage.

"And I won't let them harm you," she told him, reaching into the slit at her skirt and drawing her distaff. There were serpents throughout the gardens, and she bonded with them, using their vision to see how close the defenders were. She saw them carrying weapons—some curved swords, others short bows with sharp arrows already nocked. Some were dragging nets with lead balls attached. Coming from every direction.

Then another idea came to her. Serpents were expert at camouflage. They could be in plain sight yet invisible to predators or even their prey. She pushed Azra against the nearest tree and used the distaff to imbue both of them with that trait. To blend in with the trees so well that the defenders could not see them. She felt an innate resistance within Azra to this kind of grafting, felt the prickles of pain he was already feeling from his previous graftings intensify, but he clenched his jaw and endured it. She noticed herself that the red silk of her entari became mottled like bark. Her arms and legs looked like branches and roots. Azra transformed before her eyes as well, his face looking like bark, his clothing colors blending with the surrounding woods. She could still observe his heat, though. The little firavun faresi climbed up the tree and nestled in the branches.

She held the grafting effortlessly, feeling perfect stillness, hearing no sound. She'd never known she had this ability before, and it made her feel alive and free.

The searchers were all approaching the grove where the serpent symbol was. She and Azra held still, hardly even breathing, yet she could smell the sweat from the soldiers and taste the leather of their armor with extraordinary senses. The serpents would have bit the men if she'd asked them to, but they were defensive creatures by instinct and avoided human contact, fearful of getting stepped on.

The men converged in the gardens that Roque had brought her to and when they met, their faces showed dismay. Lord Roque was among them, his calm demeanor transformed to one of agitation, and she could feel the fear wriggling inside of him.

"You saw him fly this way?" Roque demanded.

"Absolutely, my lord," answered one of the defenders carrying a torch and blade. The torches were the kind that hissed and exuded frothing light. She could see herself and Azra mingled amidst the tree, but none of the defenders had noticed them at all. She counted two dozen in total, which she felt would have been more than a match for Azra. However, he wouldn't have tried fighting them all at once.

"Open the serpent hole," Roque snarled. "Maybe he went inside."

One of the soldiers nodded, then pulled on the heavy lid and dragged it away. Another approached with a torch and looked down. "She's gone!"

"Impossible!" Roque bellowed. He seized the torch from the man's grasp and crouched by the edge of the hole. His expression altered again, transfixing with dread.

The man who had looked down first whispered to one of his fellows. "There's just a snake in the cage. Did she transform into one?"

"She doesn't know metamorphistry," Roque said in rebuke. Then he rose and stamped his foot. "Search the gardens, you fools! I want them found before sunrise, or it'll mean your heads!"

The threat stung them into action, and they began to search the grove. A man with a torch walked right by them, gazing everywhere else but at them. Roque stayed by the opening, rubbing his bottom lip in a nervous gesture. One guard stayed by him, holding a torch. She felt Azra's inclination to slit both of their throats. The search of that area went on for a quarter hour or more, but there was nothing to find.

"What should we do?" the man by Roque asked in a deep, worried tone.

"I'll warn the guards at the mansion to keep an eye open for them," Roque said. "Though I doubt they'll return."

"Has the king made his choice?"

"He has," Roque said. "He will choose Trinati. We need that kishion out of the way, though. He's the greatest danger we face."

"What of the wolves at the gates?"

"The angel sworn have a cure. If one of their own is infected, they will reveal it, I assure you. I want that kishion behind bars so he cannot disrupt the ceremony. The crypt *must* be opened."

"As you say, my lord."

Roque looked at the man earnestly. "Have these guards poisoned by dawn. I don't want any witnesses to what happened here tonight."

"Agreed." The man with the torch nodded and walked away, leaving Roque by himself at the opening.

Roque stood there and then shoved the lid over with the toe of his shoe until it scraped into place. "Where did you go?" he muttered to himself.

Then she saw him reach to his belt where that brass cylinder was and grip it with his hand. Instantly he vanished, leaving only a residue of heat, which dissipated in seconds after he was gone.

***

ONCE THE DEFENDERS had dispersed their search, Cimree removed the disguise from herself and Azra. She remained linked to the serpent down in the lair as well as to the ones infiltrating the gardens, keeping them bound to her so they wouldn't be surprised by anyone.

Azra walked over to where Lord Roque had been standing and crouched, examining the ground.

"I've not seen that kind of magic before," he said, gazing up at her. "There's no mark of him leaving. He just...vanished."

"Did you see that cylinder in his belt?" she asked.

Azra nodded. Of course he had.

"When he brought me to the golden wall, I saw him grasp it just as we were crossing the threshold. It made me dizzy and took us to another gate. It wasn't the same one we'd entered from."

Azra rose, giving her a curious expression. She could see his features plainly with the heat radiating from him. "I noticed that your position changed after you had been with him."

"He told me they were called teleportation portals and that it was passing through the portal that made us change places, but I think it was that device he has."

"You met the king," Azra said. "I felt it when you did. You were troubled, though. What happened?"

Cimree briefly related her experience and how the king had implied that she might be the hetaera known as Tanaquil and that Azra was a kishion, also explaining what that meant.

Azra gave her a perplexed frown. "I've not even heard that word before."

"Do you think it is possible, though? That instead of killing Tanaquil, the Queen Mother used the fruit of the Gallows Tree to make her a child again? Maybe I *am* Tanaquil?"

"It would explain why you don't remember it, but surely what good would it do to remove all her memories? It seems more likely that the Queen Mother killed her rather than invent this elaborate scheme. She was more apt to eliminate a threat than to safeguard one. That's been my experience anyway."

"And you remember your childhood," Cimree said. "The

kingdom you came from and how it was destroyed by the angel sworn."

"I do remember my youth. But that wouldn't preclude the same thing happening to me. I could have been reverted back to an infant as well and would have lost those memories."

"So did Roque capture me in order to get to you, then? That's how it looks to me now. The king offered me the role of tyrant queen. I'm sure Trinati would have told us if he'd offered it to her."

"Roque is a liar and a schemer. I don't trust anything he's said. And I don't trust the king either."

"Roque is a treacherous dog," Cimree said with disdain.

"Agreed. We can't go back to the mansion yet. But while we're here, we should find the tree that Chrys is afraid of. We won't get another opportunity like this."

"That makes perfect sense. How are we going to recognize it, though? Especially in the dark."

"Something is easier to find when you already know where to look," he said with an enigmatic smile.

"Stop being so secretive. Do you know where it is?"

He nodded.

"How?" she demanded. But then she remembered. "You sent the firavun faresi to find it."

He gave her a pleased smile.

"But...how can you do that? It can understand you?"

"When I bond with something, I bond with it completely," Azra said. "I don't hold back. I want to understand its experience. To assimilate everything about it into my being. It creates a sympathy between us. An exchange. It knows that I care about it. And it wants to help me find what I'm looking for. That's what a true affinity means, Cimree. It means being totally and truly as one."

She felt the pain in his heart as he spoke. The suppressed memory that caused him grief and anguish.

"You didn't learn that as an angel sworn," she said as the realization struck her. "That's the kind of closeness you had with your wife. Delara."

Even hearing the name pained him. But he nodded slowly. "I learned more about grafting magic being with her than I ever learned in Clairvaux."

She felt the pangs of despair in him and longed to soothe them. He had raced through Ecbatana to free her. Had willingly put his life in danger to save hers. She felt bound to him in ways she didn't understand but that were compelling and powerful. And she knew that with the Tanaquil medallion, she could make him feel the same away about her. She could make him succumb to his feelings.

"Don't," he pleaded with her, his eyes showing fear and longing. They were standing very close. She could corrupt his resistance, make him desperate to please her. It was a heady feeling, one that made her aware of her own weakness for even thinking about compelling him to do that. To violate his trust.

"I told you I won't," she promised. She reached out and took his hand again. "Let's find that tree and see why Chrys is afraid of it."

Azra sighed with relief. Then he looked over at the tree branch where the firavun faresi had fallen asleep.

Its head popped up, and a chittering noise came from it. It scrambled down the trunk and shot like a dart into the grove.

Seventeen

The Forbidden Garden

Judging by the stars and the angle of the moon overhead, Cimree could tell it was nearly midnight. As they'd walked together searching the royal gardens and evading Roque's guards, who were still looking for them, she'd told Azra the rest of what she'd learned. She told him about her interview with King Diyako and how he'd offered her the role of tyrant queen. About Lord Roque and his treachery. About the cage beneath with the serpents and the type of venom they possessed. He asked questions to gather more details. And she could feel his distrust and apprehension growing stronger and stronger.

"We need to get out of here," he said at last. "I told you this place was corrupt. Now the gévaudan prowl around the city. It's just like Montheron all over again. We've been driven here and trapped inside."

"Do you think the grimalkin are coming next?" she asked.

"No," Azra said. "This golem seems to prefer using creatures that are already in place. And if I were to hazard a guess, I think it will use all these snakes against us. They're everywhere!"

He said it in a tone, and with so much feeling of disgust, that she couldn't misunderstand the level of his revulsion. They'd been following the little firavun faresi as it scampered through the garden, sniffing and darting about, and they hid whenever the searchers got too close.

She hadn't really considered the snakes a threat, but she realized he was probably right. He had a history of being right. Of discerning threats and trying to counter them. If the golem transformed the snakes into something more dangerous and deadly, it would cause a panic.

"How do we get out, then?" she asked him. "They'll hardly let us go free."

"The device that Lord Roque has might be a way," Azra said. He paused in his walking and rubbed his mouth. "I'm unfamiliar with that kind of magic, but I imagine I could persuade him to reveal its secrets if I hurt him enough." He gave her an arch look, wondering if she would oppose that.

"He's been disingenuous since we met him outside Ecbatana," Cimree said. "I'm certain you'd be a terrifying interrogator. I wonder how far it works? Do you think it could bring us all the way to Tirich Mir?"

He looked surprised and then gave her an appreciative smile. "I like your thinking. I'd need to surprise him and take it before he could use it to slip away. Most men are cooperative with a knife held to their throats."

"He'll have guards," Cimree said.

Azra shrugged as if that weren't a significant obstacle. His brow wrinkled. "We're nearly there."

Not much farther, they came to a fenced section of the gardens. The bars were solid, sheathed in gold, and pointed like spears at the top. The firavun faresi was already through and chittered at them.

"In there?" Azra said, nodding to the creature.

It chittered again.

Cimree touched the cool metal bars. Gold was a supple metal

and these bars were firm, so she imagined they had only a layer of the precious metal.

"I don't sense any birds nearby," Azra said, gazing up at the tall fence. "I'm still grafted with one, but I can't carry you. Maybe I could help you climb to the top."

"I can get through," Cimree said. She angled herself sideways and then slipped through the bars, squeezing herself internally to fit.

Azra gazed at her with another look of surprise and admiration when she finished and gave him a sidelong look.

"Coming?" she quipped.

He rose like a bird and came over to land on the other side effortlessly.

With her sensitivity to the heat spectrum, she spotted a guardian patrolling the fence, headed toward them. She touched her finger to her lips, and the two of them walked deeper into the protected part of the garden. There were fewer trees, but each one bore a different kind of fruit. The guardian had not changed pace, and it was dark enough she felt they didn't even need camouflage to conceal themselves. They just waited and observed, and the guardian continued on his patrol around the fence. He hadn't heard or noticed them.

Once he was gone, they went farther in. She paused to study the different types of fruit and then she saw a stunted tree with thick green leaves, pointed like arrowheads. It was thick with fruit that reminded her of the persimmons she'd seen earlier, though she could see they were slightly different.

She went closer to study it.

"Do you recognize it?" he asked her.

"I think this is the coptic fruit," she said. "Khaf warned me about it. He said the rind is tough and tastes like salt. If you eat it, the fruit will turn you to stone."

"That sounds rather horrible," Azra said. He examined the fruit with a look of unrecognition.

"I'd like to bring one with us," she said. "Can you pluck one? This dress doesn't really have any pockets."

Azra used his dagger tip to cut one of the fruit loose. He brought it to his nose to sniff it. "No smell," he said, before putting it in a pouch at his waist.

They passed other trees bearing other fruit. So many varieties. Were they all dangerous? She didn't dare eat from any of them. They passed one tree, devoid of leaves and fruit, that butterflies clung to. Looking at it made her skin crawl, so she quickly passed it.

The firavun faresi waited by another tree, gazing up at it. It chittered to Azra, and he paused to examine it. It looked like a cherry tree, except that the fruit wasn't red but blue. It was full of fruit hanging from long stems.

"Is this the one?" Cimree asked.

"No," Azra said. "But it wants me to take one of the fruit." He hunkered down by the firavun faresi and stroked its pelt. It made a purring sound and then chittered again. It stood up on its hind legs, reaching up to the fruit.

"Maybe it's hungry," she said.

"Maybe so. I can sense it trying to communicate, but I can't make it out. It's so faint...like a whisper." He rose and drew closer to the tree. As he reached out to pluck one of the blue cherries, he jerked his hand back.

Cimree was startled until she saw a little white serpent clinging to the branch. It was so tiny it looked harmless. She drew her distaff and joined minds with it. Then she realized that the serpents were everywhere, so small and subtle they were barely noticeable, even to her.

Do you defend the tree? She asked it in her mind.

It did not speak but she sensed that it did. And that it would not harm Azra if she permitted it.

"You can take the fruit," she said to him. "It won't bite you."

Azra looked at the white serpent with revulsion and fear. He wanted to reach for the fruit, but his terror overrode his impulse to touch it.

She put her hand on his arm. "It's all right."

"I'm not sure why I'm afraid," he said in confusion.

"Don't be," she said. She didn't use the power of the Tanaquil medallion. She sensed that just her touch was enough to calm him.

Azra reached out and plucked one of the cherries. He was relieved when nothing happened. Then he squatted down again and offered the fruit to the firavun faresi.

The little animal chittered and dashed off, leaving the fruit pinched between Azra's finger and thumb. He gazed at it curiously a moment and then stuffed the fruit into his pocket.

"What a strange garden," Cimree said.

"There's a fence for a reason," Azra said. "These aren't just ordinary fruit trees. I feel different here."

He was right. She felt it too. It felt forbidden.

They followed the firavun faresi deeper into the garden, which they discovered was not very large. They had reached the center where a formidable tree stood that looked ancient. The trunk was gnarled and deformed with gaps and holes that made it seem like the puckered face of a very old man. The roots were plump and contorted and the leaves were distinctively shaped. But some type of fungus grew amidst the leaves, with little white fruits growing in bulbs, and it looked like an infection that was killing the tree.

"I've never seen this kind of tree before," Cimree said, feeling an urge to touch the bark.

"It's a pedunculate oak," Azra said, gazing at the tree with interest. "They don't grow in the Arvadin but in the lowlands. The boglands are full of them."

"Where are the boglands?"

"West of Clairvaux. Always flooding. Miserable place for the Long Patrol to visit. Just wild and untamed and full of streams and muck. The hardy trees like this oak had deep roots. Sometimes we'd camp up in the branches to get out of the muck."

"This one looks very old," Cimree said, feeling her heart quicken with interest.

The firavun faresi had clambered up into its branches. It squeaked at them and rushed back with something small in its paws. The creature gave it to Azra.

"Is that a fruit?" she asked him.

"It's an acorn," Azra said. "And yes, you can eat them if you prepare them right. But they're the seeds of the pedunculate oaks. If you plant it, it will grow another tree."

Bring her.

Cimree startled when the thought came into her mind.

"What's wrong? You flinched." Azra still cupped the acorn in his palm.

"Did you hear that?" she asked him.

"Hear what?" He looked around, searching.

Cimree did not see any heat other than from Azra and his affinity animal. A nervous feeling wriggled in her stomach.

Bring her to me.

Cimree stepped away from the oak, worry blooming in her chest.

"Cimree?"

"Get away from it," she warned.

Azra stepped back from the tree as well, gazing at it in concern. "I can feel your worry. What's wrong?"

"The tree is talking to me."

"Trees don't talk."

"This one does," Cimree insisted.

"What is it saying to you? I can hear whispers, but I can't make out any words. This whole garden is whispering. Not just this tree."

"I don't hear any of that. But I did hear, quite distinctly, to bring her here. I think it means Chrys."

BRING HER TO ME!

The thought was urgent and nearly a shriek in Cimree's mind.

She summoned the magic of the Tanaquil and subdued her own fear. And she felt the oak respond to the magic, felt the sentience shrink. She could tell her eyes were glowing as she saw the silver light reflected in Azra's eyes as he gaped at her.

Her breathing began to slow as the fear melted away. She approached the tree, reaching out and touching the rough ridges of its bark. The sentience shrank farther away, afraid of her. No more whispers came. She caressed the bark with her thumb.

"Chrys was afraid of this tree," Cimree said, feeling certain she was right. "I think she could hear it in her mind."

"That far away?" Azra asked.

"I think so. I think she knows what kind of tree this is. It's odd, even the whisper...it felt like a woman's voice. We should go back to the mansion."

"I'm not sure it is wise to go back yet," Azra said. "There will be guards posted there."

Cimree lowered her hand. "We need to tell Trinati what's going on. This place is corrupt. I wouldn't want to be the queen of anything here."

"Do you think she'll be easy to persuade?"

"All we can do is try," Cimree said. "Let's go back before dawn. I think it won't be as easy to hide from them during the day. And if they caught us here, we'd probably be punished. They don't want anyone coming here."

She just wished she knew why.

EIGHTEEN
THE WATCHERS

There were guards posted on the street leading to the angel sworn mansion, but Cimree and Azra slipped past them without trouble in the dark. There were also some angel sworn patrolling the rooftop, but with her serpent vision, she saw them easily, and they were evaded as well. They crept to Cimree's window. Azra sent the firavun faresi ahead to make sure no one was in the room awaiting them, and it soon returned with a small chittering noise.

"No one is inside," Azra whispered to her.

Cimree climbed up the wall without any difficulty and entered her room. The animal gave a little hiss at her, but then it went over to her bed, climbed up, and curled down to fall asleep. She gazed around the room, her senses dulled with fatigue. She also wanted to fall asleep. Azra climbed up to the window and then dropped onto the floor with hardly a sound.

Cimree walked over to a changing screen, bringing her normal clothes. Behind it, she quickly disrobed and then changed back into her usual tunic and trews. She sensed Azra on the other side of the screen, trying to quell his thoughts. It felt good to wear her own clothes again. Taking off the jewelry was difficult, but she managed it and left it on top of the heap of silk on the floor.

"I'm exhausted," she said after stepping out from behind the screen. She strapped her belt and dirk to her waist. "What's our next move?"

"Stay out of sight," he replied. "They don't know we're back, and we should keep it that way. Hide the entari and jewels under a pillow and sleep in the anteroom. The firavun faresi will wake us if someone comes."

Cimree nodded. She collected the bundle from the changing screen and then hid it under the pillow. Azra examined the anteroom and then motioned for her to join him there. He moved a small padded bench away from the wall, and then he motioned to the floor.

"Where will you be?"

"I'm going to have a look around."

"Azra, you haven't slept either."

"I take what rest I can. I want to check on Andrin and his family. See what I can learn. I'll be back soon."

She touched his arm in concern, and he stepped closer to smooth some hair from her cheek. Then he nodded to her to lie down and she heeded him. Even though it was a floor, it was comfortable, and she felt she was out of sight. She lay her head on her arm and released the grafting, which even after all those hours still barely tickled her arms and legs. Azra disappeared in the gloom of the room. She closed her eyes and immediately felt herself falling asleep.

She wasn't sure how much time had passed, but she awoke to the firavun faresi chittering on the bench. Her head throbbed and her eyelids felt scratchy, but she heard men's voices coming from her room and a jolt of panic struck her. She realized one of them was Azra and that began to calm her. The brightness revealed it was morning.

Cimree rose from behind the bench, and the firavun faresi

darted out of the anteroom. She gripped the hilt of her dirk and sought out a serpent. She didn't find any nearby. With a cautious step, she approached the main part of her room.

Azra was stalking the other man. It was Khaf, and he was trying to keep furniture between them. His eyes were darting right and left, and his expression was one of fear, his hands held out placatingly.

"I caught him sneaking around in here," Azra said to Cimree as she entered. She saw the pillow had been moved, exposing a swath of red silk.

"I mean no harm," Khaf said.

The door was closed. The firavun faresi hissed at the intruder. She felt Azra ready himself for violence. But he wanted information and wasn't intending to kill the courtier...yet.

"Did you know we'd returned?" she asked him, keeping her distance. She felt strange not being grafted to a serpent. Her reflexes were slower without that bond.

"Yes," he said to her. "I knew *you* had."

"How?"

"If I tell you, will you call off your wolf?" He made a little head nod at Azra.

"Your loyalty is to Lord Roque," Cimree said. "And Lord Roque tried to imprison me last night."

"You are mistaken," Khaf said.

"I was the one in the cage," Cimree answered curtly.

"No, I mean you are mistaken about my loyalties. I could have found you last night and led them to you, but I didn't. I know you were in the forbidden garden. And that they searched for you in vain. I did not help them."

"If you want to earn our trust, you will need to be more forthcoming," Azra said. "How did you know she'd returned?"

"The jewels. There is one with a green gem. I will show you."

Cimree was curious, but she shared the feelings of distrust she felt coming from Azra. Since she was closer to the bed, she went there and moved the pillow. She found the necklace with the green gem. It was about the size of her thumbnail and encased in a gold trinket.

"This one?" she asked him.

"Yes," he said, pointing at it. "That is how I found you."

"You'll need to do better than that," Azra said.

"I am a sihiribaz," he said. "A conjurer. There is a djin trapped inside the gem."

Cimree felt confused. "A what? A *sin*?"

"A *djin*. They are powerful spirits capable of magic." The firavun faresi made a growling sound and hissed at him. "That is a djin too," he said, pointing at the creature. "A powerful one," he whispered.

"The firavun faresi?" Cimree asked.

Khaf nodded slowly, but his eyes stared at the creature with interest. "It is disguised in a mortal form. They can take other forms as well. Like serpents."

"It doesn't like you," Azra said warningly.

"Because the sihiribaz know how to capture them. But I won't. I am your ally." He turned his gaze to Cimree and then to Azra.

"You say there is a djin trapped in the jewel. Can you release it?" Azra said.

"Yes, but—"

"Do it." Azra's voice was forceful.

Khaf's wince showed he was reluctant. "It is very valuable in its current form. And useful."

"Do it," Azra insisted.

Khaf sighed. He opened his hand and held it out to Cimree.

She felt a warning from Azra and turned to see him shaking his head. He walked to her, took the necklace from her, and brought it to Khaf. She saw Khaf's eyes tighten with fear but he kept his hand outstretched.

Azra put the jewel in it. He was holding one of his daggers in his other hand, the blade aimed toward Khaf.

The other man looked at the jewel with interest. "I chose this jewel so I could find where they'd taken you," he said to Cimree. "I knew they were going to take you to the serpent lair. I was coming myself to rescue you. But I did not come swiftly enough, for you were already gone when I got there. Roque has been searching for you all night. He even killed the guards who failed to find you." His voice had an edge of contempt to it.

"Why didn't he kill you?" Cimree asked.

"He doesn't know I was there yet," Khaf said. "I am part of an order of sihiribaz called the Watchers. I can disguise myself and pass unseen by many."

"Free the djin," Azra commanded.

Khaf gazed at the stone again. "Ah, it is difficult for me to waste such a worthy creation. The emerald alone would fetch five thousand in the grand souk. With the djin trapped inside, it is worth thirty thousand. And it was borrowed, so I must repay it."

"How much is your life worth to you?" Azra said tonelessly.

Khaf grimaced. "I see your point." He began to mutter an incantation, a string of words that Cimree did not understand, which was followed by a flash of green light and a cracking noise, like that of an icicle breaking loose from the edge of a roof in winter. When Cimree looked again, she saw a dragonfly was perched on the gem. Its four wings began to flap furiously, and it soared out the window. The firavun faresi made a crooning noise.

"The charm is broken, the djin is free," Khaf said. "Did that prove my allegiance?"

"Hardly," Cimree said. "Lord Roque has something like that. A cylinder of brass, like a scroll case. Is he a sihiribaz?"

"Yes. A powerful one. But he is not a Watcher. He is allied with the revenant."

"He said it was gone," Cimree said.

"It is not truly gone. It can only be destroyed once its bone is destroyed," Khaf said. "That is our cause. Our purpose. The Watchers seek to destroy Asmodeus." His voice throbbed with hate. And it was strong enough that she felt it through the medallion's power. "It is a being of tremendous evil. Lord Roque is its puppet. But the revenant is gone and now Roque seeks supremacy as Grand Wizr. I seek his downfall."

"You risk your life by telling us this," Azra said.

"I risk my life every day by my disguise," Khaf countered. He looked at Cimree. "You are not as you seem. You seem like a hetaera. But I do not believe you are." He looked at Azra. "You seem like a kishion. There is something deeper happening here. I wish to understand."

"Hand me the jewel," Azra said.

"It is broken. It is worth nothing now except for the shards."

Azra held out his hand. Khaf scowled and dropped the jewel into it.

"It is proof that you have betrayed your master," Azra said. "I think I'll keep it with me."

"Go ahead," Khaf replied. "It is a token of trust, then. You hold my life in your hand. And I hold yours."

"Tell me of the brass cylinder," Cimree said. "It can make Roque vanish."

"It is a powerful magic," Khaf said. "And not easily broken. By touching it, Roque can take a person anywhere he has been. Anywhere, no matter how far away. He never goes anywhere without it. If he were standing here before you, he could touch it and be back at his manor in an instant."

"Anywhere *he* has been before?" Azra asked. His voice was calm, but she sensed an eagerness inside him. A thrill of discovery. Another way to escape Ecbatana. Another way to get to Tirich Mir.

"Yes. Or whoever is the possessor of its magic. It was created by Asmodeus. And it can be summoned by the revenant. Roque is bound to it and it to him. It is a devious magic. The magic of the Tay al-Ard!"

A scream sounded through the mansion. A woman's scream. It sounded like Perreta. Cimree's stomach clenched at the sound.

Khaf gave them both a knowing look. "They just discovered she's gone."

"Who?" Cimree demanded angrily. But she already suspected. And she anticipated his answer with dread.

"The little girl who can heal," Khaf said. "They took her during the night."

Cimree looked at Azra. His face was calm except his eyes. She felt the murderous rage begin throbbing inside him.

Chrysopoeia.

NINETEEN
IMPRISONED

"D o you know where they've taken her?" Azra asked simply. His calm demeanor belied his internal fury.

"I do not," Khaf replied. "My assignment was to watch for Cimree's return."

"How did you know she was to be taken, then?" Azra demanded.

"It was Trinati's doing," Khaf replied. "She revealed too much about the girl who won't speak and her powers. The only reason you are not all in cages is because Roque wants the fruit of the Gallows Tree. He will get what he wants, and he will use whatever leverage he must to do so. Including taking the girl."

Azra took a step toward him and Khaf shrank back.

"If you want to earn our trust, then you find out where they took her," Azra said. "If any harm comes to her, believe me that the gévaudan will be the least of your problems."

Cimree felt that the threat was indeed a promise. But it might not ensure a willingness to cooperate. "Please," she added, drawing Khaf's attention to her. "She's just a child."

"I will find her for *you*," Khaf said, meeting Cimree's eyes meaningfully. "But do not leave Ecbatana without me. For the help I have given already, my life will be forfeit."

"We're not leaving without her," Azra said.

"Very well. You are already trapped in Roque's web. Be careful what you do next. There are poisons here that will kill even the angel sworn. I will find the girl."

Azra nodded and allowed Khaf to leave through the door. As it opened, they could hear a commotion happening deeper inside the mansion. Andrin was shouting.

Cimree's heart panged her. Everything sat on the verge of violence: conflict with Trinati, conflict with Roque, conflict with Andrin's family. She regretted again her decision to come to Ecbatana in the first place.

"What are we going to do?" she asked Azra. She was still weary from the long night and frightened at the danger they were in.

"We must be very careful what we do next," Azra said. "Roque is behind all this treachery. His position might not be as solid as he likes. The king chose you and offered you the role. Possibly against Roque's wishes. He may be reacting to counter the threat by endangering someone we care about. That is how men like him operate."

"I remember the boulder fields we had to cross to leave the mountains of Clairvaux. A boulder could look stable until you stepped on it and things shifted. I'm worried about making the wrong step."

"Life is full of risk, Cimree. Never let fear or uncertainty stop you from making the right move in the right direction. I'll find Roque. You find Chrys."

"Me?"

Azra gripped her shoulder. "You are uniquely capable of doing it. You were the Queen Mother's spy. You have the instincts, and I saw last night what you're capable of. If Chrys is with Roque, we'll both end up in the same place. If she isn't, then we use what we can to bring her back one way or another."

"I've no idea where to start," Cimree said, feeling a flush of pleasure that he had so much confidence in her. But it was equally terrifying.

"There are snakes everywhere here. Use them."

He glanced down at the firavun faresi. Its head was perked up, the amber eyes shining with a look of cunning. Then it leaped off the bed and scampered up the wall to the window and darted outside.

Another shriek came from the other room. Cimree hugged Azra tightly, feeling they were both going into danger. She worried about him but could feel his confidence in her. As she pulled back, he lifted her chin. All he did was gaze into her eyes, but it was more of a promise.

He reached into his pocket and pulled out the coptic fruit. "This might have a purpose," he said. "It's always better to have options."

She took it from him and gazed at the fruit. Then she put it in her own pocket.

He went to the window. She, to the door. They both paused before leaving, looking back at each other and basking in the warmth and strength of their connection. It gave her confidence in herself. She wished all her memories hadn't been lost. That she weren't so inexperienced.

She left the room and went to the common hall where she found Andrin on the ground in pain, blood staining his shirt. Trinati was standing over him with a bloodied blade held down at her side.

"He drew his sword and attacked me!" Trinati said. "I could have killed him."

"You almost did!" Perreta shouted at her. She was kneeling on the floor by Andrin, whose face had gone pale. Their three children cowered nearby, staring at Trinati in terror.

Cimree hurried over and knelt by Andrin. "Let me see the wound," she said. Andrin was pressing his hand against it, but blood was seeping between his fingers. She added her own hand and increased the pressure.

"I tell you, it's not my fault!" Trinati said.

"You're saying they were able to sneak past us while we slept, abduct our daughter, and then slip past your angel sworn and they were oblivious?" Andrin said with a grunt of pain.

Cimree felt the anger, the accusation—a swarm of feelings in the hall. Wegner was standing to one side, obviously troubled by the scene. Beside him was Captain Odeon, who was equally disturbed at the turn of events. Other angel sworn had gathered as well.

"Wegner, I need some woad and the pack from my room. Can you get them for me?"

Wegner nodded and hurried away.

Trinati huffed. "And where have you been all night, Cimree?"

"You don't already know?" Cimree answered. "Lord Roque threw me in a cell. Azra helped me escape."

Perreta looked at her in shock.

"What?" Trinati said with a startled look, and her tone was incredulous.

"I need to stop the bleeding," Cimree said, turning to Perreta. "Get me a linen napkin and some water."

Perreta obeyed and returned quickly. In the meantime, Edwina had approached and began stroking her father's hair. Andrin's mouth was contorted as he fought against the pain.

Wegner returned with her pack and held it out to her. She looked at him. "Help press the wound, please." Wegner crouched down and did so, adding his strength to Andrin's. With the rag and water, Cimree cleaned her hands and then delved into her pack until she found the healing herbs she needed.

"Lift his tunic," she said to Wegner and Perreta, and they removed his scabbard belt together and lifted the bloodstained garment carefully.

Cimree added some ground woad to the wet cloth and for a moment, pressed it to the cut, which was about the width of a dagger's blade. The wound wasn't as deep as it could have been, so Trinati *had* shown some restraint. The cut impacted just muscle, not internal organs, and Cimree was grateful for that. Andrin winced as she examined the wound and then re-covered it with the woad-treated cloth. Andrin grimaced but didn't cry out. Perreta's expression was one of anguish.

"Will he be all right?" Perreta said through her tears.

"He should be," Cimree said. She asked their son, Cyrill, to bring her another linen napkin, which the little boy did, and she cleaned her hands twice more, per her training. Milena had always warned her of the importance of cleaning her hands before and after handling blood and treating the wounded. It prevented infection.

Cimree rose to her feet and faced Trinati, who was looking more subdued, though she could discern no remorse in the archangel's demeanor.

"Where is Chrysopoeia?"

"I don't know," Trinati said curtly. "Lord Roque sent for her, and I agreed."

"Why would you agree to that?" Cimree demanded. She wanted to say that Trinati had no right to do so, but she knew that would only make Trinati more defensive and rouse her anger once again.

"Because of the urgency of the situation," Trinati said evasively.

"If it was urgent, you should have woken us!" Perreta said, her voice throbbing with resentment.

"What was the 'situation'?" Cimree pressed.

"During the night, a gévaudan made it into the grand souk. It killed a dozen or more people before it was subdued. The dead were mostly guards. More people have the bite marks now, including several of Roque's defenders, who were bitten during the attack. Now do you understand? The gévaudan are inside the city now."

Or maybe Roque had let loose the bitten man who was already inside. She would not put it past him to do something like that. Especially after what she and Azra had overheard in the gardens.

"Lord Roque poisoned me and imprisoned me after my interview with the king," Cimree said. "I find the timing of his request suspicious."

"Why would he imprison you?" Trinati said hotly. "What did you do?"

"Why do you always assume it's my fault?"

"The Ecbatanans have helped us. They've offered us shelter. They've—"

"For their own purposes," Cimree interjected. "They've captured us. And we've been accomplices to our own imprisonment."

"Now you are being dramatic," Trinati said. But there was a haze of doubt in her eyes for just a moment. A glimmer that her self-certainty wasn't entirely intact. "And if we are going to stay here, then it serves our own interests to help rid them of the wolf bites. She will cure them and then she will be returned. I have confidence that Lord Roque will do as he promised."

"I have no confidence in him at all after what just happened to me," Cimree said.

"And what happened to you, Cimree? I was told that you *used* the powers of the medallion against the king. That you tried to subvert him into choosing you when he'd already made up his mind to choose me as the new queen!"

"He chose you?" Captain Odeon said, his face betraying his surprise.

"Yes," Trinati said, straightening and flashing Cimree an indignant look. "Lord Roque told me all the other interviews were just a formality."

Cimree saw that not only was this news to Odeon, it was appalling to him.

"The king chose me," Cimree said softly. "He offered it to me last night. And it was after that when Roque knocked me unconscious with a poison and put me in a cage."

Trinati's look of triumph slowly melted away. Replaced by fury. "Cimree, be very careful what you say next."

"I don't need to be careful," Cimree said. "I've told the truth. Roque is the liar. We are his captives. And unless we band together, none of us is safe."

"Did you use the medallion's power on the king?" Trinati demanded.

"No."

"I wish I could believe that," Trinati said.

"Cimree has never been dishonest with us," Wegner said with concern.

Cimree was grateful he'd spoken on her behalf. Judging by the look on Trinati's face, she was more than just furious. She'd been promised the role of tyrant queen. And she looked determined to see that promise fulfilled. She'd become accustomed to the idea of staying in Ecbatana, enjoying the riches and power and influence of the position. Cimree's confession had caused the boulder of confidence she'd had in her future to shift suddenly.

"It comes down to this," Cimree said, raising her voice so that all could hear her. "You must all decide whether to stay or to go. I am determined to continue to Tirich Mir with Azra."

Andrin and Perreta were still on the ground, surrounded by their children, and they nodded their heads solemnly at Cimree's words. The angel sworn had varying expressions. Some looked at Cimree with distrust. Others with concern. What she'd told them had been shocking. But they had to judge for themselves whom to believe.

Cimree looked back at Trinati. "You can become the tyrant queen. I think you'd do very well at it. But do not force people to stay who do not wish to. This place is full of treachery and deceit. Don't let your ambition rob you of good judgment."

"What if I forbid you to go?" Trinati said, her voice taut with warning. "I won't let you take the seed. It belongs here."

"I don't have it," Cimree said. "You've made your choice. But do not choose for everyone else."

She looked at Captain Odeon again, and the only way she could describe the expression on his face was anguish. He was gazing at Trinati as if he were about to lose her forever.

TWENTY
IMPOSSIBLE CHOICES

With Wegner's help, Andrin had been carried back to his room and set on the bed. Cimree checked beneath the bandage she'd made for him and was relieved to find the bleeding had stopped. Perreta sat at the bedside, holding his hand, her mouth drooping in a frown of worry and concern.

"Will Papa get better?" little Blanka asked Cimree, tugging at her sleeve.

"He will, but he needs to rest," Cimree said as she stroked her soft hair. Blanka had grown a lot since they'd left Clairvaux, but she had always been affectionate, and she kissed Cimree's cheek.

Edwina and Cyrill sat in the corner of the room where there were blankets for beds on the floor. Cimree looked at the children, her heart panging for them and what they'd just endured. They looked frightened and Edwina seemed to be comforting her brother.

"I'm worried, Cimree," Perreta said in a whisper. "Is Azra trying to find a way to escape?"

"He is," Cimree said, reaching out and patting Perreta's arm.

"I wish we'd never come here," the other woman said with a sigh. "It feels like we're trapped."

"I know." Cimree agreed. "But we will find a way to escape."

"But how can we know that Tirich Mir will be any better?" Andrin offered, keeping his voice low. "Azra said it was destroyed by the angel sworn, but that doesn't mean others haven't laid claim to it."

"You think we should stay here?" Perreta said in a challenging tone.

"No. I don't like it here either. There is too much deceit. False smiles. But if we try to leave, they will turn on us. I've no doubt of that. We won't get out as easily as we got in."

"There are tunnels beneath the city," Cimree said to them. "And there may be another way to get to Tirich Mir."

"Truly?" Perreta asked, her expression altering with a hopeful smile.

"I won't say more yet. The best thing to do right now is wait. To heal."

"If they've hurt Chrys..." Andrin said, his voice throbbing with anger.

She squeezed his wrist. "I'm going to find her. What I meant was that it's best if *you* rest."

Perreta hugged Cimree tightly, then pulled back. "She's like one of ours now. I can't believe Trinati allowed them to take her."

"Trinati has her own plans at the moment," Cimree said. "I will try and reason with her. But regardless, I am going to find Chrys. If Andrin gets a fever, ask for some yarrow. It will help him sweat it out."

Perreta nodded, and Cimree rose from the bed. Blanka had wandered over to her siblings and was sitting by them. Cimree glanced their way, noting the sad looks on their faces, and then she left and went back downstairs. What they had witnessed happen to their father had shocked them and frightened them. And it never should have happened among their own group.

People were eating in the dining hall, but not Trinati or

Odeon. Cimree walked up to Wegner and asked where they'd gone.

"They started to argue and left," Wegner said. He looked ill at ease. "I think they went to her chamber."

Cimree nodded to him and started to go, but he caught her sleeve. She paused and looked back at him.

"I don't approve of what she did," Wegner said softly. "Not with Chrys. Not with any of this."

"What are you saying?" Cimree asked him, matching his low tone.

He looked around the dining hall and shook his head. "I'll tell you later." He hesitated before meeting her eyes again. "I would just advise you not to perform any rash actions yourself."

She patted his shoulder, then went in search of Trinati and Odeon. The door to Trinati's chamber was closed, but she heard their voices behind it. They were arguing, but she could not make out the words.

Cimree twisted the handle and pushed it open.

"...but what does it matter to you? I don't understand why you're so adamant about it!" Trinati said in a severe tone.

Both of their heads swiveled to the door. Trinati stood midroom and Odeon was pacing back and forth, but he halted as soon as he saw Cimree there. She entered and shut the door behind her.

Trinati's eyes blazed with anger. "I don't want to see you right now."

Cimree leaned back against the door, trying to judge what the argument was about.

"The bleeding has stopped," Cimree said. "I thought you'd want to know." Actually, she didn't think Trinati wanted to be reminded at all, but it felt a more innocuous way to start the conversation.

"He drew his blade first," Trinati said tightly. "Maybe he will think first next time."

Not even a flicker of remorse. Cimree sighed.

"Please leave us," Trinati requested, though it was more a tone of command.

"I wanted to know how things stood between us," Cimree said. "And then I admit I'm curious why the two of you started arguing in front of the others."

"And what makes you think this is any of your concern?" Trinati shot back.

"If I'm not mistaken, it's very much my concern," Cimree said. She looked at Odeon, saw the turmoil in his eyes. "King Diyako offered me the title. And you say that Lord Roque has offered it to you. Are you not the least concerned that someone is lying? Do you think *I* am lying?"

Trinati pressed her lips together. She was practically trembling with anger. "No. I don't."

Cimree looked at her in confusion.

Trinati turned to face Cimree. "They've lied to us along the way ever since they met us." She held up her hands and gestured to the room. "This mansion isn't a gift. It's a ploy. The food, the clothing, the jewels. It's all an elaborate subterfuge. I thought, at first, it was just about the Gallows Tree. But there is something else going on. There is more about the connection to the golem than what they've revealed."

Cimree was pleased that Trinati had not been duped. That she was evaluating the situation in so clearheaded a manner.

"I even think they let the gévaudan they'd captured loose in the grand souk to change the situation. To force us to help. I was willing to sacrifice Chrys's healing gift to learn more about what they want. But I'm not giving her up. I'm just distracting them."

Captain Odeon looked frustrated as he spoke. "And how do you know that they haven't prepared for what you're planning to do?"

"What are you planning to do?" Cimree asked.

"It's clear to me that Lord Roque has the most influence here," Trinati said. "Not the king. Lord Felaket, who was also at our feast, is a rival and wants to take Roque's place. Didn't you see how he treated Roque's servants by giving them contemptuous commands? Diyako wants to use *you* to throw down Roque," she said, pointing to Cimree. "Roque wants to use me to achieve his ends and ensure his future. I won't be any man's puppet." She gave Cimree a derisive look. "You don't want to become the tyrant queen. I do. We didn't have time to stage a proper defense of Montheron. And that led to the fall of Clairvaux. I intend to make a stand here against the golem. We're going to kill it *here*."

Odeon wiped his brow, which caught Cimree's notice. He looked exceedingly vexed. She turned back to Trinati.

"And you think Roque will be easy to topple?" Cimree asked.

"Yes!" Trinati said in an affronted manner. "He's a sniveling weakling. A courtier. His power comes through patronage."

"And you know this how?" Cimree asked, feeling that there were gaps in Trinati's knowledge. She didn't know that Roque was a shiribaz. And that she had no idea about the magic of the Tay al-Ard. Or the other magic jewels he likely had.

"He is openly disparaged by his own servants," Trinati scoffed.

"And you believe them because a courtier *assigned* to you told you this?"

Trinati's cheeks flushed with anger. "Do not say I'm being naive."

"I'm glad you already realize it. And is this the source of contention between the two of you? Captain, have you tried persuading her to abandon this scheme?"

Trinati looked incensed. "And what does Azra advise? To sneak away and fly to some angel-forsaken mountain? And we wait there until this creature, this golem, finds us there instead? No, Cimree. We fight it here. We destroy it here. Can't you see that it was made here and that it should be destroyed here?"

"We have no idea how it was made," Odeon cautioned. "Our graftings fall apart when it comes near. It is impervious to our magic, and we are defenseless against what it can do. It's created the nightmares that have attacked us. But if we can cage it, if we can lure it here and bury it beneath stone, then the world will be rid of it. We *need* Diyako's help! We need the obedience he alone commands."

There was something he wasn't saying. Maybe Cimree had been with Azra too long, but she sensed it. There were motives at work.

"And is that why you want Cimree to become the tyrant queen?" Trinati said to him, her eyes blazing with fury. "To give him what he wants?"

Cimree stared at them both.

Captain Odeon glowered at Trinati. He was clearly upset that she had revealed something he didn't want her to. He looked furious enough that he probably couldn't speak without shouting, rather he bristled and remained silent.

"I won't be part of this," Cimree said. "Power is like fire. And you are playing with it and will get your hands burned. Those who want to stay and fight here should do so. But let the rest of us go."

"No," Trinati said, shaking her head. "We stand together and see it through. This city is more defensible than the valley of Clairvaux. We can grow fruit here. There are animals in pens ready for the slaughter. With the right leader, we could prevail against this demon-spawned golem." She took a step toward Cimree. "I know some of the others are sympathetic to you. They feel you were slighted, but this is for the best. A leader must be willing to make sacrifices to do what is in the best interests of the community. You don't have that temperament, Cimree. I do." She turned and looked at Odeon. "And I am willing to sacrifice myself if need be to save us. The tyrant queens of the past were betrayed from within and met their fates. It won't be the same with me."

There was an anguished look in Odeon's eyes. Cimree wasn't sure what was causing it. Was it that she was agreeing to marry someone in order to become a queen? Cimree knew the two of them had a deep loyalty to each other. Had that loyalty become something deeper on his part? Cimree wasn't sure, but she saw how Trinati's words had hurt him. She didn't care when her words hurt others. She was motivated by outcomes. By control.

"You are not the leader you once were," Cimree said to Trinati.

"But I'm the one I am needed to be," Trinati said self-righteously.

Cimree didn't believe that for a moment. The Trinati of the past had counseled with others before making decisions. She had welcomed different viewpoints. Had asked others to share their thoughts. Cimree had information that Trinati would have found valuable. Things about Roque, about his magic. But she wasn't going to offer it up, not when Trinati was acting so irrationally. She'd stabbed Andrin! In front of his family. And she was acting as if that wasn't very serious at all.

Cimree looked at Odeon again. The pain in his eyes and in his expression stirred her pity. He deserved better than Trinati.

Cimree turned and opened the door, leaving them together in that awkward silence. When she arrived back at her room, she found Khaf there, pacing.

He turned and looked at her with a triumphant smile. "I know where they've taken the girl. Come with me."

And I, of the Watchers, according to the records that have been passed down to us, must suppose that an angel of the Oldknow, according to the written word, had fallen. Wherefore, he became a demon, having sought that which was evil. And because he had fallen from heaven, and had become truly miserable, he sought also the misery of all—even the First Man and First Woman. Wherefore he said unto Lilith, yea, Asmodeus, who was the father of all lies, and spake in the guise of a pale serpent, "Partake of that fruit, and ye shall not die, but ye shall become as the Oldknow, knowing good and evil."

And the man partook, according to the will of the flesh and the urges therein, which giveth Asmodeus power to captivate, to bring him down to sheol, that he may reign over him in his own benighted kingdom.

— BOOK OF THE WATCHERS, THE TALE OF THE
FALLEN ANGELS

TWENTY-ONE
TREACHERY ABOUNDS

C imree followed Khaf down to the bathing pools beneath the mansion. The smell of wet stone filled her nostrils, and her eyes picked out the heat imprint of Khaf. Before going with him, she had excused herself to visit the garden and found a serpent to graft with. She needed to exploit all her advantages, and the added senses would be helpful.

Khaf checked first to make sure no one was using the pools and then motioned for her to follow him to the stone edge that covered the entrance to the catacombs Azra had shown her. He lifted the stone, revealing the stairs, and stepped over the edge to go down himself. Cimree had her dirk, her pack, and even the coptic fruit they'd taken from the forbidden garden. She could sense Azra moving with purpose and determination. He wasn't near, and she didn't think he'd found a way to get to Roque yet. There had been no feeling of triumph.

"Pull down the slab after us," Khaf told her.

"Earlier you said we were forbidden to use these tunnels."

He sized her up. "That was when I let on that I was still loyal to them."

"You aren't loyal now?"

"I'm loyal to you, Cazibe."

She wasn't sure she believed it, even though he sounded believable and there was no betraying emotion in his heart. She stared at his sincere expression, could sense the urgency of moving quickly on before it would be too late to save Chrys. She'd trained enough with Azra to believe she could remove him as a threat if necessary. She decided to see where this new option led.

She stepped down and lowered the slab which plunged them into darkness. However, she could still see him perfectly well.

He withdrew a gem from his pocket, a blue sapphire that began to glow as it lay on his palm. She stared at it curiously, tilting her head and giving him an inquisitive look.

"A spirit is trapped in servitude here," he explained. "It will guide us to her."

Cimree nodded without speaking and followed as he led the way through the narrow catacombs, barely wide enough to walk side by side. The entire tunnel was made of inlaid stones: the walls, the floor, and the ceiling too. They passed several branches off the path they were traveling, each leading a different way, but Khaf kept along the main tributary.

"Who made these tunnels?" Cimree asked him, fascinated by the craftsmanship.

"A race of servants created for that purpose. The Cruithne."

"Where are they? Have I seen one?"

"No. They were all destroyed after the catacombs were built to prevent them revealing their knowledge to anyone."

That was simply awful and her mouth twisted in distaste.

"These lead to the other mansions?" she asked him, feeling disgusted by what she'd been told.

"Every one of them," he said, turning back and nodding to her. She could feel his nervousness and concern. He was risking himself to help her. But he'd done so willingly.

"Was the city built first or the catacombs?" she asked.

"The catacombs. They've been here for ages. This was a place where kings were buried. Where treasures were hidden."

"Why?"

"It was Asmodeus's design," he said. "When he rose again with a new form, he could come and take the riches to aid him in his next plot to subdue kingdoms. He could preserve magic to be used in other lifetimes." He glanced back at her again. "He values lifeless things over living ones. He values slaves over free thinking. And since he was cast out of Clairvaux, he has learned that the promise of wealth is enough to chain men's hearts."

They continued on the path for a distance and then stopped at a four-way intersection. He held the glowing blue stone higher, and she saw markings, runes carved into the stone. "This is a crossroads. We are about to enter the ocher sector. That symbol represents the color. That one, which points to the way we've come is 'blue.'"

"What of the other two?" she asked, pointing to the tunnels on the right and left.

"White—that is a shortcut to the grand souk. And that one leads to the black."

"What about the crimson?" Cimree asked. "I know white and black and crimson were before blue."

"When we entered the tunnel from the mansion, if we'd gone down any of the other paths, we would have found the crimson rune since it is adjacent to blue."

"Do the paths go all the way to silver and gold?"

"Yes, but those entrances are guarded."

She felt vibrations coming from the ground. They were so subtle that she wasn't sure at first what they were, but when she shifted her focus down the shaft leading to white, she sensed the vibrations coming from that tunnel.

"Someone is coming," she said, pointing that direction.

Khaf frowned. "If you are seen with me, it will raise suspicion. We must flee."

She gripped his arm and shook her head. "I won't be seen."

"How is that possible?" he asked her.

"Trust me." She glanced down the passageway and felt the vibrations growing stronger. Her snake senses were so useful.

She lowered her hand and began to concentrate. Since she had bonded to that snake in the garden, she was able to camouflage herself, blending in with the colors of the stone. Khaf gaped in surprised as she seemed to disappear.

"Where are you?" he whispered.

"I'm here," she answered. Then she saw the heat coming from the white tunnel as a man came treading forward at a fast pace, one that would soon bring him to them.

Khaf lifted the stone and held it out, gazing down the tunnel until the man arrived. He was wearing a fine tunic and had a fragrant scent, something different from Khaf's, but strong enough to show he also wore a scented oil.

"Khaf?" the man asked.

"Where are you headed, Ahmet?"

"I was sent to the souk to get some ground nightshade," Ahmet said, holding out a small velvet pouch.

"Who are we poisoning?" Khaf asked with a crafty smile.

"Hamza Kerem. Roque wants to know who he is going to side with."

"Hamza Kerem is a fool," Khaf said dismissively.

"Indeed. And he won't remember even telling us. I'll wager six denarii he chooses the pretend king."

"That is hardly a wager, Ahmet. I could have told you that without the nightshade freeing his tongue."

"You boast," Ahmet said with a flare of his nostrils.

Khaf shrugged.

Ahmet gave him a little bow, always keeping eye contact, and then scurried down the pathway marked with the orange signal rune. Cimree waited until his heat had vanished from sight and the tremors had left before releasing her disguise.

Khaf gave her an appreciative look. "That would be helpful in my profession," he said.

"What did Ahmet mean about the 'pretend king'?" she asked.

Khaf's eyes narrowed and his lips tightened into a frown. "We typically do not speak of it."

Cimree cocked her head and just stared at him.

Khaf sighed. "The Diyako you met is an imposter."

Cimree blinked with surprise.

"He was another courtier. Do you think the real Diyako would risk his life meeting strangers, any one of whom could plunge a knife into his heart? Very few know what Diyako even looks like, so they do not know they're being duped. The courtier wears a gem that allows the true king to hear what is said around him and to him. And because of his close relationship with the king, he knows what answers to give."

"So was the offer I was given truly given?"

"Of course. The courtier cannot act against the king's will. You were chosen before you even went there. We should go. Before anyone else comes."

Cimree could tell that Khaf wasn't glad to reveal what he had, but his words felt truthful. The royal court of Ecbatana was interlaced with varying schemes. Even the offer to bet on a particular outcome seemed part of the culture among courtiers.

They also went down the corridor leading into the orange section of the city. Cimree paid notice to the path they were taking so that she could return back to the angel sworn mansion. Every time they took another side passage, she looked for something to mark the way, a little pattern in the stone or a crack in one of the rocks.

At last they reached a tunnel that ended at steps leading up. She could smell wet stone.

"Do all the tunnels end in the baths?" she asked him.

He nodded. "They are a convenient place to kill someone and then remove the body," he answered.

Then with a quiet tread, he went up the steps and slipped the sapphire into his pocket. He gently pushed on the stone lid, just to observe. He set it down.

"Someone is bathing," he murmured.

He checked again, but they had to wait longer. She was amused at his sighs of impatience. Finally, the bather was finished, and Khaf lifted the lid so light from the baths illuminated the entrance. Khaf went through and then motioned for her to follow. She did, finding watery footprints on the stone floor, but the bather was gone.

Khaf went to the stairs and looked up carefully, staying out of sight.

"If you can turn invisible again, do so now," he told her. "It will be easier that way."

Cimree felt hardly any tingles at all from the grafting magic. "It doesn't work as well if I move," she said. "If we see someone, I'll need to hold still."

"Agreed. Just follow me as best you can." His eyes were furtive and shifted nervously. Beads of sweat had formed on his brow.

Cimree wondered whether he was worried about his own life or if he'd planned some treachery for her.

"Lead the way," she said to him, still wondering at his motives.

Khaf walked up the steps, adopting a manner of ease as if he belonged there. Cimree followed but stopped when a servant came in sight carrying a tray of food. The servant passed her without seeming to notice her at all while Khaf continued down the corridor. It was another fancy mansion, with pillars and flowering plants and a living fig tree growing in a pot in a room that had no ceiling but was instead open to the sky. She sensed serpents in its branches.

She followed Khaf at a distance as he maneuvered through the palatial residence. Several times she had to stop to avoid being seen, but the grafting enabled her to remain unobserved. Oh what she wouldn't give to have the memories from her past lives restored!

As she continued, she sensed a serpent following her, attracted to her presence. She felt its curiosity as it slithered on the smooth marble floor after her, and she connected minds with it to dismiss it. The tiny snake obeyed and went back to the fig tree.

Khaf reached a door, one with a shiny lacquer on it, and paused, listening. Cimree approached and revealed herself.

"This is where I was told she'd be," he whispered to her. "I don't know how many will be guarding her. I hope just one. I will have to kill him or else he will report me." He gave her a look that questioned her intention.

Cimree nodded. She felt a little tang of venom as she swallowed nervously.

Khaf breathed in through his nose and then put his hand on the knob. Cimree vanished again.

He opened the door. It was a guest room, similar to the kind that Cimree and the others stayed in, except the room was darker, the curtains drawn to block out the window light. Cimree noticed a cage in the room. An empty cage. Her heart began to beat faster.

Khaf entered the room, and immediately someone pounced on him. Another man. Khaf seemed surprised by the attack, and the two began to wrestle each other, each huffing for breath.

Cimree saw the man lift a knife, ready to plunge it into Khaf's neck. She darted forward and grabbed the man by the wrist. Then using a subduing technique that Azra had taught her, she wrenched his arm behind his back, torquing his wrist in a way that caused excruciating pain, making him drop the dagger. Applying even more force, she made him gasp and drop to his knees.

Khaf quickly shut the door and drew his own weapon. The man lifted his head.

"Khaf?" the man grunted in pain.

"Greetings, Ersin," Khaf said. The man tried to look back at Cimree, but she increased the pain and pressure until he gasped again and bowed face-first to the floor. He was bigger than her, but she was using both hands to control his wrist, which gave her the leverage she needed.

"The cage is empty. Where's the girl?" Khaf demanded.

"I can't...tell...you," Ersin said against the anguish.

Khaf knelt by him. He drew out a pouch and emptied some powder into his palm.

"No!" Ersin said, trying to struggle, but Cimree increased the pressure.

Khaf blew the powder in the man's face. He shook his head, his eyes shut, sweat trickling down his cheeks. The man wheezed and grunted and then his breathing began to slow. The resistance to her grip lessened. Maybe he wasn't feeling the pain anymore.

"He's subdued," Khaf said. "But take his knife, just to be safe."

Cimree didn't want to release him, but the man's steady breathing and subtle moaning made her believe he was intoxicated somehow. She released her grip and his arm dropped to his side, slack. She took his curved dagger, and when she looked at it more closely, she saw a resin of sorts on its blade.

Khaf crouched by Ersin and lifted his chin. "Where's the girl?"

"Ilayda came for her," Ersin said, his voice sounding dazed.

Khaf's eyes widened with surprise and fear. "When?"

"Not long ago. She bribed me to let her go."

Khaf looked at Cimree and back at Ersin. "Why would Roque's *concubine* want the mute girl?"

"I don't know."

"Do you know where they went?"

"The forbidden garden. She said she would not return with the girl. And that I wouldn't be punished."

Cimree's stomach clenched with dread. She'd been to that garden with Azra. She knew exactly where the concubine was taking Chrys.

Twenty-Two
The Dryad Tree

K haf looked horror-stricken. "There are no tunnels there. If I were to go, I would be killed on sight by the guards."

"I know where the gardens are," Cimree said. "I will go alone."

He reached out his hand to her, shaking his head no. "It is too dangerous, even for you."

"I will not let them harm her," Cimree said forcefully. "I must go. And we cannot let this man tell anyone about us."

"I will slay him," Khaf said with a nod.

Cimree reached into her pocket and withdrew the coptic fruit. She handed it to Khaf.

His eyes bulged again with surprise. "Where did you get that?"

"From the forbidden garden." She handed it to him.

"I just need a piece of it," he said, taking the fruit. Drawing his own blade, he sliced a wedge from it. The fleshy part had a leathery texture with variegated coloring, and the core was gray. It gave off no odor.

Khaf wrapped the remainder of the fruit in a bit of cloth he drew from his pocket and handed it back to her, then crouched before Ersin with the bit he'd cut away. Ersin swayed slightly, his expression still vacant.

"Eat this," Khaf said, bringing the slice to the man's mouth. Ersin obeyed without hesitation, but he made a face as he chewed. Cimree watched his swallow reflex, saw the bulge in his throat. His involuntary reaction to its taste made him grimace. And she watched in amazement as the rictus fastened on him. His fingers curled, his back arched slightly, and then his skin turned to stone. The transformation happened in seconds. She heard his last exhalation and then he, and his clothing, had transformed into a statue.

"What devilry made that fruit?" she asked Khaf in a bewildered fascination.

"It is a form of metamorphistry, the highest form of magic that a Wizr can perform. The fruit must be swallowed in order for it to perform the effect. Hence the warning taste to spit it out."

"You said earlier it cannot be reversed. Was that true?" Cimree asked.

"If there is a way, I do not know what it is."

It made her think of the blue-tinted fruit that Azra had picked from the garden the previous night. Not knowing what a piece of fruit could do was potentially very dangerous. Much like the story of the First Parents in the garden. And how the man had been tricked to eat a fruit that turned him mortal.

"In the garden, there was a tree that had a blue-skinned fruit, about the size of a cherry," Cimree said. "Have you heard of it?"

Khaf frowned and shook his head. "I would be wary about eating any fruit found there. There are worse fates than turning to stone."

"Truly?"

"One of those fruits induces leprosy."

"What is that?"

"It is a fatal illness that attacks the nerves. It takes a very long time to die. You lose your sense of touch. I've seen lepers missing fingers and toes. Scabs form across the flesh. It is truly a hideous way to die. This was merciful in comparison," he added, nodding to the statue of Ersin.

"Do you know what that fruit looks like?" she asked.

Khaf shook his head. "I do not. It may be the fruit you found."

That knowledge made her desperate to warn Azra not to eat it. Not without understanding its risks. She believed that the fruit of the Gallows Tree might be able to reverse any such affliction. But not until the seed was planted, nurtured, and grew into another tree. And it could take years before it was able to bear more fruit.

"I'm going to find Chrys," Cimree said, touching Khaf's shoulder. "Get away from here. I will return to the mansion. But I'm going to hide her first."

Khaf nodded in agreement and rose to his full height in front of her. Then he surprised her by bending forward and kissing her hair softly. "You truly are Cazibe." He gave her a teasing smile, showing that he'd enjoyed startling her with the kiss. She wasn't sure if she should be offended by his forwardness—wasn't sure if that reaction was entirely her own or from a sudden surge of resentment coming from Azra.

He checked the door. "No one is there. Hurry to your friend."

Cimree watched him leave and then left the room and the cage behind. Once she was outside, she began to walk quickly in the direction of the silver wall. A drab-colored rosefinch caught her attention in a tree branch. Grafting with birds had always been challenging for her, but she needed speed in order to get to the forbidden garden quickly. Birds were afraid of snakes, which she imagined explained their reluctance to bond with her. What if she could turn that instinct around in her favor?

I can help you.

The thought came to her from a snake hidden within the foliage nearby. It was keenly intelligent and had noticed her leaving the mansion. Not all serpents communicated with her, but this one had. She sensed it and, with her distaff, connected with it. It was a horned viper, one that blended in perfectly with its surroundings. Its tail had protuberances that looked like insect legs.

I will lure the bird for you.

Cimree felt excited by the notion of being able to bond with the bird more easily. The viper slithered into place, nestled amidst some decorative rocks until it was nearly invisible. But its tail began to flick slowly, and it appeared to Cimree to be like a spider. Another rosefinch spotted it first and swept down for a snack.

The viper stung it with its fangs, injecting its paralyzing venom into the bird, which flapped and fluttered until its paralyzation was complete.

Now graft with it.

Cimree wondered at the snake's intelligence. *Are you really a snake?* she thought toward it.

I am not. But I am a spirit creature. And I serve you willingly because your friend insisted on releasing one of us from bondage. There are many others seeking freedom as well.

Cimree thought about how Khaf had followed her using the jewel he'd given her and how Azra had forced him to break the magic and release the dragonfly. Or at least it had appeared to be a dragonfly. She wondered if the serpent from the legend had been a spirit creature in disguise.

You must hurry, the serpent warned her. *I must resist my instinct to feed. Bond with the bird.*

Cimree pointed the distaff at the rosefinch and tried to bond with it. It responded instantly and with terror, begging her to help it escape from becoming a meal.

I will if you help me, Cimree thought to it. The bird was eager to do so, and she felt the grafting slip easily into place.

Cimree rose from the ground, feeling the wonderful sensation of flying, a disconcerting constant inhalation, and the quickness and subtleness of the bird. She shot like a dart.

Cimree knew the guardians were searching for her. Many archers had tried to shoot her as she flew over the walls, but the instincts of the finch gave her agility and maneuverability that helped her stay hidden among the treetops. Horns had been sounded in warning, which made her thrill with excitement, but she passed over the golden wall effortlessly before racing into the gardens. She knew her destination since she'd been there, and flying through the treetops enabled her to reach it quickly and stealthily. She landed close to the oak tree with the growths clustered in its upper branches, hiding herself by another nearby tree.

Cimree dropped down into the garden. Her shoulder blades were tingling from the grafting, but she was not out of breath, even though she'd been flying very fast and had dodged the enemies shooting at her. She released her connection with the rosefinch and then admonished the serpent to let it go.

Very well, she heard it in her mind, a bit begrudgingly, and then saw the bird fly away through the serpent's eyes. She'd always relied on others to help her bond with birds. Suddenly, she had a way, a possibility, of being able to do it herself. The added insight thrilled her.

Thank you, she said to the serpent. Without its help, it would have taken her a lot longer to reach the garden. She was about to release the horned viper, but the snake clung to her.

Don't look at the tree too closely, it said in warning, *or the Dryad will steal your memories.*

She wondered at its meaning, confused but eager to learn more about it.

What are you saying—

The connection was cut between her and the viper. She hadn't released it. A sickening feeling came into her stomach. The last time that had happened to her she was in the sky above Lake Beatriz, and the golem had severed the grafting. Her pulse quickened with fear. She gazed around the garden, unable to see any sources of heat.

She realized that *all* her graftings had been severed.

She felt Azra's consciousness prick with worry. He felt her fear. Felt its familiarity. He was going to cease what he was doing and come to her immediately.

No! she thought in her mind. She summoned the magic of the Tanaquil medallion and used it to capture her fears and worries. And she would use it to take away Azra's as well if she needed to. She knew she could drive the golem away if it came for her. When she'd encountered it in Montheron, it had fled from her. It could not break the bond of the medallion's magic.

She gazed around the garden. Where was it? Another warning horn blew. She didn't know what it meant, but it was a foreboding sound.

Then she heard the sounds of cracking twigs coming her way. Instead of fear, she felt defiance. The movement was coming from the direction of the oak tree.

Look at me.

The thought whispered in her mind. The impulse to look was strong. Overwhelming even. Cimree squeezed her eyes shut and sent a blast of fear in its direction.

Don't take her away—I need her! Please!

Cimree pushed away from the tree she had leaned against and started walking away from the oak tree. The terrible urge to turn around and look chafed inside her, casting her mind into a frenzy of doubts and curiosity. Just look back! She knew if she did, she would see something wonderful. Exotic. Life-changing. There was knowledge to be gained. An understanding of the world that she could get no other way.

Go! Cimree shrieked in her thoughts at it, increasing her pace and using the magic to send more waves of emotion. She tried different feelings. Worry, despair, anguish, sorrow. Nothing seemed to work against it. Still the thoughts tugged at her, demanding her to look back.

And she knew if she did, she would lose her memories. And something about that was familiar. An instinct, deep down, reminded her that it had happened to her before.

"Quit struggling!"

It was a woman's voice. This didn't come from behind her but ahead, nor was it in her head. In her frantic state, she'd failed to hear the sound of others approaching. She was far enough from the tree that its compulsion was lessening but still present. It still had her attention but she felt stronger against it.

She opened her eyes, looking straight ahead, and saw Chrys, her arm clenched violently in the hand of a woman who was exposing exceedingly too much skin and wearing a shocking display of jewelry: a tiara that had feathers made from gold, with a gemstone at the forefront and another jewel dangling from a chain of precious metal centered on her forehead; large gauges that had insects set in amber in the centers along with multiple other earrings and a necklace that wrapped almost her entire slender neck. Her golden dress was made of silk, and the stays pushed up her bosom, exposing an obscene amount of the most ample breasts Cimree had ever seen. Sleeves similar to the Ecbatanan fashion clung to her upper arms in a billowing purple fabric that was threaded with golden designs. Her face was so youthful that she seemed to be Cimree's own age, with paints and kohl around her eyes and her lips an unnatural hue.

The woman was dragging Chrys by the arm and stopped short when she saw Cimree in front of them.

"You're one of the angel sworn!" the woman hissed at her, her expression turning to one of fear and hatred.

When Chrys turned and saw Cimree, she started to weep with relief. Her tunic sleeve was torn, and the grip on her arm was clearly causing her pain, but her relief at seeing Cimree overshadowed all else.

"Let her go," Cimree demanded, attempting to snatch away

the woman's feelings and replace them with the abject terror caused by the presence of the Fear Liath.

Cimree saw the jewel on the woman's forehead begin to glow.

Her mouth curled into a frown. "I'm not so easy to compel, tyrant queen!"

TWENTY-THREE
GOLEM'S BREATH

C imree acted on instinct. This must be the concubine Ilayda who Ersin had told them had stolen Chrys. She might use her weapon to threaten the mute girl or she might use it against Cimree, but holding a hostage made more sense.

Cimree rushed forward, using the edge of her hand to strike at the concubine's throat. Her opponent blocked it with one arm while drawing a thin blade from her bodice, slicing it against Cimree's outstretched arm. A sting of pain flared.

Cimree kicked at the woman's knee, but the other backstepped to avoid the blow. Her reflexes were exceptionally quick. But at least the combat had caused Ilayda to release her grip on Chrys, and the young girl darted out of reach.

Ilayda scowled and went on the attack, sweeping the blade in the air in front of Cimree to drive her backward, but Cimree used both hands to block the blow and swiveled around. She stepped inside the other woman's legs, pivoted her hips, and they both fell on the garden floor. Ilayda kicked her off and they both rose, breathing hard, and began to circle one another, each looking for an advantage.

"I must bring the girl to the tree," Ilayda said with anger in her eyes.

Cimree invoked her magic again, trying to draw the anger out. She saw the jewel dangling from the other woman's forehead flicker again with power.

"Tell me why," Cimree said, feinting a punch, causing the other to react.

"I cannot speak it," Ilayda answered. "My tongue is bound. But it must be freed!"

"What must be freed? The Dryad?"

Ilayda's eyes widened with surprise. "How can you speak of it!"

"Why won't you speak of it? I won't let anyone harm the girl."

"I don't want to harm her! She is *needed* by the tree! She is Dryad-born!"

"She's afraid of it."

"Fear is part of life. You are not my queen yet!" she said obstinately, making Cimree wonder if the concubine feared what would happen to her if Cimree came to rule.

Cimree swiveled to the left, as if she were going to strike, but then reversed suddenly and attacked the other way. The ruse worked, and Ilayda slashed in the wrong direction, overextending herself and allowing Cimree to catch her wrist above the thin blade. She stepped over the arm and wrenched, to give herself control of the other woman, but Ilayda was equally skilled in evasion and hoisted Cimree off her feet, throwing her to the ground. Cimree landed on her back and instantly the concubine straddled her, pressing her thumbs into the indentation on Cimree's throat.

Cimree felt sharp pain and couldn't breathe as the woman choked her. She reached up and grabbed the ornate tiara and wrenched it off the concubine's head, bringing locks of hair with it. The concubine gasped in pain. Cimree stabbed Ilayda in the chest with the tiara, and the feathered edges cut into the woman's skin, but still she choked Cimree, trying to knock her unconscious.

Cimree sensed the snakes in the garden and tried to reach out to them in her mind without the grafting wand. Azra had told her that with animals of affinity, the distaffs weren't even required. But darkness began to dance in her vision as she struggled to remain conscious. With a final surge of strength, she sent another gush of fear into the woman, and this time it worked. The concubine's eyes filled with terror and she let go of Cimree, freezing instead of fleeing.

As the welcome air rushed into Cimree's chest, the dizziness began to fade. She heard a deep crackle of branches coming toward them. Limbs began to rain down. Something hulking and heavy was passing through the treetops.

Ilayda still straddled Cimree, pinning her to the ground, and she tried to buck herself free. Many serpents swarmed them, hissing and beginning to strike at Ilayda, piercing her legs with their fangs. The concubine screamed in terror and revulsion. The snakes bit her legs again as she rose and began to run away. Cimree still clenched the tiara in her hands, lying on her back, watching in fascination as the serpents did her will and continuously bit the other woman.

Suddenly the concubine was hoisted into the air, as if jerked by an invisible rope. Her terrified scream was cut off instantly.

Cimree scrabbled backward and gained her feet, ignoring her minor injuries. She hooked the tiara into her belt to free her hands and cast her gaze around. Chrys was gazing at the trees where the concubine had disappeared into the foliage, her mouth gaping with fear. Cimree ran to her, grabbed her by the wrist, and pulled her away. They began to run as fast as they could.

The canopy creaked again, and more limbs began to snap off and drop behind them. It had to be the golem. Cimree's own fear would have drowned her without the power of the Tanaquil amulet. She barely managed to keep it subdued as they fled. They dodged through the trees of the garden, determined to escape the golem and the oak tree at the garden's center. She didn't care if they encountered Roque's guards. She'd welcome it! But the creature quickly overtook them, able to leap from tree to tree faster than they could run. As more branches came down, she glimpsed something overhead, something that blended in with its surroundings. A natural camouflage just like Cimree could use. It only increased her dread.

She couldn't invoke those same grafting powers to hide her and Chrys from its sight. No, not when the golem could sever the connection so easily. Or even prevent her from doing it. This creature seemed designed to destroy angel sworn.

A branch struck Chrys and knocked her down. It hadn't been a large one, but it was enough of a blow to stun Chrys and send her sprawling. Cimree halted and gazed around at the canopy, trying to figure out where the golem was, even though it was invisible to her eyes. Her breathing was fast and hard. She sensed Azra coming to her—he was in the garden. Moments before, he'd been far away. Suddenly he was there, racing toward her. The sudden change in distance felt like the teleportation effect when Roque had brought her through the portal. Did that mean Azra had the Tay al-Ard?

That would give them a way to escape.

Cimree pulled Chrys up, trying to revive her so they could run again and close the distance with Azra. Then she smelled something. Something awful, a foul and horrid stench. And she heard the golem breathing. The skin on the back of her neck tingled in anticipation of being touched.

Cimree whirled and sent a blast of fear at it. She knew her eyes were glowing silver. Magic churned through her, a river of power that overwhelmed her emotions, boiling them raw. The feeling of imminent touching departed, and she saw the tree just overhead trembling and swaying. A piercing shriek sounded. No, a voice.

"Cim-reeee!" it hissed. It was a crooning sound. A greedy sound.

She sent another blast of fear at it, and the power of the magic intensified as Azra drew nearer. The trees continued to writhe overhead.

Cimree watched the trees shake as it thrashed up there, though she was still unable to see it. The golem was fighting against its instinct to flee. It wanted her. What did her magic make it feel? Did it enjoy the fear she sent to it? Was it relishing these irrepressible human feelings?

A branch sailed toward her head—thrown, not fallen. Cimree dived to the side, covering Chrys with her body, and the limb struck Cimree's back.

"Cim-reee! Cim-reeee!"

The tree shook as if the huge creature was bouncing up and down in it. Branches were cracking and falling, and then it leaped to another tree, coming at her again.

Cimree used the magic to force it back.

Hurry, Azra, she pleaded in her mind, feeling the drain from the magic sapping her strength. When she'd faced the Fear Liath near the Gallows Tree, overusing the magic had made her black out. And then she realized, in horror, that the golem probably knew this. It wanted her to become helpless. Powerless.

A cracking sound. Then another branch hurtled at her and struck her again. She gasped in pain at the blow, but she bundled Chrys to her, protecting her, the instinct to preserve and protect so deep inside her that she couldn't do otherwise. She continued to summon her magic, desperate to protect Chrys and herself until Azra could get there.

He was almost there. She could feel his presence, his fear for her and Chrys's well-being motivating him to greater speed. The golem would sever his grafting like it had in Montheron. Even with all his fighting prowess, he was no match for such a creature.

Cimree heard a clucking sound. Smelled the stagnant breath once again. It was on the forest floor, creeping toward her. She gazed around in terror, sending another blast of fear, but the magic was half-hearted. Dizziness made her topple over.

"Cim-reee," it whispered. She felt it touch her hair. It had fingers, but they were inhuman.

Then a jet of blinding blue flames struck the golem. A harsh barking of rage accompanied the smell of burnt skin. The golem shrieked in rage and fury and leaped back into the trees. Angry smoke churned in the air. The creature roared in thwarted fury and pain.

Azra slid up to them, his hands shimmering with blue flames, a look of fierce determination scrunching his face. He wrapped one arm around her and Chrys.

Magic sucked them from the garden.

It felt as if she were falling off a mountain and plummeting to her death, the feeling so visceral and frightening that she fainted.

Twenty-Four

Alcove

Cimree had passed out before when she had overused the Tanaquil's magic, and she knew the thickheaded grogginess took some time to wear off, but as consciousness was regained, she felt cold on her bare skin and realized she wasn't wearing her tunic.

Cimree forced her eyes to open. She was lying on her stomach in a darkened place. She smelled must and stone and then heard the chittering of a firavun faresi.

Azra's presence was immediately discerned, which caused an intake of breath. Everything was a blur in her mind, but then she remembered the golem, and her heart had an involuntary spasm of fear that made her sit up quickly only to hit her head.

"Careful," Azra cautioned.

A wreath of blue flames appeared, the fire illuminating his hands and casting away the shadows. She had an instant's time to grab her tunic, which she discovered she'd been lying on, to cover herself. Her back was sore in two places. Using one hand to hold the tunic against her breasts, she reached with the other and felt the bruised skin around her shoulder blade, wincing at the tenderness.

Azra was sitting cross-legged beside her. The little shelter of broken stone pieces made for tight quarters. Chrys was sitting against a tilted bit of sculpted stone, the firavun faresi coiled in her lap while she petted it.

"How long have I been unconscious?" she asked, her voice thick. Thirst clawed at her throat.

"Hours," Azra said. The light from the blue flames danced over his fingertips. He held one of his hands aloft, bringing more light to her face. He was looking at her cheek.

"I was focused on your other wounds. I missed one," he said.

The feelings she experienced from him were tender and full of longing. There were memories in the mix, feelings he'd had long ago when he was injured and being helped.

Cimree switched hands to remain covered and looked at the other arm where the concubine had sliced her. It was bandaged, and she sniffed the fragrance of the poultice he'd used.

"Did you use woad?" she asked him curiously, feeling self-conscious and wanting to pull the tunic back on, but not with him just gazing at her in so intimate a way.

"It was in your pack." He pointed with a flaming finger at her pack, which was nearby. The space barely fit the three of them, and it looked like a wall had collapsed.

"Are we underground?" she asked, trying to make sense of their location. The tightness of the space was unnerving, and she felt as if the walls were going to shift and collapse and bury her alive. Her insides wriggled with apprehension.

He shook his head. "Listen and you'll hear the grand souk. We're inside the outer wall of the city."

She lifted her eyebrows in surprise.

"When they built this wall around Ecbatana, they used these tunnels within the walls to transport material, and then it seems they backfilled the tunnel with debris to make it impassable. Well, except for pockets like this. I found this spot when I first came. It's a good hiding place. They couldn't get to us even if they knew we were here."

"I think I prefer the mansion," Cimree said. "Do you have anything to drink?"

Chrys scooped the firavun faresi from her lap and produced a waterskin that she handed to Cimree. She savored a few sips and then handed it back.

"I noticed your hand is on fire," Cimree said, arching her brow.

He nodded. "That blue fruit we found in the garden. It's changed me."

She gave him a worried frown. "I was worried what it might do to you."

"It's connected to my emotions somehow," he said. "The flames are fed on anger and other similar feelings. Pride. Ambition. Wariness. It's strange. The flames come when I focus on those feelings. It's the same magic that Roque's defenders use at the inner walls."

Cimree nodded. "I saw them when we first came," she said. She was relieved they were out of immediate danger, but she did not like the cramped quarters and the feeling of being enclosed. The underground tunnels she'd walked with Khaf hadn't disturbed her this much. She wasn't sure why.

"You're uneasy," he said, tilting his head slightly.

"I am," she agreed. "It feels wrong here."

He nodded in understanding, but she was confused by this. "When I first came all those years ago, this was used as a den by a pack of firavun faresi. Your affinity is revolting against their lair."

That made sense. She'd always wondered how Azra had endured being in the dungeon of Montheron for so many years, but understanding his affinity, she realized that it was comfortable to him to be in cramped places. The close walls offered protection from attack. He was, in his way, able to relax in a place like this. To feel safe.

"Are there more of them about?" she asked him.

"About twenty, I think, but I've asked them to stay away. They felt threatened by you. A serpent in their warren."

Maybe that's what she was feeling. All their little eyes glaring at her in the darkness. She saw him reach into his belt and withdraw the brass cylinder—the Tay al-Ard.

"You found Roque," she said, smiling at him.

He nodded. "I waited a while for him to show at his palace. He'd just had an argument with one of his concubines, based on what I'd heard him complain to his servant. I was hiding in his wardrobe, watching through the decorative slits. After he dismissed the servant, I was able to sneak up on him and steal it from his belt. He knew instantly, and a knife to his throat provided some much-needed information about it."

Cimree would have enjoyed seeing that, and she relished the feeling of satisfaction in Azra's chest as he told her what he'd done.

"He, of course, babbled and made threats and promises. I could have named the tyrant queen if I'd cared to, but I wanted information about the device. There is only one and it is a powerful magic. The power is called teleportation, and it can take the holder anywhere they have previously been. You cannot use it to go somewhere you don't know about firsthand. It requires time to rest between frequent uses. It can be invoked multiple times in a row, but with the risk of breaking the gem that traps the entities therein. According to Roque, these entities prefer this servitude and are incredibly difficult to capture. In their natural form, these entities cause enormous whirlwinds and can devastate entire cities. Being in the Tay al-Ard is a blessing to them, he said. Otherwise they do nothing but destroy."

"I'm not sure Lord Roque is trustworthy," Cimree said.

Azra snorted. "We're in agreement on that score. We can use the Tay al-Ard to go to Tirich Mir. It can transport multiple people at once, but the more people you bring, the more it taxes its powers. I'd like to get Andrin, Perreta, and the children to safety and then see who else will go with us. We can leave the mayhem here and be done with it."

"I haven't felt you use it," Cimree said. "Until you teleported to the garden and then again when you brought us here."

"I was with Roque when I felt your danger. So I used the Tay al-Ard to go to the garden and followed our connection to find you. My intention is to travel to Tirich Mir alone first and make sure it is safe for us. They are scouring the city for us as we speak. And I didn't want to use it to return to the angel sworn mansion without letting the device rest for a while and until I was sure that you'd awakened naturally and were all right. Now we know that the golem is here. We need to leave right away."

Cimree noticed that Chrys began nodding vehemently when he said those words. He looked at her curiously and then back at Cimree.

"I've learned something about her," Cimree said, gazing at the mute girl. Chrys met her eyes. The girl was staring at her intently, her gaze fixed and studying.

Cimree looked back at Azra, unnerved by the intensity of the child's gaze. "We can speak of it later."

"Tell me now," Azra said firmly.

Cimree quickly told him about the snake she'd encountered, one that was probably like the djinn Khaf had spoken of, which had spoken in her mind and could communicate more articulately than other serpents. How it had lured a bird with the feature embedded in its tail and how she'd been able to graft with it to rescue Chrys.

"The snake told me that the tree in the forbidden garden was a Dryad tree. That Chrys is Dryad-born."

Azra frowned in confusion, his forehead wrinkling. He turned to Chrys. "I don't know what that means. Do you?"

Chrys nodded slowly, her eyes riveted on Azra's.

"You are Dryad-born?"

Chrys nodded again.

"Is that why you were afraid of the other tree?" Cimree asked her gently.

Chrys turned her gaze to Cimree and nodded slowly once more. She looked too reticent, distrustful even. Like she didn't want to reveal too much.

Cimree touched Azra's arm to get his attention. "I don't know if the concubine was acting under Roque's orders. She might not have been. He'd put Chrys in a cage in a palace in the ocher quarter, and the concubine had bribed the guard to steal her away. We ended up turning him into stone."

"With the fruit we took?" Azra asked in surprise. "I remember having a certain feeling from you several hours ago. I couldn't make sense of it, like you were seeing something that disgusted you but also intrigued you."

"For certain it conjured many abhorrent feelings," Cimree confessed. "I have the rest of the fruit with me. What about the seed from the Gallows Tree?"

"I hid it there," Azra said. He leaned closer to her and pointed a flaming finger to a gap in the stone beams nearby. "Where I knew no one would find it."

"They might have found it," Cimree said. She quickly told him about the nightshade powder that Khaf had used on Ersin before they'd transmuted him into stone. The powder blown in his face had made him willing to say anything.

"That's helpful to know," Azra said. "Why don't you get dressed. I think I've rested the Tay al-Ard long enough. I'll go back to the mansion and tell Andrin's family that we'll be leaving. I'll ask Perreta to bring people to their room where I can talk to them. I think we should invite Wegner first."

"Agreed. And Uorsin."

Azra made a face, and she felt his hesitancy.

"I thought he was your friend? Don't tell me he wouldn't be useful."

"He is. But he cares for Darcia, and she's loyal to Trinati."

Cimree gaped at this. "I didn't know."

"Neither does she." He gave her a wry smile. "He was very... melancholy after she left Montheron. Angel sworn are rather timid about expressing certain feelings, especially those that go against the rules. As if Odeon and Trinati aren't examples of that!"

Cimree agreed. She'd felt, for a long time, that there was something between those two. "So fleeing Ecbatana is complicated," she said. "We can't move everyone at once, or we might break the Tay al-Ard. Some won't want to go. Some might betray us to Trinati if they knew. And Roque is going to hunt for us until he gets back what you took from him and the seed of the Gallows Tree as well. Nothing angers a deceiver more than being tricked."

"I think you've articulated our dilemma well enough. I knew your instincts would be helpful in solving our problems. You got *her* back." He turned back to Chrys and put his arm around her, and she hugged him closely, a look of tenderness in her eyes that had always been there but was incomprehensible to Cimree.

"Thanks for tending my injuries," she told Azra as he hugged the girl.

"You have two bruises on your back that will turn rather ugly by tomorrow. I don't know what hit you, but you took some hard blows."

"They were tree branches," Cimree said. "The golem threw them at us."

Azra's brow narrowed again, and she felt his natural curiosity. "Really?"

"Does that surprise you?"

"It reminds me of an animal. They aren't native to these parts. I encountered a pack of them when I was on a Long Patrol. The beasts were very strong, with a sophisticated social structure. They fought over fruit trees and had deep territorial divisions. They even looked similar to us. Fingers, toes, ears like ours. Highly intelligent. I grafted with one, and it was nightmarish in intensity. It did not like the grafting at all and fought the loss of its freedom, so I released it. Very curious."

"What did you call it?"

"When I described it to my mentor, he said they were called troglodytes. Or just trogs."

"What Odeon saw, what I've seen, this golem is like no animal in existence."

"But it may have started as one," Azra said. "And it was transformed into something else." He gave Chrys another hug and then reached out and touched Cimree's bare shoulder. She looked down, noticing the whorl-like tattoo on her chest had grown considerably since she'd last examined it. The stain made her feel embarrassed that he could see so much of it.

When their eyes met again, he shook his head slowly. The feelings between them surged with power. Azra was sharing a part of himself with her again. Feelings he'd known since he'd lived in Tirich Mir. They made her ache and swelled her heart with tenderness and excitement. He always held back, but this time, he'd lowered the barriers. The flame in his hands was warm. It didn't burn her.

She wanted to hold him, to stop the rocking maelstrom of their world and just be together again. Somewhere quiet and safe. Not this cramped debris field.

"I'll return soon," he said, and it sounded like a promise, his eyes full of shared hunger.

She reached forward and caressed his cheek. He sighed and let her, but she felt his disappointment, his longing for something more.

Too soon, he pulled his hand away, and the flames extinguished, plunging them into shades of darkness. And then he was gone, whisked away by the magic of the Tay al-Ard. His sudden absence only caused the pangs of longing to intensify. She could still sense him, within the city, deeper within its boundaries. He'd likely gone back to the angel sworn manor.

Light shone through the debris farther off. Enough to barely see her own hands and the edge of her skin as she pulled on the tunic she'd been pressing to shield herself. It took time for her eyes to adjust to the gloom. But then she saw a glow coming from a spot near her bag.

It was coming from the gems in the tiara she'd torn off Ilayda's head.

Twenty-Five
Escape

C hrys gently shook Cimree's shoulder, awakening her in the darkness. With the limited ambient light, it was difficult to see anything, so she reached for the faintly glowing gemstone set in the concubine's tiara and held it closer so she could see Chrys's face. The mute girl pointed up.

Cimree concentrated and finally heard and felt the thrum of a hammer and chisel. Little wisps of stone dust came from above, several paces from where they were.

She'd taken the tiara because its magic had helped the concubine deflect the full power of the Tanaquil medallion, and she had wanted Khaf to show her how to break it and free the creature trapped inside. But she was realizing that the gem brought additional trouble. Through a gem, Khaf had been able to follow Cimree. Were they trying to find her, or did they think it would lead to the concubine?

"We should probably leave," Cimree said as the noise continued. She imagined men up on top of the outer wall trying to make a way to get down, removing the stone blocks one by one to excavate an opening. She still felt the oppressiveness of being in the firavun faresi's lair.

Chrys nodded and pointed another way.

"Is that the way out?"

Chrys nodded.

"How do you know?" Cimree asked.

Chrys just stared at her. There was no way she could offer an explanation.

Cimree sighed and hurriedly gathered her pack, using the tiara to provide light to see what she was doing. She gazed at the pocket in the debris that Azra had pointed to, where he'd hidden the seed of the Gallows Tree. Should she take it or leave it? Bringing it along would save another use of the Tay al-Ard to find it. But taking it also risked it going to their enemies. She rubbed the edge of her nose when a trickle of stone dust fell on her face and tickled her skin. Choices had so many consequences. It just wasn't possible to foresee the outcome of every single one.

She reached into the little hole, felt around for the pouch with the seed, and pulled it out. After tugging open the drawstrings, she emptied the seed into her hand. She hadn't looked at it in a long time, but its distinctive shape was familiar to her. The seed was long and flat, tapered at one end to a kind of point with a stubbier lower half. It was cold and all the desiccated strands had rubbed off during their travels, so it was smooth, like a piece of wood. She slipped it back into the pouch and tied it up again before stuffing it in her pocket. Grabbing her pack with one hand and holding the tiara with the other, she nodded for Chrys to lead the way.

The smaller girl made a little clapping sound with her hands. Cimree frowned, not sure what that was about, and then a firavun faresi appeared from the gloom, its banded coloring barely visible in the dark. Was it the same one that had been with Azra? Cimree couldn't tell, but Chrys smiled at it and stroked its sleek fur. The firavun faresi chittered a moment and then darted through a dark gap in the rubble. Chrys followed it and Cimree followed her.

The tightness of the space made her intrinsically fearful that she'd get stuck down there. It was an irrational fear, because Azra could get in and out easily enough it seemed, but just the idea of being trapped beneath the rubble made her shiver in fear. This caused a worried sensation from Azra far away, but she tried some deep breaths as she maneuvered through the gaps in the debris. More light came from ahead, revealing Chrys as she effortlessly went over and under and between the thick pieces of broken stone. Cimree had to crouch most of the way, suppressing the growing terror that they were trapped and would never escape. But the firavun faresi, despite its smaller size, was able to lead them to a breach in the wall. The opening was ground level and would require squirming through it on their stomachs.

Chrys reached it first and gave the little creature an affectionate pat on the head. It seemed to like that. She knelt by the gap, the light from outside revealing her dusty self. Cimree struggled to make her way through the final twist and realized that anyone peeking inside the gap wouldn't have believed there was a void deeper in that was big enough for people. Listening carefully, she could still hear the tapping of the hammer on the chisel farther back.

Cimree set down her pack and the tiara and then knelt by the gap and lowered her head so she could peer outside. She could hear the noise of the grand souk, the voices clamoring for a sale, the haggling over prices. But just through the gap in the wall was an alley of sorts. There were large chests and barrels stacked near and on top of each other. It was a place where cargo was stored. Not a soul was in sight.

If they went into the souk, it was more likely that she'd be discovered. Her tunic and trews marked her as one of the angel sworn. After drawing her distaff, she reached out to feel for serpents. There were several in the bazaar, but they were all confined. That wouldn't preclude her from bonding with one, though. Judging by the brightness of the light outside, it was late afternoon.

"Maybe we should wait here and see if Azra returns," she said to Chrys.

Chrys pointed to the tiara stone and shook her head.

"If they try to sense for it again, they'll learn we moved, and then we'd be trapped," Cimree said. Chrys nodded gravely.

"If I go out into the souk dressed like this, I'll be noticed more easily. I need to find a way to disguise us."

Chrys pointed to her pack.

Cimree wrinkled her brow. "I have another tunic, but it's the same problem. It's not the fashion of Ecbatana. And I don't have any money to trade, nor would that help avoid notice."

Chrys shook her head and pointed again to the pack.

Cimree hadn't opened it, so she did so and found, to her surprise, the red silk garment that Khaf had chosen for her. The one she'd left back at the mansion. She hadn't taken it. Who...?

Azra had done it. It was the only answer that made sense. Chrys made a gesture for her to put it on.

"After we're outside," Cimree said. The firavun faresi darted through the gap and began to explore around the chests and barrels. Chrys scrabbled through the opening easily enough and reached her hand back for Cimree's pack. Cimree crawled on her stomach, feeling the aches in her body from the golem's attack still, but the pain had subsided considerably. Her back was the sorest part.

After she'd emerged from the gap, Chrys motioned for her to hide in a small space between some chests. There she was able to quickly change into the silk entari and rolled up her dusty clothes and stuffed them into the pack. Before she did, she'd taken out the seed and set it within reach. The stains from the medallion's magic were very visible and she found, deeper in the pack, the jewelry that Khaf had brought her and hastily put that on along with the sandals.

Chrys was staring at the symbol on her chest, her eyes looking intently. It was not the first time Cimree wished the girl could speak. She seemed wiser than a child. She'd always been like that.

Cimree reached for the pouch with the seed, but Chrys took it and shook her head. She patted her own chest.

"You want to carry it?" Cimree asked.

Chrys nodded long and slow.

"Can you keep it safe?"

Chrys nodded slowly again.

Cimree nodded for her to take it and then tucked the dirk into the pack, but she kept the dagger she'd taken from it earlier and put it in the girdle around her waist. She also took the pouch with the coptic fruit and tied that to the girdle. The billowy sleeves hugged her upper arms, hiding the wound she'd received from the concubine. Before heading out, she wanted to have her instincts honed and heightened. It was a relief to be out of that dismal place, and even though the streets of Ecbatana felt dangerous, she also felt better suited for that kind of danger.

She drew the distaff and sought a serpent to bond with. A fat boa constrictor slept in a basket. A sleek, shiny, banded venomous cobra was in another, chafing at its long confinement. Cimree chose that one to bond with using the grafting magic. Immediately she felt aggressive instincts, quick reflexes, and a venom that made her salivate involuntarily. Her ability to see heat came along with sensing all the tremors. What surprised her was this snake's maternal instincts.

The firavun faresi growled at her, and Cimree hissed back at it. Chrys looked at her in surprise. It had surprised Cimree too. She took the jeweled tiara and tucked it behind the crate. If they were following the gemstone, it would lead them to a dead-end alley.

Chrys took Cimree's hand, and they walked to the edge of the alley and joined the crowded street. Although she was unfamiliar with the bazaar, she used her internal sense to head the direction she felt Azra was. People brushed against her in the thick throng, but she felt that in her new attire, she wasn't really remarkable at all. Some merchants tried to sell her things, but she just looked to the next one with a half-interested expression. A short time later, the crowd was interrupted by several warriors on horseback who came from ahead of them. Cimree immediately turned away and examined some beaded necklaces at one of the nearby stalls. The merchant engaged her in conversation, pointing out the quality of the beads and how the coloring would match her eyes.

Cimree waited until the horsemen passed—there were six of them—and noticed that they stopped at the alley she and Chrys had come from. Two dismounted and went down that way.

Cimree looked at Chrys and saw her somber gaze fixed on the soldiers. Cimree shook her head and they started to walked away. She wanted to create more distance between them and the soldiers. Chrys tugged at her hand a moment, halting her.

Cimree looked and saw the mute girl was looking at the merchant intently.

"Would you like one of the necklaces, little one?" he asked her eagerly.

Cimree saw her blink slowly, and then the man's expression suddenly changed to one of confusion. Chrys gave Cimree's hand a squeeze and started to walk away. Cimree was curious about what had happened. The merchant just stared absently, as if he were talking and couldn't remember what he was supposed to say. Chrys tugged at Cimree's hand, pulling her from her study of the merchant's sudden bemusement.

What had just happened?

Cimree led them way, but she wondered at the strangeness of what she'd observed.

A memory flickered in her mind. *Don't look at the tree too closely. Or the Dryad will steal your memories.*

It was a warning the viper had given her. A warning about the Dryad tree in the forbidden garden. Her stomach began to tighten with dread. When she and Azra had faced the Fear Liath by the Gallows Tree, she couldn't remember how Azra's wounds had been healed. There had always been a gap in her memory. That was when they'd discovered Chrys.

The Dryad-born.

From somewhere deep inside Cimree, the idea suddenly sparked that some of her own memories had been taken away just like the merchant with the bead necklaces.

Watchers, beware the great imitations of goodness. Those are the handicrafts of Asmodeus. Truly the prince of darkness can be gentle. Persuasive. Reasonable. He does not rush into acts of violence, but lays traps of secret hurts. He convinces in the delay of good deeds, of generosity postponed until another time. Procrastination is a subtle thief who robs not coin but opportunity. Sheol is full of good wishes and desires.

Beware, therefore, of smiling eyes, of subtle coaxing and reasonable explanations. The drowsy lion seems tame until it is close enough to bare its fangs.

— BOOK OF THE WATCHERS, THE TALE OF THE
FALLEN ANGELS

TWENTY-SIX

HELP OF A STRANGER

As Cimree led Chrys through the grand souk seeking the nearest gate to the next wall, Cimree's mind was so caught up in her thoughts of stolen memories that she didn't realize the man was following them until he'd caught up.

"Sultana, if you please!"

The man wore costly attire and had a groomed goatee. Cimree, startled at being addressed, gave him a wary look but continued walking.

"May I speak with you, sultana? Do you go to the azure quarter? Are you and the little *preya* going there?"

"Where we go is our business," Cimree said, increasing her speed. She increased the pressure on Chrys's hand. The well-groomed man increased his pace as well.

"I mean no offense, sultana, but if you are going that way, may I accompany you? My chit was stolen. The guards at the gate will not let me through. If you would help me, my master would reward you. Please, sultana! I beg you to have pity on your lowly servant."

Cimree felt nothing but distrust for the man. But he was keeping pace with her, weaving effortlessly through the crowd to keep up. Her instincts warned her that he was a thief, looking at her as a possible victim.

"I can't help you," Cimree said, and finding an alley leading deeper into the city, one that looked vaguely familiar, she quickly took it.

The fellow was on their heels. "My master is very rich. You've heard of him, no doubt, Master Alak Kozumbay, the merchant of ivory! His palace is one of the finest in Ecbatana. Would you help me, sultana? Surely you are from that quarter."

"Leave us alone," Cimree said in a warning voice.

"Is that man troubling you?" shouted another man. A fellow with a deep paunch and a jeweled saber hanging from his side had also followed them. He had graying hair on a balding scalp and a billowy silk shirt, open at the chest. He was probably fifty years old, judging by the wrinkles and liver spots.

"Do not interfere in our business, old man," said the one who'd accosted them, in an angry tone.

The older man drew his jeweled saber and brandished it, and the other fellow ran on ahead, his eyes blazing with fear.

The older fellow approached, shaking his head and clucking his tongue. "The deceivers grow more bold each day," he said and then offered a humble bow. "I saw him watching you in the crowd and thought I might lend assistance."

"Thank you," Cimree said, feeling relief.

He gazed briefly at Chrys, gave her a tender smile, then focused back on Cimree. "I'll escort you to the gate in case that ruffian decides to circle back. He won't bother you now that I'm here." He wagged his jeweled saber. It had a broad, curved blade about the length of his arm.

"Thank you. Just to the gate," Cimree said.

"Your accent is curious," said the man as they began walking again. "That's what I savor about Ecbatana. People of all sorts have come to live here. Have you listened to the wolves howling each night? Very unnerving." He frowned and shook his head.

"Where we live we cannot hear them as well," Cimree said.

"And they continue to attack the caravans relentlessly! There are wagons of spoiling goods abandoned on the roads."

A few others passed them from ahead, going to the souk, but the foot traffic had lessened considerably. She could hear the scrape of the man's sandals as he walked. She kept her eyes open for the man with the goatee who had accosted them, but he'd disappeared. There were fewer stands and things being sold, the structures looking like tiny living quarters. She smelled a fragrant thing cooking, a meat of some kind, and passed a window where she heard sizzling.

Cimree didn't want to talk to the man, but she felt obligated to since he'd come to help. "I've heard some of the wolves have made it inside the city."

"I have as well," he said with a worried frown. "That even these cannot kill them," he said, brandishing his sword again. "These are evil times. Have you heard the news, though? That the tyrant queen has been chosen?"

Cimree felt a startled jolt in her chest. "Who?"

"King Diyako has chosen one of the angel sworn refugees," said the man with certainty. "The one with golden hair and the regalness of a true queen. She was chosen and brought to the royal palace for the ceremony. Have you seen her? They say she is very beautiful."

Cimree did not allow her face to reveal any reaction. Rather than lie, she thought it best to answer the question with a question that implied she hadn't. "Is she?"

"I have not seen her," said the cheerful man. "I was elsewhere when her entourage arrived with Lord Roque, may the sun favor him. It has been many years since a tyrant queen was last chosen. She will be blamed for all our misfortunes." He chuckled to himself.

They passed a gap between two houses and suddenly Chrys was yanked away from Cimree's hand. She turned in surprise, seeing the fellow who had troubled them before pulling her deeper into the side alley.

Cimree was shoved into the alley, and the old man, his expression twisting with menace, brought the edge of his saber to her throat as he pinned her against the wall.

"Scream and you'll lose your head!" he said darkly, all look of friendliness gone. He gazed back at the alley entrance and then gripped her arm tightly, right where the wound from the concubine's knife had scored her, making her wince in pain. He kept the tip of the blade poised at the edge of her neck.

The two men were accomplices. She realized her mistake too late, that the first had been a diversion, while the second had been designed to win her trust. A surge of outrage and fear mingled in her stomach.

"That girl is worth many coins," said the older man, nodding ahead to the others. "Lord Roque is gathering all the little girls throughout the city and paying handsomely to see each one. She doesn't have the mark on her wrist, so she hasn't been seen yet. We'll take the reward you were intending to claim."

"Take her jewels," said the man holding Chrys.

Cimree stuck her leg between the older man's, hooking her foot around his ankle. She dropped, grabbing his wrist, and disarmed him in a fluid motion while he lost his balance and fell down on the street. Her reflexes outmatched his easily, and he was on the ground, staring up at her in surprise.

She felt the instinct to strike him, her bonding with the cobra was so strong, and suddenly she'd drawn her dirk and stabbed his belly. Instantly, she felt a discharge of venom. It was a feeling in her mouth, like the contraction of the gland that makes spittle. The man began to writhe in pain. And seconds later, he was dead. Not from bleeding. She'd killed him with venom.

The other fellow gaped at her in dismay, still clinging to Chrys, holding her in front of himself like a shield.

Cimree sent a jet of fear at him, a mind-blackening terror that caused him to release Chrys and flee deeper into the alley. She wondered briefly why, if Chrys could steal his memories, she hadn't used that power against him. But maybe it required a prolonged gaze and he just hadn't been looking into her eyes. Cimree stared at Chrys, who rubbed her arms where the man had been squeezing her so hard.

"Are you all right?" Cimree asked.

Chrys nodded, her eyes and pout showing she'd been genuinely afraid.

Cimree gazed down at the dead man near her feet. The toxin had killed him quickly. He'd died in seconds. The instinct to strike had come so quickly, almost like a reflex. Had she done this before? Her, a healer in training? But no. Maybe it was the shadow of a past memory from when she had been a more formidable foe. She felt a little ashamed at how easily she'd done it. And how it made her feel powerful. Dangerous.

Being bonded to the cobra had an entirely different sense to it than other serpents she'd bonded with. The cobra *wanted* to attack. The aftertaste of venom in her mouth was a peculiar sensation.

Those two men had seen her as a target. Had assumed she was bringing Chrys to Lord Roque to earn some coins and had decided to intervene and rob her of the possible reward as well as the jewelry she wore. She'd just experienced the real underbelly of Ecbatana. And she knew they weren't safe walking the streets any more than they'd been in the hiding place in the wall.

But she had learned something from the men that they didn't know she'd needed. Trinati had been chosen as the tyrant queen. She'd been taken to the palace in the center of Ecbatana.

Lord Roque had lost the Tay al-Ard that morning as well. A grim realization came to her. Events were already unfolding that she had no control over.

She felt the flare of magic from the Tay al-Ard and suddenly she sensed Azra nearby, heading toward them. She motioned for

Chrys to come to her and took her hand. By the time they reached the opening of the alley, leaving the corpse on the ground behind them, Azra arrived. He glanced over her shoulder at the body and gave Cimree a smirk of approval.

"It wasn't safe staying there anymore," Cimree said.

Azra nodded. "I know. I could feel it. But it isn't safe going to the mansion either."

"Did you find Andrin and Perreta?"

"Yes. But the mansion is surrounded by Roque's warriors. He's going to kill Trinati unless we hand over the Tay al-Ard and *you*."

Cimree looked at him in surprise. "Wasn't she taken to the king's palace this morning? Why did she go willingly?"

"She didn't know. They tricked her and have trapped her in a room with no way in or out except the Tay al-Ard, and only Roque has been there. He said she's running out of air."

Twenty-Seven

Angel's Wrath

A sudden commotion at the mouth of the alley attracted Azra's and Cimree's attention, and they watched as several soldiers pursuing them came into view. As soon as they saw Cimree and Chrys, their hands began to glow with blue flames.

"It's them!" shouted one of the guards with a groomed beard and an intensity to his eyes.

She felt Azra's anger and put a warning hand on his shoulder. "Let's get away. Back to the mansion."

"I'd rather kill them," Azra said gruffly.

She squeezed his shoulder, her eyes fixed on the menacing guards.

"Put your hands on my arm," Azra said as he drew out the Tay al-Ard.

"He has it!" shouted the leader vehemently.

Chrys and Cimree touched Azra's arm, and the magic yanked them away, causing Cimree's stomach to clench as the exhilaration and uncertainty wrenched her senses. In an instant they were back at the angel sworn manor in the room the family was using. Andrin was pacing with an expression of pain, but he was dressed and armed. Perreta gasped in surprise to see them appear suddenly in their midst.

"Cimree!" Edwina called out in excitement. "Chrys!"

It was a joyful reunion, and it made Cimree's throat clench to see Perreta begin weeping as she hugged Chrys tightly. Andrin limped closer, holding his hand to his injured side. Cimree was surprised to see him up and about. Blanka and Cyrill joined in the fun, and the look of relief on Chrys's face was palpable.

"Thank you, Cimree," Perreta said, still pressing Chrys to her bosom. "May the Oldknow bless you!"

"Are we going to Tirich Mir, then?" Andrin said eagerly. "This place has brought nothing but conflict."

"If I use it too frequently, it will break," Azra said. "It might be best to let it settle."

"There's been shouting downstairs," Perreta said with a frightened look. "Captain Odeon is taking charge. He wants to send everyone to look for Cimree and bring her to Roque."

"I've never seen him this distraught," Andrin confessed. "Not even when Montheron fell."

"He's worried about Trinati," Cimree said. "We should all be."

"After what she's done to you?" Azra said with an offended look. "She deserves her fate. I think many of the angel sworn will be loyal to you. Let them choose to stay or come with us."

"It's not that simple, Azra," Cimree said.

"It is that simple. I'm not giving this back to Roque," he said, holding up the Tay al-Ard. "Not with the golem already here. We must go as soon as we can!"

"The golem is here?" Perreta asked worriedly. "You've seen it?"

Chrys gripped Perreta's arm and nodded, her eyes fearful.

"Wegner will come," Andrin said. "Those who are loyal to Trinati and Odeon should be left behind."

"No," Cimree said forcefully. "I don't want to leave anyone behind. I think we should all go to Tirich Mir. Let me try to persuade them. I don't have long before Roque's soldiers arrive."

Azra's eyes flashed with rage. "No, Cimree. They had their chance. We don't have enough time."

"No, they don't know what we know. They're acting out of fear and desperation. It's similar to what happened in Montheron, isn't it? Distrust, confusion, panic. The only difference is we don't have grimalkin killing everything that moves inside the walls."

"Well, the golem is here now, so we can expect that next," Azra said. "Trinati might already be dead. It doesn't take long to suffocate."

"I'm sure it depends on how much air was in the crypt," Cimree said. "But you're right. We can't delay. I'm going down there."

"Cimree, no!" Perreta said. "We should just go!"

"Roque is the one who has betrayed us. Who feigned friendship with us." As she spoke, Cimree felt her determination and her frustration swell. She cared about every person who had left Clairvaux to look for a new home. She couldn't bring herself to abandon any of them, not without at least giving them a chance to escape. She looked into Azra's eyes, hoping he would support her. But she did not ask him to. He knew her heart.

His loyalty was to her. To Andrin and Perreta and their children. He'd always been an outcast to the rest of the angel sworn. A fallen angel.

"I won't let them take you," he said to her in a grave tone. "If they try..." He left the implication unsaid.

"All *we* can do is try," she said, looking at him pleadingly.

He pressed his lips tightly together, then gave her a curt nod.

THERE WAS INDEED a confrontation going on in the dining hall of the mansion. From what Cimree could tell, there were three factions. Odeon had most of the warriors gathered around him. They were all armored and had weapons at the ready. Like they were going to war. Wegner had the healers and the artisans with him, and he seemed to be trying to persuade against rash action. Uorsin stood apart from both groups, and Darcia stood near him, looking fearful and confused.

"It's Cimree!" she shouted, the first to notice her enter the room, and her yell caused an immediate uproar.

"Take her now!" Captain Odeon demanded.

Cimree invoked the power of the Tanaquil and crushed the feelings of hostility in the chamber.

"She's using her magic on us!" one of the warrior women, Salisha, said in alarm.

"Look at her," said another with disdain. "She looks like one of *them*."

"I'm wearing this because I needed to escape Roque's minions," Cimree said. She knew her eyes were glowing silver because she saw Azra's eyes glowing. He stood at her side, hand gripping a dagger hilt. She felt him ready to attack.

"Where have you been, Cimree?" Wegner asked worriedly.

"I went to rescue Chrys. Everyone, please listen. We will discuss this calmly."

"Do not listen to her," Odeon said forcefully. "She'll lead us to our doom. We cannot delay or Trinati will die!"

"Captain Odeon," Cimree said firmly, staring at him. He seemed reluctant to meet her gaze. "I know how you feel about her. We need to come up with an answer all can agree on. We are more powerful when we counsel together. When we listen to one another."

He met her eyes, his face showing his conflict. But he remained silent.

Cimree spoke clearly and hopefully no one noticed her tremor. "Lord Roque is a deceiver. From the moment we arrived, he has done nothing but manipulate us and turn us against each other. Now he's taken one of our own and is using her to control our actions. He's using Trinati for his own ends."

"And now you propose we abandon her. Because she tried to become the tyrant queen," Odeon said stiffly.

Cimree shook her head. "No. I say we rescue her."

Her words were met with looks of surprise. Even some of the warriors had an altered countenance.

"I thought you were going to suggest we escape without her," Wegner said.

Cimree shook her head. "We need her. We all need each other. I've seen the true face of Ecbatana. It is corrupt, conniving, and disgusting. Azra was right. We should have avoided coming here. But I will not leave anyone behind unless they wish to stay here. We have another way of getting to Tirich Mir now. Azra can take us there quickly. This latest ploy is to turn us against each other. To make us fight each other and not them. I say we turn on him."

"He controls all the defenders," Odeon said. "He has power here. Why don't we give him what he wants, and he'll set Trinati free!"

"What Cimree is suggesting is more reasonable," Wegner said. "Roque may be powerful, but he's never faced the wrath of the angel sworn before."

Cimree felt a surge of relief when he said that. When he defended her. She glanced at Azra and saw just a little smirk on his mouth.

"The crypt cannot be opened," Odeon said. "The device that Azra stole can do it, but only in Roque's hand. We did not come here to steal!"

"If the crypt can be opened, and I believe it can, I'm convinced Wegner can figure it out," Cimree said. "Can't you see that they want us to make a rash decision? To succumb to panic. I propose that we go on the attack. The golem is here. They're already frantic."

Odeon gaped at her. "How do you know this?"

"I've seen it," she said. "These bruises came from it." She turned and showed him the bruises on her shoulder and back. "We need to go, but I don't want to leave Trinati behind. If Wegner cannot figure it out, then we take Roque and *make* him free her. His life for hers."

"This is the best idea we've heard all day," Uorsin said, raising his fist. "We must stop arguing amongst ourselves. Cimree has always been a voice of reason."

"I tell you, it may sound reasonable, but it is the path to our destruction," Odeon said emphatically.

"Explain yourself," Wegner said in a challenging tone. "Your argument is only appealing to emotion. After what Trinati did when we got here, I'm frankly surprised Cimree is suggesting we rescue her. But I think it is wise."

"It is not wisdom," Odeon said, his mouth contorting with anger.

"We must be united," Cimree said. She looked to the captain. "We must trust one another again."

"But I cannot trust *you*," Odeon said flatly.

She felt confused and hurt by his words. Azra's fury began to seethe.

"What injury have I done to you, Captain Odeon?" she said. "I healed your wounds in Montheron. We faced a similar situation then. What has changed?"

His lips quivered with disdain. "Everything has changed. The world has changed. It wasn't until after Clairvaux fell that I learned the truth about you from the Queen Mother. And why I cannot trust you." He cast his eyes around all of them. "And why none of you should."

Twenty-Eight
An Hour Only

Odeon's words were a blow that disoriented Cimree momentarily. Judging by the surprised looks on the faces of the others in the room, she could see they were all disturbed by his pronouncement.

"What did she tell you?" Cimree asked, trying to keep her voice from shaking. "And why have you been keeping it until now?" She felt everyone was looking at her, and it made her want to hide from their eyes.

"I was dragged back to Clairvaux by those evil creatures, and I found the Queen Mother wounded, chained to the floor, and in such a ruined state it was truly pitiable. When she gave me her distaff, she said that you had betrayed her in your previous life. You'd been one of her most trusted servants and then schemed to overthrow her. To make yourself ruler of the angel sworn." His voice had a hard edge to it. He didn't look like he was lying. His expression was full of earnest conviction.

His words had stunned everyone.

"I have no memory of this," Cimree said. "I was turned back into an infant."

"She said that you did it to yourself," Odeon retorted, "to

avoid punishment after she discovered your treachery. You'd managed to keep this secret, even from her. But she knew you were in league with Azra. Both of you conspired to bring down the Queen Mother. If I had known this when I governed Montheron, I would never have allowed you out of that cell." He directed this final statement at Azra with a spiteful look.

Cimree felt Azra's confusion. That he felt he was being accused of something he hadn't done.

"I'd never met Cimree until Trinati brought her to Montheron," Azra said. "My banishment was long ago."

"You were banished because of your past treachery," Odeon said, pointing his finger at Azra. He shifted his stance, holding out his hand imploringly to the rest of the angel sworn. "I speak the truth from the Queen Mother's own lips. You'd put your faith in a fallen angel and a spy? She ate an entire fruit from the Gallows Tree in order to wipe away her guilt. The Queen Mother, in her benevolence, chose to give her a new start as an infant. Not even Trinati knew of this. But I've told her. And now, she is suffocating to death unless we surrender these two to Lord Roque."

Cimree saw some of the armored angel sworn turn to her with frowns. Many seemed confused or wary because of what Odeon had said. She was confused herself, but knowing that Chrys was Dryad-born, that she could steal memories—surely it played a part in this, at least explaining Azra's amnesia. Chrys had always been close to Azra. Yet she couldn't speak and reveal what she knew.

Cimree tried to step forward, but Azra put out his hand to block her. He could also sense the shift in the tension. They were about to be attacked and violently subdued.

"I do not know whether what you've said is true or not," Cimree said boldly. "I have no memory of it. And I know that Azra doesn't either. We have not intentionally misled any of you."

"Your words ring hollow," Odeon said stiffly.

"But they are true, nonetheless. Our aim is the same right now. Trinati must be freed. We must unite, or we suffer ourselves to be in bondage to the Ecbatanans. They are motivated by greed. Their city is on the verge of collapse, and all Roque can think about is how to manipulate the outcome to get what he wants." She shook her head. "We cannot tolerate this. We must set her free."

"But if we can't, she dies!" Odeon said in desperation.

"Let us try," Cimree countered. "And if we cannot free her, I will surrender myself."

Azra's heart lurched with concern. He looked at her as if she had lost her senses. She put her hand on his shoulder. There was much she wanted to say, but it wasn't the right moment.

"You will?" Odeon chuffed incredulously.

"I will," she said. "But I think my plan is better. I have faith that Wegner can open the door and free her. Let us at least try." She looked around the room. "Can we agree on this? Can we cease this division?"

"I support Cimree's plan," Wegner said, raising his hand in a gesture of acceptance. "Whatever she may have done, I had no knowledge of it. It must have happened long ago."

Uorsin raised his as well, giving a nod to Azra. Their bond of friendship was now absolute. Cimree gave him a proud smile.

Darcia looked startled at his vote, but she, too, raised her hand. "I've known Cimree as long or longer than any of you. She is trustworthy. And very brave."

Cimree felt a jolt of surprise at Darcia's kind words. Others began to lift their hands until the only ones who hadn't were Captain Odeon and his guards. They were looking to him. It seemed they'd be bound to whatever he decided.

"We cannot delay," Cimree said to him encouragingly. "For her sake."

"How much time will you allow Wegner?"

"An hour," Cimree said. "Someone bring an hourglass. When the sand runs out, I will surrender. You have my word."

Azra's eyes flashed. He looked furious, like he was about to swear at her.

Trust me, she thought to him. She wasn't sure if he could hear her thoughts, but hopefully he sensed her intention.

"Then I agree. I will follow your orders for one hour. We all will. But when that hour passes, Azra better come and deliver the Tay al-Ard."

Cimree felt like sighing in relief. They were all staring at her. "He will. Azra, we need a diversion. You must lead their guards on a confusing chase and draw them away from the palace. Be unpredictable. Odeon, you will lead Wegner to the palace with your guards so we can breach the door. Uorsin. Your strength and knowledge will also be helpful. We might have to break it down."

"With pleasure," Uorsin said grimly.

"But where will you be when the sands run out?" Odeon asked.

"I'm coming with you," she told Odeon. "I will honor my promise."

"Fetch an hourglass. It comes with us," Odeon said. The room became tumultuous as everyone began to act on her orders. Odeon's warriors had already prepared for action, but instead they would turn against Roque and his henchmen.

Amidst the chaos, Azra turned to face her, incredulous at what she'd committed to do. She put her hand on his cheek. "I'm going with them," she said softly. "But I'm not defenseless. I'm going to bond with a serpent first. I can disappear out of sight."

She felt the surge of relief inside him.

"I was afraid you'd chosen the martyr's path," he confessed.

She shook her head and lowered her hand. She leaned closer as if to press a quick kiss to his cheek. "Chrys has the seed," she whispered.

"Now," Cimree announced to those gathered around her in the gardens in the rear of the mansion. She'd summoned the spider-tailed horned viper to help tame one of the garden birds so she could fly more easily. She was still connected to the cobra from the souk, and she felt rather dangerous with the combined abilities.

She was waiting for Azra to cause trouble and for the alarm horns to sound. She heard them in the distance and felt Azra's heart beating wildly as he fought Roque's soldiers. He was bonded to many different creatures, giving him added abilities, and joined with his own cunning, she knew that he alone could wreak havoc on Roque's defenses.

"Fly!" Odeon commanded, and all the angel sworn, including Wegner and Uorsin, rose together into the dusky sky. She suspected that the golem was lurking in the gardens in the center of the city still. Its presence was another threat that Roque hadn't counted on.

Her heart sang as they soared quickly over the rooftops. Odeon had several angel sworn with bows and sharp arrows leading the way, prepared to shoot down any defenders who opposed them. But they met no resistance. It seemed Azra had already drawn off many to come fight him. And since he had the Tay al-Ard, he would be even more difficult to catch.

They had passed over the ocher and silver walls in minutes, bypassing the streets and open estates. Then they reached the gold wall, the final barrier, and raced toward the impressive palace citadel. Shouts came from below as they flew past. Her lungs remained full of air the entire flight, and she savored the interesting feeling of being bonded with a bird. The rock viper had come to her eagerly, seeming to anticipate some sort of pleasure in bonding with her and experiencing, vicariously, what she was doing. She recognized the landscape of the forbidden gardens where she'd had her interview with the pretend king. A thicker copse of woods showed her the place Roque had taken her to before putting her in the cage beneath the round lid.

Odeon began to swoop down inside the outer walls of the palace, choosing to land on the balcony of an upper floor. Several angel sworn with him touched down, swords drawn, and they smashed through the balcony windows to lead the way.

Odeon waited on the balcony for Cimree and Wegner, who'd been flying together, to land. Darcia had come too, and she was the one holding the hourglass. It was more than half full of sand. Odeon looked at it and then nodded.

Cimree quickly followed the wake of destruction left by the angel sworn. They were deep in the heart of the palace, yet there were no servants. It was eerily quiet. The beautiful, tiled hall led to a wide set of stairs.

A cry of alarm sounded from below, followed by the clang of metal on metal. By the time Cimree had hurried to the bottom step, there were guards sprawled on the floor.

"That way!" Odeon commanded, pointing to the main corridor.

"How do you know the way?" Cimree asked him.

"I came here with Trinati," he said. "I saw the door she entered. When Roque made his ultimatum for me to go find you before she died."

Cimree nodded, and they hastened down the corridor. The doorway was huge, made of metal, and probably weighed as much as a herd of milk cows. Instead of being rectangular, this double door was tapered at the top. The doors appeared to be made of iron with intricate patterns of square and diamond shapes. There was no handle. The hinges were all on the inside. Stone supported it on all sides, providing a sturdy barrier.

Wegner came up to it and began to rub his hand on the iron. He examined the seams. Darcia arrived last, holding the hourglass and watching the sands trickle in a stream. Cimree felt Azra flying again before rushing into another conflict. She wished she could see him fight, to watch the dexterity and abrupt attacks and blows she felt him giving. Her own heart was racing a little at the adventure.

"Well?" Odeon demanded.

"Give him time," Cimree scolded.

"It would take a battering ram the size of a tree to break that open," Odeon said disdainfully.

"Every door has a weakness," Wegner said. "Be it the hinges or the lock. There must be a way to open it on this side. No one would design something that couldn't be opened another way." He closed his fist and began knocking on the door, listening to the sounds made as he tapped on various parts.

Odeon's lips were twitching. He looked uneasy. He wasn't even looking at Wegner. Instead, he was gazing at the tall, vaulted corridor with its resplendent decorations and mosaics. That was not the reaction she'd been expecting from him. If he didn't believe Wegner could open the door, he'd be watching the sand escape the upper chamber of the glass.

"Uorsin, would you tap higher up?" Wegner said as he squatted at the crack between the doors. "It has to be along the seam. This is the weakest part of the door."

"What are we trying to find?" Uorsin asked.

"Doors like this will have rods that rise vertically and sink into the stone at the base to hold it closed. When the door is pushed closed, the rods will sink into the footings. The pivots will be a metal disk with a latch of sorts. If we can pry them up, the bars will lift and the door will open."

"You can't know that," Odeon said over his shoulder. "It could be a crossbar."

"I've designed hundreds of different kinds of doors, Captain. A crossbar requires brute strength to lift and put in place. This door is a trap and must be reset in order to open. Just knock along the edges until you feel more resistance. That would likely be the spot."

The two men continued to knock, their ears pressed close to the metal.

"Cim-reeee!"

She recognized the sibilant hiss from the golem, and her

stomach fell as if the Tay al-Ard had whisked her away. It was in the palace.

"What was that?" Darcia demanded fearfully.

"Hold her," Odeon ordered sharply.

Two angel sworn defenders, Salisha and Angheld, grabbed Cimree's arms before she could react.

"Captain Odeon," Wegner said in outrage. "There is still time left on the hourglass!"

"I'm not turning her over to Roque," Odeon said. "That was never my intention."

"Cim-reeee!" The creature seemed eager with anticipation.

She felt her heart begin to quicken. Azra felt her fear. Felt the sting from Odeon's betrayal. She sensed his determination to come after her.

"You didn't bargain with Roque, did you," Cimree demanded. "You had a bargain with the golem all along."

He turned to face her, looking anguished and torn. "What I told you was true. You had betrayed the Queen Mother. The golem promised to let her live. But you were the price."

TWENTY-NINE
RECOMPENSE

"What were you to gain from this?" Cimree demanded, her mind whirring. She could not see the golem, but since it was close enough for her to hear it, it was too close. She began to summon the magic of the Tanaquil amulet, bringing in a lulling and peaceful feeling. The way she felt walking among the wild-flowers in the valley of Clairvaux ,with the lazy drone of bumble-bees. The gentle rush of the Silver River.

"She's still alive, Cimree!" Odeon cried avidly. "The Queen Mother is still in Clairvaux. The golem will free her if I bring you to it. I was ridden with guilt for not having obeyed her when Montheron fell. It fell anyway. At least I can atone for that now."

"You've no idea what you've done," Cimree said. "And now you've killed Trinati."

Cimree looked at Darcia and sent a blast of fear into her chest. She'd been holding the substantial hourglass in both hands, and the sudden impression of danger made her instinctively drop it before she whirled to run. The bulb of glass shattered, spilling the sand onto the floor.

Cimree wrenched an arm free from Angheld. She struck

Salisha with the heel of her palm, a stunning blow to the chin that Azra had taught her, which caused that one to let go as well.

She saw Captain Odeon's face fill with sudden determination just as he rushed to seize her himself, but she evaded his lunge.

"Get that door open!" she shouted to Wegner before taking flight down the same corridor Darcia had fled down. She didn't know which corridor the golem was coming from; its sibilant voice had echoed off the stone walls in such a way that she couldn't know. But there were only three ways to go, so she picked one and hoped the odds were in her favor.

"*Cim-reee!*" shrieked the golem from behind her. She'd hoped the lulling magic she'd created would have confused and slowed it down. She hadn't flown far before her graftings were suddenly severed and she dropped to the stone floor.

She'd been expecting it and tucked her arms close as she landed, doing a front roll to disperse the painful impact and jumping to her feet to begin running in earnest.

Her intent was to lure the golem after her, to allow Wegner and Uorsin time to open the door and save Trinati. Odeon's betrayal was too momentous to think about, but she could see that she'd been missing information all along. Azra was racing to the palace; she could feel his presence getting closer.

But the golem began to attack the others. She heard the cries of terror, the sound of iron blades clanging as they fell. She turned and paused, watching one angel sworn guard get thrown into the iron door like a puppet, then slump to the floor.

Cimree still couldn't see it. Its camouflage disguised it. She used the magic of the medallion to reach into it, to draw it to her. To fill it with the instinct to hunt.

Odeon was swinging his sword in swaths, trying to find the golem, but his efforts were fruitless.

She heard a clucking noise coming toward her. She ran.

Knowing it could outrun her, she went to the nearest door and pulled at the handle. It swung open, revealing a study filled with books and scrolls. And a balcony.

Cimree rushed through the room and opened the glass door of the balcony just as the door she'd hurried through was ripped off its hinges with a roar of rage. She drew her distaff as she ducked through the glass door and ran to the edge of the balcony, springing up on the decorative stone railing and then leaping off. The silk of her garment whipped as she fell, plummeting fast.

Cimree used the grafting wand to snag an unsuspecting bird in one of the many trees. It was dusk, and many of the birds were resting, but she found a little starling and the sudden bond with it gave her the power of flight just before she hit the ground. Cimree felt the excitement well inside her as she zipped away from the palace, heading to the forbidden gardens.

A cry of rage sounded from the balcony, and her grafting was cut again. She landed on the turf and rolled onto her back. Looking up, she saw a bulky shape up on the balcony and then a shadow of movement as it dropped down to the ground. It was moving like a giant spider, rushing at her.

Cimree scrabbled to her feet and sprinted into the trees. She was near the place where her interview with the false king had been. She dashed through the woods, heading to where she remembered it was thickest. That would make it difficult for the larger golem to chase her, and it was close to the garden with the metal lid, which opened to the underground area housing the cage and all the snakes hidden inside the walls.

Unexpectedly, the golem caught her around the middle and hoisted her into the air, making her scream in fear and surprise. Its speed was startling! She smelled its rank scent and then shoved at it with her thoughts, sending a hurricane of emotions at it with the amulet's magic. Azra was drawing near, but even he was no match for it.

Her power made it drop her, and she started to flee again while it let out a booming cough. She only knew where it was because it was thrashing against a tree. She focused on the shuddering branches and sent another jolt of terror at it. The power roared through her, filling her with a sense of fulfillment and the desire to invoke more of it. Maybe it wanted her because she had power it could not banish.

It let out a mournful cry and began to flee, so she turned and sprinted through the woods again. But as soon as her attention was diverted, it came charging back at her. Branches snapped and came tumbling down. It was coming over the treetops again.

Cimree recognized the spot, the opening in the woods where she'd found the lid with the serpent symbol on it. Her breaths came in gasps. Azra was approaching even faster, speeding to her so he could use the Tay al-Ard to take them both away.

The golem made a clicking noise, and she felt Azra's surprise as he fell from the sky, crashing into the trees not far from her. The golem must have severed his graftings.

Her feelings were in her throat, but she didn't have time to worry. She rushed to the metal circle with the symbol and heaved it open.

"Cimree!" Azra called out to her. She couldn't see him, but she felt him. He was too far away, and the golem was nearly on top of her.

"Get out of here!" she called to him. She jumped down into the pit and landed on the stone below.

Instinctively, she leaped away, temporarily blinded by the darkness. She heard a snuffling noise. A monstrous muscled arm came through the opening, groping for her. Cimree backed away from it until she collided with the bars of the cage. She panted for breath, but she realized that her plan had worked. It couldn't get down there. It was too big.

She felt Azra's panic and worry, but she began to slow her breathing, tamping down the raging magic inside her. Dizziness was coming. The golem hissed down the shaft, reaching for her still, but she was beyond its grasp this time.

Azra charged at it.

No! she thought to him. He couldn't use grafting magic against it, which meant his speed and strength were lessened. He was just a man.

"I'm safe, get out of here!" she yelled up to him.

"Not without you!" she heard him say. The golem made clicking noises again. She heard Azra grunt in pain.

"Go!" she begged, staring up at the hole. He was trying to get down to her so he could use the cylinder to escape with her. But the golem protected the entrance. There was no way Azra was going to get past it. He would die first.

The dizziness was getting worse. She'd used the magic too much, too soon. Her vision began to blur, and the backlit circle on the ceiling of the underground chamber began to wiggle.

I can't faint. Not now. Her breathing came in panicked gasps.

She saw a wreath of blue flames explode over that circle. Azra was sending it against the golem in waves. The golem snarled, and she felt Azra's pain as the golem struck him. She felt him also beginning to lose consciousness.

Her heart was in agony, and then she felt the Tay al-Ard's magic snatch him away, sending him far, far away. It felt like he was on the other side of the world. The connection was still there between them, but the distance muted it. Where had he gone? How far had he gone?

The only answer that made sense was Tirich Mir.

But he was safe. He was away from the golem.

Cimree's knees trembled, and she was afraid she'd collapse, so she hunkered down against the cell that Roque had put her in. The bars pressed against her back. She was so thirsty. But her pack was back at the mansion. Other than her daggers, she had no other weapons except the coptic fruit. Would that turn it into stone? She felt so dizzy she was afraid she'd fall over. The swirling thoughts were meaningless. She didn't need other weapons. The magic of the Tanaquil amulet was the only thing that had resisted the golem so far. She tried to swallow, but her throat was too tight.

The hiss of a serpent greeted her. She remembered them and their venom that could make the victim listless as if dead. One of the serpents approached her with curiosity. Cimree drew her distaff again and bonded with it. She saw the iridescence of the golem's arm. It was exploring the ceiling of the chamber. He was studying it, trying to find a way to get to her.

At least she could see part of it. The arm withdrew. More serpents were coming, joining her. But she felt no threat from any of them. The noise and her presence had attracted them.

The golem's hand emerged again. This time, it had an open palm. She saw something moving in the palm, which confused her. Set into the center of the golem's palm, she saw an eyeball protruding from the flesh. The eyeball swiveled and then looked at her.

"Cim-reee," it crooned.

She felt nothing but disgust and revulsion. And determination to destroy it.

"Leave," she murmured, still near fainting, sending a tendril of magic at it, making it share her feelings for it. Her loathing and detestation.

The golem hissed at her, and the hand and its macabre appendage withdrew.

The fatigue was too great. Cimree stretched out on the floor, surrounded by a dozen or more serpents. They felt strangely warm. She could see them in the growing dark. And their presence was comforting. They'd watch over her while she slept.

Wake me if someone...comes, she thought to the serpents. Then she passed out.

WHEN SHE WOKE UP AGAIN, her arms were fully stretched out, her shoulders aching. Her wrists were sore as well, and she felt tingles up her arms, as if she'd been grafted to a bird for hours. Her head felt strange. Foggy.

She tried to open her eyes, but every sense was disoriented. Then she realized she was sitting down, not lying down. Cimree lifted her head. She was still grafted to the serpents, but they weren't the source of the poor circulation in her arms. Her wrists were shackled in iron cuffs. The serpents were all gone. Attached to the cuffs was a chain mounted to a hook on the ceiling of the cage.

She was *inside* the cage.

"The poison is wearing off. You're awake again."

It was Lord Roque's voice.

THIRTY
THE REVENANT OF ECBATANA

C imree turned her head and saw Roque in the shadows, the heat emanating from his body in a red blur. He closed a stone door in the wall, and she watched him touch a part of the stone and then she heard a click. The grogginess of sleep faded instantly as wariness and the first tremors of fear arose. Azra was still far away, but she could not feel anything from him. Was he unconscious? Asleep? She looked down at herself and saw that her distaff was gone. So were her daggers. She had the silk entari to cover her, and the pouch with the coptic fruit still dangled from her girdle. That was all.

"You have proven a poisonous thorn in my side," Roque said as he left the stone door and approached her. He held a glowing crystal in his hand. "A vicious weed." All pretense at civility was gone. His voice throbbed with hatred.

"And you are a coward and a thief," Cimree spat back at him. Her knees and hips were aching from her uncomfortable position, so she shifted and tried to stand. Her joints hurt.

"Recognize this?" Roque asked, holding out the feather-designed crown that Cimree had taken from the concubine and stashed in the ally in the grand souk. The soldiers had retrieved it.

"A pretty jewel," Cimree said dispassionately.

Roque stopped at the door of the cell. He looked over his shoulder at the gaping hole in the roof with fear in his eyes.

"At least it cannot get down here," Roque said. "It's killed every defender we've sent against it. Magic doesn't work on it either. Except yours, it seems."

"What do you want?" Cimree asked, hating the way his eyes began to roam her body.

"I want Ilayda!" Roque roared at her. His eyes flashed menacingly as he tossed the decorative crown on the floor, which made a metallic sound. She heard a guttural noise coming from the ceiling hole. The golem was still there.

She noticed her distaff was tucked into Roque's belt. And a dagger. She deliberately did not gaze at either, not wanting to reveal her intention. The golem hadn't severed her bond with the serpents yet, and she could feel them nearby. They were repelled from the room it seemed. Something about Roque's presence had driven them out. A magical artifact perhaps?

"The golem killed her," Cimree said after the echoes of his shout had faded.

"I know. But I blame you. I blame *all* of you."

"We did not create the golem," Cimree said. "Our magic does not work that way. It only shares abilities temporarily with consent. It is your people who dabble in an unnatural magic that creates unwilling abominations."

"I know the Queen Mother didn't create it," Roque said. He gripped one of the bars and slid his hand up and down it. The fierceness in his eyes hadn't diminished. He gazed at her, squinting slightly. She felt his blood stirring with heat and tried to banish his feelings with the power of the medallion, but she was too spent to control anything. All she had was a vague sense of his emotions. Hatred and something she didn't understand. He was used to getting what he wanted. And there was something about her he wanted.

"You've told us nothing but lies since we came here," Cimree said, trying to engage his eyes again. To have him look her in the face and not ogle her body.

"Ecbatana's foundations were built on lies," Roque said, flashing her a dangerous smile. She could see he wanted to harm her. "Just as Clairvaux was." He released his grip on the bar and then sank his hand into his pocket where he removed a key. It was a strange key. One end had a circular shape with two little nubs on it. Then a shaft and then a rectangular shape at the other end with a pointed hook on the last part. He inserted it into the lock of the gate and twisted it, producing another noise before releasing the lock. The key looked ancient, its iron shaft speckled with rust.

He then slid the key back into his pocket and set the glowing crystal on the ground.

"What lies?" Cimree asked.

"Ecbatana is a lychgate. Catacombs were built to hide Asmodeus. That is the name you call him in your fables."

"He tried to seduce the Queen Mother," Cimree said.

"No. That's just another lie you were taught to believe. He took her by force. She stayed in Clairvaux out of shame." Every intonation of his voice sounded terrible in her ears. He was gloating, reveling, threatening her with his words. Fear crept into her stomach. Fear of what he was going to do to her.

"Everything you've said has been a lie."

Roque laughed without mirth. "Then you will believe what I do. We thought you were a hetaera, come to rule us once more. But you are not one. Yet."

He opened the gate of the cage.

She heard the distinctive growl of the golem. The creature's arm had lowered again, and she saw the eyeball embedded in the center of its palm. It was watching.

"Where did the golem come from?" she asked, trying to distract him from his purpose. Because she was standing, she had more blood in her shoulders and the pain had ebbed. She felt the venom of the bond still within her. It was a venom that would make Roque seem like he was dead for days. But she needed something to activate the ability. Something sharp. Her teeth? Her fingernails? He would need to be close to her.

"Why do you care where it came from?" Roque said, pausing at the threshold. "Don't you want to know where *your* kind came from? You are the seed of Asmodeus."

"'The seed'?" Cimree said, wrinkling her brow.

"The progeny. You claim to be angels, but you are all demon spawn. Ecbatana is your true home. Asmodeus, your true father."

She did not believe his words. But they still rankled inside her. She could discern the difference between the idyllic life she'd lived in Clairvaux and the gluttony and depravity of Ecbatana. But did his words explain some part of why the Queen Mother had never left? Had she been taken by force, as some desperate or violent men did, and created laws to prevent the abuse of women ever after? To give women the power to judge and condemn? What was true and what was a lie?

"And what are you?" Cimree said to him derisively. "Nothing but a servant."

"Oh, I am more than a servant," he said, his eyes flashing with rage at the insult. "I have ruled Ecbatana for years. My word compels obedience. Until you came. And you began to twist my own against me."

"Twist your own?" she demanded in confusion.

"Khaf. You think I don't know of his betrayal. I've known it. My men are looking to find him and to destroy him in the most painful way you can imagine a man can endure. I'll not kill him. I'll make a eunuch of him and teach him his place. Lord Felaket is attacking the other nobles right now, trying to get force on his side to overthrow me. All I want from you is to know where you've hidden the seed of the Gallows Tree." He reached to his belt again and produced a small pouch. She watched him untie the end and sprinkle some dust in his palm.

Nightshade.

"What is that?" she asked, making her voice tremble on purpose.

"A special herb we grow in Ecbatana. A rare flower."

"I won't taste it," Cimree said, turning her face away as he entered the cell.

"You will do anything I say," Roque demanded, his eyes widening with a threat.

She kicked him in the groin. As his eyes bulged in pain, she blew the powder in the palm of his hand into his face just as she'd seen Khaf do.

He sank to his knees in agony, his spine crooked with the pain she'd caused him, hunching over, his fists pressed against his lower abdomen. And then the pained look transformed to one of relaxation as the nightshade began to take over his mind.

He really was a power-hungry idiot.

"Roque, can you understand me?" she said

"I hear you," he said with a soft, pleasured voice. She wondered how long the nightshade would last. With Ersin it had begun to wear off after a few minutes.

"How do you open the door where Trinati is trapped? There must be a way from the outside."

"I like you," Roque said, giving her a grimace-like smile.

"Answer me," she demanded.

"It's already open. The angel sworn opened it."

Cimree sighed in relief. "Is Trinati all right?"

"She's fine," he said playfully. "I made sure there was plenty of air before trapping her inside. She was wise to hold still and control her breathing."

Cimree lowered her head, grateful for that outcome. Roque made a playful gesture at her, which disgusted her. "Did the revenant create the golem? Tell me how it came to be."

"We don't know," Roque said. "No one does."

"But it came from Ecbatana, did it not?"

"Yes, it was created here. Created to destroy the angel sworn. To be immune from their dominion over all living creatures." He reached out to touch her, but she swatted his hand away. A little pout came to his mouth, like he was a naughty child.

"What gave it that power?" she demanded.

"Asmodeus only shares slivers of his wisdom and knowledge of good and evil."

"Did the golem kill him?"

"He cannot die. His essence is trapped in a finger bone. If I knew where it was, I would have destroyed it and become the true master of Ecbatana." He gave her a sly grin.

"Where is the revenant now?"

"We don't know," Roque said with a sigh. "When its corporeal form is destroyed, it seeks another. That takes time. He will come again in the form of a man seeking power. The tyrant queen rules during his absence."

"So he is gone."

Roque blinked a few times, a look of confusion on his face.

"The revenant is gone?" she pressed.

"We don't know...where," he said, blinking more rapidly. The nightshade was beginning to wear off.

She needed to get out of the chains. She tugged at them, but they were very tight. Earlier, she'd used an attribute of the snake to slip through the bars. She focused on the manacles at her wrists and began to twist and pull her arm. Even though it was tight, her wrist and hand came through, freeing one of her arms. She shook away the pain in her hand.

"What is happening," Roque mumbled. He sounded nauseous. His pain was returning as well.

Cimree focused on the other cuff and slid her hand through that one as well.

Roque was kneeling before her at the opening of the cage. Horror flashed in his eyes as he realized he'd been duped by his own nightshade. He reached for a ring on his finger, and she saw him twist it, exposing a needle. The poison that knocked her out earlier. All he needed was to score her skin, and she'd be helpless again. And her skin felt very exposed in the entari.

Roque lunged at her, even though he was in obvious agony. His hands grasped at her, trying to catch her, but her snake reflexes helped her dodge his hand. She coiled the dangling chain with the empty manacles around his neck to stop his breathing. His arms flailed at her, but she ducked around behind him and hoisted him on her back. A garbled choking sound came from his mouth as he struggled against her hold.

She felt the needle slash against her arm. Her chest filled with panic. The poison only took a second or two to work. If she fainted, he would be able to do whatever he wanted with her.

Cimree uncoiled the chain from him. Dizziness flooded her mind. Her vision began to warp.

"You...will...suffer," he panted, backing away from her, backing toward the cage opening.

Cimree's legs twitched, and she felt she would collapse. She lunged forward, making him howl in fear as she struck him in the chest with both hands just as Azra had taught her. He was knocked backward as she collapsed.

She saw the heat of the golem's arm as it reached forward and grabbed Roque by the back of the neck. Her vision went black as she heard him hoisted through the hole in the ceiling.

And she fainted as his screams resounded in her ears.

Be vigilant, ye Watchers. Be diligent. Cower not. Because we do not wrestle against blood and flesh. Asmodeus can shed these like a garment. Daggers cannot kill him. Arrows will not pierce him. Legions of unseen hosts are arrayed against us. To defeat him, we must wrestle against rulers, against the authorities, against the cosmic powers of darkness that steal hope and weaken thought and strain resolve. We wrestle against forces spiritual, of evil from the heavenly realms. But fear not because those that are with us are more than those that are with them.

— BOOK OF THE WATCHERS, THE TALE OF THE
FALLEN ANGELS

Thirty-One

The Golem's Magic

"Cazibe? Are you down there?"

The voice coming from above woke Cimree. She recognized the speaker as Khaf. Her muscles were sore. Her back still ached. Her head felt heavier than normal. She was lying on the stone floor of the darkened pit. The crystal that Roque had brought had gone out.

"I'm here," she said in response. She pushed herself up on her hands. The bodice of the entari was sagging, and she pulled it higher to cover herself.

"I can't see anything down there," Khaf said.

She could see him perfectly well, as if shrouded in fire with all the heat he gave off. She smelled him too. She was grafted to a dozen snakes, which were all around her. With Roque gone, they had returned.

"There are snakes down here," she said in warning.

"I hear them," he answered with a chuckle. "I'll light a lamp. Where did the golem go?"

"I'm surprised it's not up there with you," Cimree answered. She rose to her feet, and feeling her muscles pull strangely, she massaged her shoulder.

"There are dozens of dead warriors up here," Khaf said. "And what's left of Lord Roque."

"The golem pulled him up," Cimree said. She felt the serpents give way as she walked over to stand below the hole.

There was starlight behind Khaf, barely visible beyond the burning heat of his body. She saw him pull out a little oil lamp and set it down at the edge of the hole.

"I lack the ability to summon fire with my hands," Khaf said. "I need a flint and spark. Give me a moment."

"There is a secret entrance down here," Cimree said. "I saw Roque touch a stone."

"It leads back to the palace," Khaf said. "I don't know the way, for it was forbidden my rank."

She felt surprisingly comfortable temperature-wise. The dank cold of the pit wasn't affecting her. Or maybe it was the bonding with the serpents and sharing their cold-bloodedness. She didn't remember grafting with so many serpents. She touched her abdomen and waist. Her distaff was still gone. Roque had stolen it.

"Roque had my grafting wand," she called up to him. "Is it up there?"

"I'll try to find it," he said. She heard the snick of a blade against flint, and some sparks showered down on the wick. It took a few tries before the wick began to sizzle and then brighten.

Khaf lifted the lamp by the tiny handle and began to search around aboveground. She felt her stomach growl. She was hungry enough to eat a mouse. That thought wasn't right. She'd never craved eating a mouse before.

"He was...torn apart, it seems," Khaf said with a tone of disgust. "I don't see your wand anywhere. The golem was guarding this place until about an hour ago. Then it left. I was fearful it had found a way to get down there with you."

"No," Cimree said. "It reached for me, but it couldn't get down here."

"Lucky that," Khaf said. "The angel sworn have taken over the palace. Everyone has been brought there. I volunteered to find you."

"They don't want me," Cimree said with a sigh.

"Trinati insisted. She wants to leave and go elsewhere. She said Ecbatana is cursed."

"I thought she wanted to become the tyrant queen," Cimree said, gazing up at the hole.

"I think the only thing she wants is to make sure Roque is dead. He betrayed all of you."

"He knew you'd betrayed him," Cimree said.

"I kept up the pretense as long as I could," Khaf said. "I do wish to join your group. If you'll have me."

"We'll take anyone who wants to go from this place," Cimree said. "Azra has the Tay al-Ard."

She could sense him very far away still. He was awake. Worried. But she felt he was resting. And in pain.

"The Tay al-Ard is a powerful artifact," Khaf said. "A weapon made by Asmodeus to conquer. With Roque dead, there will be factions who go to war to take his place of dominance. There will be no tyrant queen now. I'll pull you up."

"Thank you," Cimree said. She was relieved that Trinati had had a change of heart. That staying in Ecbatana had lost its attractions. No doubt she'd been told about Odeon's duplicity as well. That he had been part of the subterfuge.

The glow from the lamp reached the edge of the pit. Khaf knelt down on one knee and set the lantern on the lip of the hole so it shined the lamplight down to her. He saw her looking up at him and then his face twisted in horror and shock at seeing her.

"Your hair—" He started to speak and then stiffened. His body began to twitch. The look of pain and terror froze on his face. And she watched in disbelief as he turned to stone in front of her. The body heat extinguished. The soft flesh was gray. His clothing was gray. Every part of him had become stone. And that horrible expression on his face was made permanent.

Cimree felt a salty taste in her mouth.

"Khaf?" she said in a whimper.

The lamp he'd lit continued to glow at the edge, the light rippling off the stone statue he'd become.

"Khaf?" she called again, feeling on the edge of panic. The pouch at her side was missing.

He'd said something about her hair before he'd been transformed. She reached up and instead of finding hair, she discovered a nest of serpents. They weren't *in* her hair, they *were* her hair. Each was sentient, a denizen of the lair. With venom that could paralyze a victim for days. She felt that venom as part of herself. This wasn't grafting. This was an abomination.

She could feel Azra becoming aware of her distress. How was he interpreting her raging feelings? Fear, shock, self-hatred, despair. This was not grafting magic. Well, part of it was. She felt the union with the serpents, but this time it was physical. This was a different kind of magic. It must be the dark power of metamorphistry that Roque had mentioned. Odeon had said the golem had created the grimalkin and gévaudan and kobolds. He had seen it take on parts to itself.

The golem had turned *her* into a monster. That was the most probable explanation.

She swallowed, trying to subdue her panicked gasps. She'd been unconscious. And it had changed her. The coptic fruit. That was the taste in her mouth. It must be. It had fused her with it and with the serpents. She tried to release the grafting mentally, to sever the connection. But the bonds held fast. When she closed her eyes, she realized that she could see in every direction. The nest of serpents on her head gave her that ability. No one could sneak up on her.

Then Azra was there. She felt the magic transport him from Tirich Mir—or wherever he had been—right to the opening of the pit. His immediate arrival terrified her, and she fell back to the corner of the chamber, turning her face away from the lamplight.

"Cimree!" he called down.

"Don't—come—down!" she pleaded emphatically.

"What's wrong? I can't understand all that you're feeling."

"Don't look at me," she said. Even though she was closing her eyes with her hands covering her face, she could still see the entire chamber in detail.

"What has happened?" Azra demanded angrily.

"Do you see Khaf? I did that!"

"The statue? I don't care that you killed him."

"I didn't do it deliberately. He looked at me and then he turned to stone."

"I'm coming down there."

"No!" she shrieked. "The golem transformed me. I have snakes for hair. I'm...I'm hideous. When it was dark, when he couldn't see me, nothing happened. But when the light of the lamp fell on me, he turned to stone. It was...it was awful to watch."

"Cimree, I don't care what happened to you. We will break the curse."

"I think only the fruit of the Gallows Tree can," Cimree said. "Don't you understand, Azra? We only have one seed. We need a safe place to plant it. It could take years to bear fruit."

"Years? What does that matter?" Azra said. "I don't care how long it takes."

"I don't want to look like this," Cimree said, feeling tears sting her eyes. "I can't bear it."

"We bear what we must," he said. "I didn't enjoy being in the dungeon of Montheron for so long. If I can bear that, then you can bear this."

"It's not the same."

"No, it's not. Not at all. But you're still *alive*. And whatever that creature did to you can be undone. I will get the seed. We will plant it and grow a new Gallows Tree."

"Why did this happen to me? I don't understand."

"Cimree. Whatever happened wasn't your fault."

"It's all my fault," Cimree said in misery. "I chose to come here. It was my decision. Only to find out that Odeon had known all along. He'd come here first. I was blind. And now what I see turns to stone."

"It's not your fault," Azra said with firmness. "You didn't choose *this*."

"And I can't go with you to Tirich Mir," she said, the realization hitting her like a thunderbolt. She wouldn't be able to look at Andrin, Perreta, or any of their children. Or Chrys. Looking into Chrys's eyes would kill her. Grief panged her heart. Roque had said metamorphistry was permanent. "I'm a danger to everyone who looks at me."

"You are Cimree, and I care for you, and I'm not going to abandon you here. There are caves in Tirich Mir. I've told you about them. I'll find a place there where you can come and be safe."

She felt violated by what had happened to her. Her free will had been ripped from her by the golem. Just as Roque had wanted to force himself on her. Anger and rage began to bloom inside her.

"Let me pull you up," Azra offered.

"We can't risk it. I can't risk harming you!"

"I can't leave you down there, and you're not tall enough to jump this high."

"There's another way out. There's a tunnel down here. I think I can open the door." She'd seen Roque close it.

"Very well, but just in case, let me leave another way out. I'll tie the end of a cloak to the statue here and drop it down."

She wanted to cry. Khaf had tried to help her. He had defied Roque. He didn't deserve his fate.

Neither did she deserve hers.

Thirty-Two
Cimree's Justice

C imree bent down and picked up the crystal that Lord Roque had used for light. When she wrapped her fingers around it, it began to glow dimly. In the light, she saw her arms were perfectly normal. The whorl pattern on her chest was still there, although it had grown so much it had begun to spread to her shoulders. With its light, she peered around the chamber and, finding nothing else of interest, approached the cloak that Azra had left hanging from Khaf's stone body.

She tucked the glowing crystal into her girdle and reached up for the fabric of the cloak. It supported her weight, and she began to climb, finding it nearly effortless to do so just using her arm strength. But it was more than that. The grafting with the serpents had rendered additional climbing power, and she felt her muscles along her body contracting and squeezing as she climbed up.

After reaching the top, she pulled herself out of the stone hole. The coolness of the night felt soothing to her. She produced the crystal and by its light, she gazed around the copse of trees, where she found the dead sprawled haphazardly. The dead gave off no heat. With the illumination from the crystal, she examined the scene. The golem had slain them all.

A thump sounded to one side of her, and the salty taste invaded her saliva. In her peripheral vision, she'd seen something fall from a branch. As she stepped closer, she spied a stone bird on the forest floor. And realized that she'd killed it without even meaning to. She bent low and touched the intricate stone wings, which were spread as if it had tried to take flight before it was turned to stone. The beak was split wide in a silent screech. Her heart panged at what she'd unwittingly done. She hadn't even seen it in the trees, but it had seen her. The realization of her predicament weighed on her even more.

Cimree went back to the statue of Khaf and untied the cloak Azra had left. She slid it over her shoulders and raised the cowl to cover the nest of her hair. She felt the serpents' disagreeableness in her doing so. They didn't want to be covered up, but it seemed there was nothing they could do but accept her decision. The covering felt unnatural and uncomfortable. She did it anyway and stuffed the crystal into her girdle again.

As she roamed the woods to escape the forbidden garden, she sensed that Azra had gone away again back to the distant location. He was evacuating people to Tirich Mir. How many trips would he be able to make before the magic of the Tay al-Ard was spent again? He'd already exhausted it once, hadn't he?

Her stomach growled again for want of food, and she realized that getting food would be a challenge. If the bird had turned to stone just looking at her, then she would have to do her foraging at night. And even then, what if she caught a fish in a river and it turned to stone before she could eat it? Would she be dependent on others to bring her food? The feeling of misery threatened to overwhelm her. She could be trapped like this for years.

So many decisions had led to this point. She hadn't chosen to become the golem's newest monster. But if she hadn't chosen to come to Ecbatana, it probably wouldn't have happened. Guilt and shame toiled inside her heart, bringing a sullen feeling of despair.

Past the copse of trees, she found herself back in the forbidden gardens and followed a footpath away from the direction of the Dryad tree. That was another mystery to be solved. Cimree felt that some of her memories had been stolen as well. Her past life had been stolen by the fruit of the Gallows Tree. Had she willingly eaten the whole fruit and reverted herself back to a state of infant helplessness? Why had she done that? Had she known about the Dryad tree, or was the Gallows Tree also a Dryad tree? Was Chrys linked to the seed of the fruit?

Noise from the footpath alerted her that men were coming, judging by their deep voices. She left the path and stood by a decorative tree. Because she was grafted to the serpents, she decided to see if the camouflage ability was still present. With a thought, she tried to disappear, to blend in with the tree.

The voices grew louder. "But do you think Roque is dead?" said one of the men.

Another man spoke, one with a deeper voice. "Lord Felaket heard a report that the golem killed him. His body is by the hetaera pit."

"By the twelve suns, if he's dead, there will be a war." That was a third man.

Cimree saw a group of five men walking briskly toward her. Two carried torches, but she didn't need the light from the torches to count the men. They stood out plainly in the night with her heat vision.

"One our master is sure to win," said the first man again. "No one is more ruthless than Lord Felaket."

"Aye, which is why he sent us to find and bring back Roque's body or be killed by the golem ourselves." That was a different voice, and he didn't sound all that willing to sacrifice himself.

They approached the point where Cimree was hiding and walked right past her. None of them saw her. And looking at them caused no reaction. It seemed the petrifaction was caused by someone seeing her.

Cimree went the other way, listening to them complain until

their voices became unintelligible. She retraced the path back to the iron fence around the garden and easily slipped through it. Shortly after, she made it to the gold-embossed wall and gazed up at it. Drawing in a breath, she began to scale the wall, which caused the same squeezing feeling she'd experienced earlier climbing the rope cloak. It was simple to climb the wall. While doing so, one of the serpents pushed against the cowl, and the hood slid off. Their discomfort had finally won out. Her senses became more alert with over a dozen sets of eyes aiding her perception. She smelled something off as she neared the top.

Cimree looked up just as a warrior with a bow peered down at her, his shooting fingers tensing the string with an arrow already nocked, his face illuminated by a lantern glare at his feet. The splash of salt in her mouth revealed instantly his transformation. He must have heard her approach the wall and had stood ready to shoot her. And upon seeing her, he had instantly turned to stone.

When she reached the top of the wall, his statue form was frozen in that position, head bent down, the bow and arrow tensed in his arms. They, too, had turned to stone. The grim frown on the defender's face moved her with pity. She swallowed the salty taste, feeling regret for having harmed another person.

"I'm sorry," she whispered, touching the stony forearm of the statue.

An arrow struck the statue's shoulder, breaking off a piece of it. Cimree flinched, realizing she was exposed on the top of the wall. The archer who'd shot at her, clearly hadn't turned to stone himself, so distance mattered.

It also meant she could be killed by an arrow at a distance.

Without a grafting wand, she wouldn't be able to fly off the other side, so she bent low and then swung her legs off the other side of the wall and lowered herself down. Another arrow whooshed by and then another. But they were all going too high. Cimree slithered down the wall quickly and then started to hurry away. Her stomach was growling fiercely.

There were manors in this part of the city, the silver district. This is where most of the lords of Ecbatana lived. And as she walked away from the gold wall, she began to see corpses slain by blades. She passed the results of two skirmishes, counting at least a dozen or so men lying dead in the street, their vacant expressions gazing skyward.

"Who do you serve?" demanded a voice not far away. She froze, wondering if she'd been seen.

"Lord Felaket now," answered another voice. It was coming from farther ahead, and looking that way, she saw some heat outlines faintly through a garden hedge.

"Wise choice, friend. He could use another with the fireblood to serve him. Go to his palace and swear fealty to him. Swear the oath of the ancients to him, renounce loyalty to Roque, and you will survive the night."

"I shall. I hear Lord Felaket pretended to make a truce to Lord Avanak and plunged a dagger into his chest instead."

"Indeed so," said the first man. "And then murdered his household. He's moving quickly to consolidate his position. You'd best hurry, friend."

"What of the king?"

"Roque had him killed hours ago."

"Now that Roque is dead, what's the point? I'll join Lord Felaket."

"Indeed so. Hurry. He's attacking the angel sworn next."

Cimree's chest clenched with dread. Azra was still far away. She didn't know how many were left. She began to increase her stride again, being careful not to scuff her sandals on the road. She'd passed the hedge when an idea struck her.

Lord Felaket was consolidating his power, seeking to become the new de facto ruler of Ecbatana. These kings and tyrant queens were merely puppets of the revenant. And they were about to unleash their full treachery against Trinati and the angel sworn.

Cimree turned back and walked to the hedge where the men

had been speaking. She entered the grounds and saw four men standing near each other, with another lying dead at their feet. One of those gathered had blue flames swirling about his hands as he stood in a defensive posture, so he must be the new recruit.

A proud-faced man turned to look at her, his brow lifting in curiosity.

"What are you doing here, woman?" he asked. His eyebrows lifted in surprise, and then horror filled his expression. All four of them turned to stone. The salty feeling in her mouth made her desperately thirsty and accentuated her hunger.

She'd killed them all as soon as they gazed upon her. The expressions of terror on their faces made her wonder what she looked like. Would she turn herself into stone if she looked in a mirror?

She couldn't know unless she tried it, and it seemed a foolhardy action to take. She'd gone to the hedge to stop these men who were under orders to attack the angel sworn. Clearly Felaket wanted all his possible enemies dead before the sun rose. This was the true nature of Ecbatana. All the hospitality, the succulent meals, and endless fruit. It was a wary truce until a time of succession. That's when the blood started. No one had wanted the angel sworn as allies. The smiles had been all been false for the most part. They'd destroy the angel sworn and hope to find the seed of the Gallows Tree among the corpses.

Well, they would have to get through Cimree.

Unless she found Lord Felaket first.

THIRTY-THREE
LORD FELAKET'S CUNNING

Cimree climbed up the wall of a grand estate thick with ivy growth. She found a series of spikes embedded in the top, but she was able to support herself on the narrow wall without losing balance if she remained in a low squat. A spherical decoration made of stone projected from the lip of the wall nearby and was repeated all along the wall she was on, which she could see silhouetted by myriad light sources in the garden below. The manor, half-hidden by a veil of trees, was fully lit and there were sentries roaming the grounds with torches and weapons.

It was, by her best estimation, Lord Felaket's manor house within the confines of the silver wall. She remembered passing it on the way into the city, for Khaf had mentioned it, and the shape and design of the walls had stood out to her. The trees were denuded of extra branches, the boughs all immaculately trimmed and with no twig out of place. A fountain burbled near the front of the estate. Judging by the position of the stars, she could tell it would be dawn fairly soon. Sunrise would increase the likelihood that she would turn people into stone. She did not desire this, and the realization that her power would be heightened in natural light was a cause for concern. She didn't want to affect any of the angel sworn if she could possibly help it. That meant she needed to succeed before it became too light and then go underground into the catacombs during daylight hours.

She had felt Azra return and then leave again. His actions held urgency and a nagging worry. He was trying to evacuate the angel sworn with the Tay al-Ard. How many more trips would he be able to do before it stopped working? Or even broke?

Cimree peered through the trees, watching as the sentries all assembled together at a single point by the main doors. She needed information before deciding how to act. Was Lord Felaket in his manor, protected by all these guards as the man had said earlier, or was he part of the attack launched against the angel sworn? Was he the kind of man who led into battle or relied on underlings? She couldn't just ask, or she would risk turning an informant into stone. But she suspected he was at the manor, since she'd overheard one of his minions tell a man to swear his fealty there.

There was no use waiting around. The enormity of her situation still weighed heavily on her, but she was devoted to protecting the refugees from Clairvaux and needed to put aside her despair until they were safe. When it swelled to intolerable proportions, she used the magic of the Tanaquil amulet to subdue her feelings and lock them away.

Gripping two of the iron spikes embedded in the wall, she slung herself around to the other side and slithered down through the tangle of ivy. She dropped the last few feet and landed deftly on the turf. Her writhing crown of serpents saw no one nearby. Due to the removal of all the lower branches that would have concealed her, she had to slip from tree to tree to get closer, using the camouflage inherent in snakes to blend in with the surroundings. She counted fifty men, and about a quarter of them held torches. They were milling about, as if waiting for further orders. She was still too far away to hear anything more than the murmuring of some of their voices.

Cimree wished she had her distaff and could use it to fly closer.

She had most if not all of the attributes of the serpents, as if grafting magic had been involved, but whatever the golem had done to her, it was not like grafting magic. This was metamorphistry, the weaving of actual animal parts and not just their attributes into other living things. Forcing sentient beings to share the same space and vie for control of the resulting chaotic form.

As she spied on the crowd of soldiers, wondering how close she could get to them, she saw a group of a dozen break away from the pack and head toward the gate, a few with torches. She stooped by the tree trunk and watched them come closer to her. The gate was on her right, but she could not see if anyone was near it. There was another tree closer to the gate, so she moved to that one instead.

She saw that one of the guards had a grizzled pointed beard and a look of wary intensity on his face and seemed to be the leader. When he arrived at the gate, he conversed with some of the guards there. Thankfully, she had gotten close enough to hear them.

"There is a band approaching, Issef," said one of the gate guards.

"Can you tell who it is?" asked the wary man.

"No, Captain."

Issef made a gesture, and the main group of sentries joined him at the gate, providing a show of force. That meant the front door was left unguarded except for six men holding giant halberds. The blades on the halberds were pristine and shimmered with the torchlight. She glanced back at the gate.

The guardians reached Issef and halted, standing in formal array with spears, swords, and torches. She decided to wait and see who was approaching the gate before determining whether to go into Felaket's manor during the distraction.

"Stand ready," Issef commanded, drawing his own sword, a broad scimitar. He had decorative armor, mostly consisting of chain mail with golden decorations on the trim and attached to the links in circular shapes. He wore a long chain hood with a diadem at the forehead. Bracers of brass or bronze were attached to his forearms, and his gauntlets were studded with spikes.

As his men quieted, she heard the sound of marching steps approaching the gate. Was it another armed force come to attack Felaket's manor? To try to do away with him while the bulk of his fighters were storming the angel sworn manor?

Issef came forward to the front of the gate himself, flanked by two large and muscular men who were similarly garbed in chain mail.

"Who are you?" Issef demanded.

"My name is Cassapan," said the newly arrived person, who was heavily armored as well. "I brought a gift to Lord Felaket. Three dozen concubines from the royal palace."

"Where are they from?" Issef asked brusquely.

"My master claimed them from the estates of Faroush, Denizar, and Kalem. They have been toppled. My master seeks an alliance with Lord Felaket."

"And who is your master? I don't recognize you."

"I am with your humble servant Dizeniyah. These are spoils of war, Captain. A tribute to Lord Felaket. May we deliver these in person?"

Cimree thought that a very bad idea. It seemed like a ruse to her, a way to trick them into opening the gate.

"How many soldiers did you bring?" Issef asked, craning his neck as if trying to count them.

"We have only fifty. Enough to protect our precious cargo. Is Lord Felaket here?" Cimree felt it was a lie. A deliberate deception.

"My master's whereabouts are none of your concern. Leave the women at the gate and retreat."

"I was authorized to hand these concubines over to Lord Felaket himself. Surely you understand."

"Back away from the gate now," Issef ordered.

"Do not be so hasty to slight my master," said the other man with a warning tone.

"Do not be so hasty to presume I'm a fool. Much blood has been spilled tonight. Traitors abound. Now back away from the gate! Leave the concubines."

"I would be a disloyal servant if I did that," countered the other. "Felaket has enemies enough right now. Dizeniyah would be a valuable ally."

"That remains to be seen. Withdraw from the gate. Leave the concubines."

"They will come with us. Flesh is worth more than gold to some."

"Leave them or tell Dizeniyah he will die next. We take your gift and make no promises."

"They're worth a small fortune!" growled the other man. Cimree couldn't see him through the crowd of men, but she could hear the fear in his voice. He'd come expecting to win the upper hand, yet he was being forced to retreat without gaining anything.

"And how much is your life worth to you?" spat Issef.

There was a pause. A disgruntled reply: "You make a fair point. Lord Felaket is shrewd. We leave our gift before parting. I've heard the angel sworn are nearly overrun. They've fought valiantly but are outnumbered. They'll all be dead in a few hours, except the ones he keeps for...sport. We obey you, Captain."

She could hear the sound of footsteps retreating from the gate and the whispering murmurs of the women left behind. The captain stared boldly at the retreating men and waited until they had gone a sufficient distance.

"Open the gate. Bring them inside." There was a tone in his voice that Cimree didn't trust. He was not done showing his dominance yet. Felaket valued ruthlessness. No wonder his servants displayed it. She suspected he was going to execute the concubines. Right in front of the men who had brought them as a gift. A bribe.

The concubines had done nothing to deserve that fate. Ecbatana was all madness and revenge.

She saw one of the gate guards produce a key for the lock on the gate. He inserted it and began to twist it.

Cimree stepped away from the tree and walked toward the assembled soldiers. She dropped the camouflage and walked right at them. If Lord Felaket intended to rule Ecbatana this way, it would mean untold suffering for everyone. She knew she could stop it.

With a thought, her crown of serpents began to hiss in warning. The noise attracted the eyes of some guards who, when they saw her, gaped in horror before turning to stone. Involuntary were the reactions. Face after face turned to look at Cimree approaching, their mouths suddenly gaping in terror as their skin turned to rock and their limbs froze in place. Even the weapons they held turned to stone. The salty taste in her mouth increased her burning thirst.

Cries of fear came from some of the men who saw their fellows succumb to Cimree's new power but didn't know the cause. It was joined by the women left at the gate, who began to scream in terror.

The gate creaked as it was pulled open by the man who had been ordered to do so. Issef whirled in confusion, his face turning fearful as he saw what had happened to his men, who had become statues around him. Then his gaze met Cimree's. He didn't stare at her in terror. His eyes widened as if she were beautiful, a brightening of wonder in his expression, which hardened until he, too, turned to stone in her presence.

Some of the soldiers, the ones opposite her, began to flee for their lives, screaming in fear. She hoped the concubines had started to run away as well. But the gate was open, and Felaket was more vulnerable than he knew. Most of Felaket's sentries had succumbed to her power, unable to resist looking at her. Unable to avoid dooming themselves with their own eyes.

She turned away from the gate and began to walk toward the door of Felaket's manor. The six sentries with halberds took attack stances, readying their weapons to face the monster approaching them. Had they seen what had happened at the gate in the torch-light? None of them fled like the few of Issef's men who had survived. The six met her sternly, implacably, courageously. And all six turned to stone as soon as she drew near enough to be seen. Their courage only sealed their fate.

Cimree heard the screams, the shouts, the panicked sounds coming from behind her. She paused at the fountain and cupped some water in her hand to drink, slaking the salty taste. Then she climbed up the manor steps and pulled open the door.

The entryway was thronged with soldiers, the wide hall crammed with another hundred or so. Issef had been deceiving with how many had been left outside, trying to provoke an enemy into attacking Felaket's manor only to discover a more sizable force awaiting within.

The hall was blazing with torchlight. And as they glimpsed her standing in the doorway, these soldiers, too, succumbed. An army of statues stood at the ready in front of her.

The feeling of saltiness in her mouth made her start to gag.

Thirty-Four
Fate of Thousands

The palatial residence of Lord Felaket was a witness to his wealth and his depravity. Climbing the wide stairs leading to the upper floors, Cimree saw on the walls decorative scenes depicting carnage against beasts, prisoners, and slaves. This was a man who had led armies and sought to glorify his past conquests by carving his exploits into the stone walls of his palace. Hunters with bows were displayed shooting down lions, piercing their necks. Images of ferocious animals recoiling in terror from the mounted warriors were on prominent display. There were scenes of conquered foes, decapitated by swords. Others held scenes of torture that made Cimree stare in revulsion. These were shadows of the tales Azra had told her.

It wasn't difficult finding Lord Felaket's chamber since she only needed to look for the centermost door with the most lavish decor. The pillars were carved into statues of humans, crouched as if holding up the weight of the roof on their hunched shoulders, looks of agony carved into their faces. The hall below, still visible from the banister, was eerily quiet, filled with lifeless stone statues that she'd created. She passed another hunting image, this one showing a humanoid beast with arms and legs attempting to fight off a charging horse. It was unlike any other beast she was familiar with, and the humanlike form struck her forcibly as it stood on two legs, two arms, and had a vaguely human face

She went to the door with its massive brass handles carved like ibex horns. She pulled and they opened smoothly. The interior was darkened, save for a glowing orb with a cloth over it.

She heard the release of a trigger, the twang of a crossbow, and with her serpentine reflexes, she dodged to the side as a quarrel ripped past her violently. She entered the room and shut the door behind her. Her eyes searched through the darkness and found a man hiding behind a bulky piece of furniture. The heat radiated from his body in waves. She could feel his fear.

"What are you?" asked a moaning voice coming from the direction of the figure.

The darkness would prevent him from seeing her fully, which gave him protection. Did he know that? The crown of serpents were each gazing a different way, looking for others in the room. But there was just one man there.

"Lord Felaket?" she asked, walking slowly toward him.

"The abomination speaks? What are you?"

"I am one of the angel sworn," Cimree said.

"Impossible."

"I've come to stop you."

"You sound like a woman, but I've heard it can speak as male or female."

"I am not the golem if that's what you've been suspecting. You feared it would come for you tonight."

"We all fear it, angel sworn. And you should fear it the most."

"You have knowledge of it. Do you know where it came from?"

"I'm the one who brought it," the man said.

"You are Lord Felaket?"

"I am. And the new king of Ecbatana. Stay your hand, destroying angel. Spare me and my people."

"We did not come here to destroy you," Cimree said. "But instead of hospitality, we received treachery." She was walking closer to him. He quietly moved to another obstacle farther away and crouched behind it. She simply changed direction.

"Come no closer," he said, his voice starting to tremble.

"Why did you create the golem?" she demanded.

"To defend us against the Queen Mother," Felakat snarled. "To protect ourselves from your vengeance."

"Why would you fear her?"

"Because if she learned what Asmodeus was doing here, she'd send her angel sworn against us."

He had information she wanted to know. If only there were some nightshade powder she could use. "Did Asmodeus create the golem to destroy the angel sworn?"

"We don't know why he created it. He'd invented a new form of magic, metamorphistry, and was using it to create new beasts to hunt. Ones that would be impervious to celestial iron. That could sever your graftings and make you vulnerable to death so that the Gallows Tree might be claimed at last. But something went very wrong."

He darted from his hiding place once more and hurried to the fireplace. She saw recently quenched coals sizzling within. There was just enough light from beneath the orb on the plinth that she glimpsed his boots and the hem of his robe as he darted there. She rushed to intercept him while he fumbled for something on the fireplace mantle. A mechanism was triggered, and the wall inside the fireplace swung open, revealing a secret corridor beyond.

Cimree grabbed him by the collar with one hand and his arm by the other. She used an arm-bar technique to drive him to his knees in pain, and she heard him suck in his breath. He'd turned his face away from her, looking down at the floor. Even though she was much smaller than him, Azra had taught her how to subdue a larger man by his wrist. She smelled wet ash and realized that he must have recently doused the fire.

"What went wrong?" she asked.

"The golem killed the revenant," Felaket said with pain lingering in his voice.

"How?"

"We don't know. It escaped, and when Lord Roque had the sealed chamber opened, all was disheveled and torn asunder. The revenant's skeleton was broken into pieces and strewn about. We can only surmise that the creation turned against its creator for some reason. We heard about the fall of Clairvaux a year later. *Agh!*" He gasped in pain, for she'd indeliberately increased pressure against his wrist and arm in her shock.

The fall of Clairvaux had been instigated by these people! They'd been secretly plotting the destruction of the angel sworn, but their avenger had turned on them as well.

"Can it be killed?"

"We don't know *how* to kill it," Felaket said. "It keeps changing. Keeps altering its form. It adapts and hunts and has even learned to speak."

"Did Captain Odeon come here before us?"

"Yes. We tricked him into a temporary alliance. He was so concerned with keeping the Queen Mother alive, but she's already dead."

"How do you know she is?" Cimree demanded, aghast.

"Because Roque sent a kishion to kill her. He returned just before you arrived. With her head in a bag."

Cimree's anger surged in her heart. This man was utterly despicable. He whirled on her suddenly, untwisting his arm, and grabbed her throat with his other hand, his eyes squeezed shut. The suddenness and violence startled her. Before she could react, one of the snakes grafted to her head lashed out and bit his hand.

Felaket gasped, tugging his hand away, massaging it. And then the venom made him powerless, and he sagged to the floor.

Cimree rubbed her throat, grateful that the serpent had bitten him of its own accord. The doors to the chamber were pulled open. She saw a man in hunter leathers like one of the Long Patrol standing there, holding the handles. Light from the hall illuminated the room.

"Lord Felaket! We've breached the angel sworn—"

She gazed at him and watched him turn to stone mid-speech, still gripping the ibex-horn handles. He and his weapons all turned to stone. The taste of salt struck her again.

She looked down and saw Lord Felaket was already stone. He'd been facing her when the doors opened and just seeing her face had triggered the reaction. She hadn't even been looking at him. There was information she'd still wanted to learn from him, and she felt frustrated that he'd been made useless. But he was a terrible man and deserved his fate.

Standing in the shadows of Lord Felaket's chamber, she realized that the fate of thousands rested on her shoulders. If she walked among the people of Ecbatana, she would destroy them whether she intended to or not. Did all of them deserve death? They'd built a society that was wealthy beyond belief, but it was utterly cruel and malicious deeper within the colored walls. Conquering such a place would have been difficult even for the angel sworn, with catacombs crisscrossing beneath the city. But if she left Ecbatana, how would she survive when every living thing that looked at her was turned into stone? If she stayed in the city, hidden or beneath the streets, she could survive a long time. She wouldn't risk her friends' lives by going with them to Tirich Mir.

Why did the golem want her? Why had it spoken her name? She'd been surprised that it had the capacity to feel. She'd learned about that in Montheron. And the Tanaquil amulet was the only magic that seemed to work against it.

Did it want her because of that magic? Because she could make it feel things? Or did it want to use her as it had used the cats native to Montheron? They'd turned into grimalkin to attack and destroy the population.

Understanding began to awaken within her. Had the golem

wanted to use *her* to destroy the people of Ecbatana? To punish them for their cruelty to animals and beasts? The golem used parts of the natural world as its weapons. Snakes. The city was full of snakes. Asmodeus was known to have dominion over serpents.

His creation had turned against him. But it was still bent on destroying the angel sworn. Maybe it was bent on destroying all mortals as well. Odeon had said that the kobolds were overseeing the destruction of man-made structures.

To the golem, Ecbatana must be the worst abomination of all. It would use Cimree to hasten its collapse. And then it could send the kobolds to eliminate all signs of a civilization having been there. The realization struck her like a physical force, and she took a step back. She couldn't be sure she was right. The golem was quick and ruthless and able to kill. Yet it had not killed her, even when it had chased her through the forbidden gardens. It had spared her life more than once.

Because it knew about her affinity for serpents? Had it learned that about her in Montheron? That she could be useful in its intention to destroy?

Cimree walked to the center of the room where the plinth and orb were and removed the covering from it. The sudden glare of white light made her wince and shy away. But as her pupils adjusted, she saw that the orb was mirroring a scene elsewhere. She could see images in the sphere of another part of the city. No, they were inside the angel sworn manor. She recognized it, saw streaks of blood against the walls. Dead bodies were everywhere. Her heart constricted with pain.

The man had just come saying that the manor had been breached. Azra was out of time. She felt him still far away.

But how could she get to the manor quickly? Her distaff was gone.

There is another where you are.

She heard the voice in her mind and recognized it. It was the spider-tailed horned viper that she'd bonded with earlier, the spirit creature. She sensed it approaching the manor.

I will not look at you, or I'll turn to stone as well. But that fool Felaket has scionwood wands. He collects them. I'll trap a bird for you if you'd like. The viper sounded a little bored, but it was encouraging.

Who are you? she asked, wondering at its sudden offer of help.

You are a marvelous creation. I'm in awe. Would you like to save them? I can help.

Who are you? she demanded again.

I am Iddawc. I am Asmodeus's serpent.

Thirty-Five
Fallen

It was nearly sunrise. As Cimree flew over the next wall, the sapphire one, she saw swaths of oranges and yellows mixing in with a gray sheen of clouds. It was bright enough to see everything and to be seen, although the first rays hadn't crested the eastern mountains yet. She was grafted to a pigeon and soared as quickly as flight could take her to the angel sworn manor. The flashes of salt in her mouth indicated she was seen and was leaving statues in her wake.

The Queen Mother was dead. A kishion had returned with her head. It meant that Clairvaux had truly fallen. If the Queen Mother had known what Ecbatana was about, would she have ordered its destruction as she had in other places? Cimree felt certain that she would have.

An arrow lanced past her, missing by several yards, but it was followed immediately by another salty taste, and no more missiles came after it. With the added vision of the myriad serpents grafted to her head, she could see evidence of the night's fighting in the streets. The dead were strewn everywhere. So much violence had been wrought that it sickened her. But it also caused worry about what she'd find at the angel sworn manor. Azra was still far away.

She'd not felt him in Ecbatana for several hours. Had the Tay al-Ard stopped working, stranding him there? How many angel sworn were left?

The mansion came into view over the swiftly rushing trees. There were dead Ecbatanan warriors everywhere, slain in the act of trying to breach its borders. She spied several armored angel sworn prone on the ground, lifeless. The doors of the manor had been broken to pieces, pulverized by the iron-plated battering ram that had been discarded by the entry. Outside there were healers treating the wounded, who had been gathered together for their injuries to be mended.

Cimree swooped down from the walls, the taste in her mouth getting more noxious as the flood of salt came. All who looked at her turned to stone, the healed and the whole. The Ecbatanan guardians left to protect the door would stand vigil permanently, or until their stone skin had been worn by wind and time.

She landed by the door and hurriedly went inside, following the trail of destruction. Fighting was still going on deeper inside. She could hear the clash of arms, the shouts of anger and frustration, the moans of the dying. As she passed one soldier lying on the ground bleeding, he caught a glance at her, and the rictus of pain on his mouth was his last living expression.

She'd brought a heavy cloak with her to hide her face with the cowl when it was time. Outside, she heard cries of terror and the sound of men fleeing. Maybe some had only barely glimpsed her and were not stricken because of it. But they'd seen the result as their fellow warriors stood in mute testament to their fate.

Where was the fighting still happening? She followed the sounds to the steps leading down to the bathing area. It would be darker there, but there were torches burning in sconces on the walls. The air smelled rank with death. The clang of metal weapons against armor grew fiercer still.

A crowd of soldiers blocked the top of the steps, each hastening to join the fight below. The noises were desperate.

"One left. We must bring their heads to Felaket!" someone shouted.

"But it's already dawn!" someone lamented, implying they believed they were too late to fulfill their mission.

"He'll show mercy if we bring the heads. Onward!"

"You'll not touch her!" roared a voice she recognized as Captain Odeon's. It was full of wrath and pain. She remembered him fighting when Montheron fell. He'd refused to abandon the fortress, even though Trinati had ordered the evacuation. Was Trinati down there as well? Already dead?

Cimree drew her dirk and stabbed the nearest man in the back with it, using the venom instinct to incapacitate him. He let out a cry of pain first, which drew surprised looks from his companions as they whirled to face her before turning to stone.

In the crammed space, soldiers began to solidify before her, the light from the torches soon shimmering over their stony visages.

"What's happening? What is this madness?" a man shrieked in terror, and then when his confused eyes fell on Cimree, he turned to stone next.

"Flee! Flee!" someone shouted. "They've unleashed a curse on us!"

But there was no room to flee. Statues with shields and curved stone swords blocked the only escape back up the stairs. And in their panic, more saw her and more were afflicted.

"Get in the water! Get in the water!" someone else screamed, only to be cut down by Odeon at the base of the steps.

Cimree raised the cowl of her cloak to hide her face. The crown of serpents on her head hissed at the obstruction, but they began to settle their writhing when they felt her insistence to be calm.

The noise of fighting dried up like an abandoned cistern. She heard Odeon's heavy breathing, the shuffle from his wounded steps. He killed another man, the last, and then slid down to the floor himself at the edge of the bathing room, leaning back against the wall, utterly exhausted.

Cimree looked down the steps that were crowded with statues in various stages of action. She couldn't see him, but she heard his breathing.

"Captain Odeon."

"Cimree? You're alive? How?"

"Do not look at me, or you will share the same fate as these unfortunates. I'm going to come down and help you."

She heard a catch in his throat. "I do not deserve your help, Cimree. Not after all I've done."

Cimree felt surprisingly detached from her previous anger at his betrayal. Was it because she could feel his remorse, or was this new form somehow to blame? She decided it didn't matter at the moment. She was needed.

"I am still coming down. Do not look at me. I cannot undo what has been done. It may be beyond the power of the Gallows Tree. Close your eyes."

"I am too weary to keep them open. But tend to Trinati first. If she still lives." He said the last part with a grunt of anguish.

Cimree maneuvered her way down the steps, having to crouch and dodge to get around the obstacles of once mortal men. The serpents were getting restless again. After she had made it past the final obstacle, she drew the distaff that she'd claimed from Lord Felaket's hoard and used it to summon serpents to defend the grounds of the mansion. She did not sense the horned viper yet, but she imagined it was coming. She had many questions to ask it still.

At first glance, she saw heat coming from both bodies.

"She's still alive, if barely," Cimree said in relief.

There were many dead warriors at the base of the steps, and she used her dirk to cut strips of cloth from their attire. Odeon's head was sagging. His wounds were plenteous and some were severe. She made two blindfolds out of the fabric and hurriedly wrapped one around Odeon's eyes.

"Please help her," he implored.

Cimree saw Trinati lying in a pool of blood near the edge of the bath. The bench that led to the catacombs had been blocked with debris. There were casks of food and supplies down there as well, hastily gathered to withstand a siege. Cimree padded over to Trinati, who was lying on her stomach, head cradled on one of her arms. Cimree began to examine the archangel, looking for any obvious wounds. The armor had protected her but not fully. She was bleeding profusely from her head. Her hair was sticky with blood. A sword had punctured the chain mail at her waist.

"Nnghh," Trinati moaned after a few prods. Cimree hastily put the blindfold on her and secured it. With that done, she lowered the hood fully so she could see and hear better. The serpents quelled their agitation and began to examine the room. She was thirsty and longed to be rid of the salty taste in her mouth.

On closer inspection, she found another wound at Trinati's neck, which was still weeping. She applied pressure to it and wrapped it up before working on the head injury. After that one had been bandaged with rags cut from the clothing of the dead, she was satisfied that she had reduced the extent of Trinati's traumatic injuries. The other smaller cuts had stopped bleeding. The bruise on Trinati's cheek would heal itself.

She turned back to Odeon and began to examine him.

"Help her," Odeon commanded. "It doesn't matter if I die."

"I did help her. But you're still losing blood. You need to be tended as well."

"Let me die. So long as she survives."

"You will both survive if you quit being so morose." She was surprised to find his armor by his shoulder had been struck by a crossbow quarrel, which had pierced it clean through. It was probably fired at close range. She unbuckled his breastplate and helped him shrug out of a mail shirt. Sweat and blood stained his tunic beneath. He hissed in pain, which roused the serpents on her head, and they looked at him curiously. She went to work, grateful for Milena's thoughtful training on handling battlefield injuries. She was by no means as expert as her mentor had been, but she knew the importance of stanching the bleeding and disinfecting the wounds. She'd need more than the bathing water to do that, and she hoped she'd be able to find what she needed in the kitchen.

Some snakes had slithered into the mansion, and one was curiously coming down the stairs, but she rebuked it and commanded it to stay away lest it die looking at her. It flicked out its tongue and then retreated.

"I'm so thirsty," Odeon said after she'd managed to wrap up his wounds.

Cimree went to the stack of provisions and found a vessel, which she emptied, and then went to the farthest end of the pool to fill it with water. She took a sip of it herself, found the water didn't taste tainted, and then brought it back to him and helped him drink from it. He did so greedily at first before resting his head back against the stone wall.

"Is Trinati awake?" he asked.

"I am," she responded in a mournful voice. "I regained consciousness a little while ago. Why do I have bandages on my eyes?"

"So you do not look at me," Cimree said. "The golem has woven its magic once again. Any who look on me in the light turn to stone."

"What?" Trinati said with shock. "That is...that is dreadful."

"But useful," Cimree said grimly. "There were still dozens more attackers coming down here. They're all statues now. Where is Azra? How many escaped?"

"He took them all to Tirich Mir," Trinati said, her voice sounding subdued and near tears.

"All the rest?" Cimree asked, confused at finding Odeon and

Trinati still there. "Why didn't you go with him? Did the Tay al-Ard break?"

"I refused to go," Trinati said softly.

"You wished to stay here? Why?" The only reason Cimree could think of was Trinati's desire to become the tyrant queen. That seemed an awful reason to stay.

"I am a fallen angel now," Trinati said with contempt for herself in her voice. "I cannot be with the others until I atone for what I did. I disgraced myself, and *you*, when I betrayed you. I put all the angel sworn in jeopardy, thinking I knew best. I cannot go to Tirich Mir until I perform a penance worthy of such a failure. Azra said they would be safe there. We would all be. But I cannot be safe from my conscience. It...it torments me."

Her words and the depths of her emotion surprised Cimree. Trinati had always been so self-assured, so decidedly above everyone else, that to hear the depth of her guilt and shame was odd.

Cimree crossed over to her and took her by the hand. "Your leadership is needed, Trinati. I cannot go to Tirich Mir with the others. Not when simply looking at me will destroy the viewer. You are needed there. I know it."

Trinati was still lying on her back in the same position that Cimree had left her in after tending her injuries. One arm was draped across her stomach.

"If I hadn't rebelled against you," Trinati said, her voice thick with tears, "none of this would have happened. I was blinded by pride. And that does not make a good leader. I don't deserve your compassion now, Cimree. If our people were still in danger, I would go and see them to safety. But the caves are uninhabited. They are just what we need, as he said they would be. Everything has been as he said, I know that now. So I refused to go with Azra when he came for us at the end. I told him I would die here or go to Tirich Mir after I'd performed my penance."

"And what penance do you need to perform? We're already

exiles from Clairvaux. What further punishment is there? The Queen Mother is dead. They brought her head here just days before we arrived."

"No," Odeon gasped in surprise and defeat. His emotions quickly overwhelmed him.

A dark smile twisted on Trinati's mouth. "At least her suffering is over. The Queen Mother would never forgive a man who betrayed the angel sworn. She could not forgive Azra, nor did he seek it from her. But before I was named the archangel, I'd heard the Queen Mother tell the story of a female angel sworn who had gone to the mortal world and been with a man. Had lived with him for several months in heathen bliss. She'd kept her sin a secret until it could no longer be kept. She was with child." She paused, her words having grown weaker as she spoke. So much blood had been lost.

"Rest," Cimree said. "I'll clean your hair."

"I don't deserve your pity!" Trinati said, her voice shaking with grief.

"We were all deceived by these people."

"Azra wasn't," Trinati said tightly. Not with anger, but with self-recrimination.

Cimree lightly brushed Trinati's forehead above the blindfold. "Can you imagine how he feels, then? To never be forgiven because of what he chose all those years ago? Because he's a man. How is that just?"

Trinati grimaced at her words. "It's true. It is not. And it was wrong of us to treat him so. I think...she just wanted him to admit he was wrong. But he never could. Because he *wasn't* wrong."

"Do you believe that now?" Odeon whispered with a groan from his spot against the wall.

"I don't know what I believe anymore," Trinati said plaintively. "But I will make amends. I will suffer the penance for my deeds in the only way I know how."

"Do you believe I betrayed the Queen Mother, Odeon?"

Cimree asked him after a small pause. She felt he had been sincere. But she still wanted to hear him say it.

"I do believe that, Cimree. I justified betraying you because of that belief. But you cannot be held accountable for something you have no memory of. Your rebirth should have purged any guilt. I, too, was blinded by what I wanted. Whether you are the same person still or are different because of how you were raised this time, I must confess that I cannot condemn you for what you may have done previously. I am guilty and in need of penance. But there is no penance for a man."

"And what is the penance?" Cimree asked. She didn't think it fair that a man could not be absolved.

Trinati sighed. "I must climb the Wilderswill with my pride. Without any graftings."

"That waterfall is clear back in Clairvaux," Cimree said, distressed by the very thought of how far they'd come to get to Ecbatana and how far they had to go to Tirich Mir. It had taken a year to get this far. The Wilderswill was the waterfall closest to the ruins of the Gallows Tree at the headwaters of the Silver River. The Fear Liath might still be there in the mist. Even Azra had been defeated by it.

"I know," Trinati said with implacable determination. "But remember, I am an Eyriemaester. I can fly there and return swiftly. And then I'll rejoin the rest at Tirich Mir. If they'll allow me. But I must atone for this. I cannot face the others until I do. Since they are no longer in danger, I will not postpone my penance. These wounds of my body will heal eventually. The wounds in my soul cannot unless I do this."

Cimree heard Odeon sigh.

THIRTY-SIX
SEPARATION

They came after nightfall. That was becoming a pattern. No one tried to attack the angel sworn mansion during the day, so that was when Cimree slept, although she was always partially awake due to the grafting with the snakes. She had enough food to last several weeks stored in the mansion. Staying put was not a wise option in that one place, for they'd find a way to trap or destroy her. They might even try to burn the mansion down, although it was mostly made of stone. She would have to change locations from time to time and to forage for food. She'd resigned herself to the fact that it would take years before a new Gallows Tree would bear fruit.

At night, she could hear the howl of the gévaudan as well. They were inside Ecbatana, ravaging and destroying. And Cimree was the threat deeper inside the city. There had been no further encounters with the golem. It had instigated the destruction of the city and disappeared. Or maybe it was watching with glee as the city was destroyed. She realized that in time the kobolds would come to begin their work of dismantling.

The men sneaking onto the mansion grounds had thick boots that went to mid-thigh, to protect them from the snakes she had surrounding the estate. There were three small groups of men, about nine in total, coming from three different sides. They carried no lights with them. They were heavily cloaked, with masks covering most of their faces, save tiny slits for their eyes. The masks were painted with savage-looking marks. Were they trying to make her afraid? She felt *their* fear as they approached the mansion and its broken windows and doors.

Trinati and Odeon had left two days before, after partially recovering from their battle wounds. They were going to fly back to Clairvaux so Trinati could train to complete her penance. Odeon refused to let her go alone. He also felt the dishonor of what he'd done. Cimree had seen they'd both changed because of what had happened in Ecbatana. The guilt they bore was painful to them, but it was a motivator as well. They would go on to Tirich Mir after completing the task. And both had promised that once the Gallows Tree bore fruit again, Cimree would be the first to taste of it.

The suspense is going to kill them, I think. She heard the thought from Iddawc outside in the garden. It sounded bored. Asmodeus's serpent had taken up residence in the mansion garden.

Maybe you could be useful and drive the intruders away? Cimree suggested.

That would require too much work.

You are a rather lazy snake, Cimree thought. She did not trust Iddawc, but at least it had provided a form of companionship. She'd also learned it wasn't fond of answering too many questions, especially about itself or its prior master. Solitude had never bothered her before, but after Odeon and Trinati had left, she'd felt her aloneness keenly.

Snakes are inherently lazy. It is our nature. And I'm lazier than most because I trick my prey into coming to me. She felt a sort of smug satisfaction in the thought.

She had positioned herself in one of the darker corridors where she could respond quickly to the threat. She'd removed the

Ecbatanan gown and was wearing her tunic and trews once again. One of the three groups was drawing near the window in the kitchen. Cimree had already cleared out the rest of the food, but she thought longingly of the taste of freshly cooked bread. It would mitigate the residue of saltiness that was ever-present in her mouth.

Cimree quietly padded into the kitchen. She reached into her pocket and grasped the crystal that could glow.

She heard one of the men kick at a serpent that had started to climb his leg. The sense of revulsion in him was strong, and she thought she heard Iddawc chuckle in her mind.

"This is the kitchen," she heard one of them whisper. "Go quickly. Go quietly."

"Yes, Haseem," whispered another.

Cimree gripped the crystal and prepared to pull it out.

"When do we go in?" asked the third man.

"We wait for the sign."

That was interesting. It was a coordinated attack. Cimree knew through the serpents that the other group had paused at the front door. And another was at one of the bedrooms on the western side of the mansion.

The sound of a horn blew. It startled her, causing a ripple of fear inside her. The first man jumped through the window, landing like a cat with a hand-held crossbow in hand. Cimree drew the crystal, summoning its light, and the masked man turned to stone immediately. The second fellow was transformed mid-jump, and his stone body landed with a thud on the kitchen floor. The salty taste in her mouth still troubled her, but she had become more used to it. The others were charging inside, all three groups converging at once. That was what the signal was for. She heard the third man whimpering outside the window, too afraid to enter.

"Haseem? Haseem?" he gasped. Neither of his fellows could respond.

Cimree heard the sound of steps running through the

mansion. Since the third man stayed outside, she hurried to the central hall and found three new intruders racing toward her. One glimpsed her and tried raising his crossbow, but he turned to stone before he could pull the trigger. The other two froze in place mid-stride.

Five of the nine had turned to stone. One was still cowering outside, weeping in fear, and the other group of three had jumped inside the windows so they were out of view of the serpents outside.

Cimree heard the sound of running behind her and turned to face it. But they weren't running at her, they were running downstairs to the bathing room. Terror fueled their feet. Cimree started toward them, knowing they'd have to get past the stone effigies blocking the stairs down. She realized what they were doing. They were trying to open up the passageway leading to the catacombs. These groups had been a diversion. The real attack was coming from below. Cimree felt her heart shudder with concern. She was alone.

"I can't see a thing!" one of the men growled in frustration and terror. Cimree hurried to the stairs and saw the heat coming from all three men as they struggled to get downstairs. One of them had made it down to the bottom. None of them was facing her.

"A light is coming. Hurry!" another quailed.

Cimree felt a shift and suddenly Azra was down in the bathing room. His immediate presence filled her chest with relief. She could sense his concern and heard the swords coming from their scabbards. She retreated back up the steps and stuffed the crystal into her pocket again to snuff out its light.

Azra killed the first man. She could hear it in his grunt.

"She's down here!" another shrieked. "Get away!"

Azra launched at the second fellow and killed him on the steps. The third was frantically retreating, clawing past the statues. She saw Azra's heat as he gave chase.

Cimree waited at the top of the steps for the man as he made it past the statues. She waited until he was almost upon her before dodging to the side and flinging out her leg to trip him. He landed on his stomach, grunted, and then fled while she watched him leave. The one who'd been whimpering by the window heard his howls of fear as he fled the mansion and ran after him. Only two of the nine had survived.

"Cimree?"

The sound of Azra's voice thrilled her.

"I'm here. Close your eyes."

"Ours are covered."

"Who is with you?"

"Andrin and Chrys."

Waves of emotion surged in her heart: relief, rejoicing, and then pain.

"I'll come down, then. If all your eyes are bound."

"They are. Come down."

The feelings of despondency she'd had just moments before were gone. He was there! Andrin and Chrys too! She could feel him so strongly, his feelings of loneliness matching her own. She maneuvered past the statues, and he was waiting for her at the bottom of the steps, his swords sheathed behind his back once more. Andrin and Chrys were seated on the stone bench by the pool, their eyes tightly bound with strips of cloth.

The serpents on her head hissed at Azra, sensing him as their enemy. She wanted to embrace him, but she suspected they might strike at him if she did. His affinity for firavun faresi made him their natural predator.

"I'm going to pull out a light crystal," she said. "I want to see you all so badly."

"I'm blindfolded," he said. "I wrapped them before I came. I don't always need to see to fight."

Cimree was grateful for his foresight. He hadn't even needed his vision to kill those men. She pulled out the crystal and covered her mouth to stop an involuntary sob when she saw those she loved so much.

"Being away from you has been torture," Azra said. He held out his hand to her. "Come closer."

Cimree closed the distance, reaching for his hand and taking it. The snakes were still wary of him, and she tried to get them to calm down because they were hissing so loudly.

"I've missed you these last few days. I don't know how I'm going to bear it for so long. Because it *will* be a long time. And I can't stay in this mansion forever either."

"I sensed you were in danger, so I came," he said. "I wasn't afraid for you. It was all the excuse I needed to come. Perreta and the other children all wanted to come and say goodbye to you," he said, stroking her hand with his thumb before coming closer. She sensed his internal clash between wanting to embrace her and the feeling of revulsion toward the snakes as her hair. "We had to compromise. Chrys especially expressed the need to come back."

She soaked him up with her eyes. He'd wrapped a long strip of cloth around his head to cover his eyes so he wouldn't accidentally see her. Instead, he used his hand to feel his way up her arm.

"Do you know why?" Cimree asked, looking at the little girl who was seated next to Andrin and holding his hands tightly.

"Not really. Come here, lass. Don't fall in the pool, though."

Andrin rose and guided the little girl by the sound of their voices. Chrys reached out hesitantly, and Cimree knelt in front of her. "I'm here."

Chrys touched Cimree's shoulder with her outstretched hand. Then she slid it up toward her neck. The serpents were totally docile. Chrys touched one of the longer ones, showing no fear at all. Then she smiled and nodded and hugged Cimree tightly around the neck.

"Azra said your hair has...changed," Andrin mentioned, sounding unnerved.

It felt so good to be hugged that Cimree didn't want to let her go. Chrys wasn't acting bothered at all by the transformation. It warmed her heart.

"I've changed in more ways than one," Cimree said. She wanted so much to go with them. But if anyone in their group were turned to stone, she wouldn't have been able to forgive herself. She felt like someone with a highly contagious disease. The proper thing to do was to stay away from others and not risk infection.

"What you did saved everyone," Andrin said. "It's not fair that you can't come."

"It's for the best. But thank you for coming. And give my love to Perreta and the children. I miss them all so much. It soothes my heart seeing you." The sadness of their impending departure rose in her like storm clouds gathering over the skies of Clairvaux.

Chrys pulled back, carefully took Cimree's hand, and opened her palm. With one little finger, she traced something on Cimree's palm. What it was, Cimree had no idea. It was a circle, a straight line, and a little hook at the end. It was a symbol that Cimree didn't recognize.

"Can you draw it again?" Cimree asked her.

Chrys did, repeating the same thing.

"What did she do?" Azra asked.

"She drew a symbol on my hand."

Azra held out his hand, but Chrys shook her head no.

"She won't do it," Cimree said. She cupped the child's cheek. "Is that for me?"

Chrys nodded resolutely.

"You can take us back now, Azra. I know you'd like some time with her alone." Andrin's voice was gentle and sympathetic.

Azra drew the Tay al-Ard from his belt. Cimree hugged Andrin and Chrys once more and then guided their hands to Azra's arm. They vanished instantly, and she started to cry as soon as they were gone. Azra returned moments later alone.

"Do you recognize the fabric of my blindfold? It's your tunic," he said with a half smile.

Once he said that, she did recognize it. "It is. Tell me, how is everyone else? Are they safe?" She reached out and gripped his forearms.

"Safe enough for now," he answered.

"What do you mean?"

"The caves were empty. No one has lived there for quite some time. But there is a village in a valley that is quite near the caves. They're not aware of us yet, but there's at least a hundred or so. They are herdsmen, mostly. Lots of goats. And they're growing a rare kind of flower in their pastures. I haven't approached them yet."

"Are they like the ones you met before?"

"Yes. They're very wary of outsiders and prone to violence. We're keeping quiet for now. Wegner is exploring the tunnels, trying to find the most defensible ones."

"Ah, Wegner! How are Perreta and the other children?"

"They're well," Azra said with a smile. "The children all miss you and asked when they get a turn to come see you."

"I miss them so much," Cimree said, her throat catching. "I see you told them about what happened to me."

"Yes. They all know. Little Blanka said she didn't care. That they should all wear blindfolds so you can come back."

It made Cimree's heart squeeze to hear it. She couldn't go back. Not until she was cured. "And the others? Uorsin? Darcia?"

"They're all safe. I don't really think about how they are doing. Tell me, what happened to Trinati and Odeon? I tried to persuade them to come, but she refused. I wasn't sure how to interpret your feelings when you found them alive down here."

"Trinati has changed. I've never seen her brought so low. They're going back to Clairvaux."

Azra snorted. "There is nothing left there worth saving."

"The Queen Mother is dead. Well, I heard her head was brought to Ecbatana."

She felt his reaction to her words. His hatred for the Queen Mother had given him purpose and fed his anger. The look on his face revealed the complexity of his emotions. She reached up and stroked his cheek tenderly.

"The First Woman is dead," Azra said with a sigh. "I suppose I thought Lilith would live forever."

"Was that her name?"

Azra nodded. "The name the Oldknow gave her after she was created."

"It feels like the Oldknow has abandoned us."

Azra let out a breath. "I don't think so. I don't think the Oldknow ever intended us to stay in Clairvaux forever. I think fear kept the Queen Mother inside the valley for far too long."

She lowered her hand and put it on his chest. "I'm glad you came back. I was feeling so lonely."

"I could tell," he said. He put his hand on her shoulder and one of the serpents bit him.

Cimree felt a surge of frustration and gave a mental rebuke to the serpent. It became more timid. None had bothered Andrin. It was probably Azra's affinity for snake-killing animals that caused the reaction.

"I'm sorry," she apologized.

"Venom doesn't affect me," he said. "Firavun faresi are immune to it."

"But it must have hurt."

"Only a little." He squeezed her shoulder and then pulled her in for a hug. The serpents grafted to her began to writhe in terror, but she willed them to calm down. She also felt their aversion to him, but she couldn't bear to let that estrangement happen.

She pressed her head against his chest, wrapping her arms around him, enjoying his warmth. Feeling his arms around her, the hopelessness and oddness began to fade. It felt good to be held by him, even though it made the snakes want to frenzy.

She pulled back. She could sense the needle pricks of pain he was enduring. Not just from the graftings he'd done before coming but from the fangs. His ability to endure pain was remarkable.

"Is Chrys happier now that she's away from Ecbatana?"

Azra reached out and touched her chin. "She is," he answered. "There's something about her so different than others. A sadness. She caresses the seed sometimes. Treats it like it is the only thing that comforts her. We're looking for a place we can plant it. A place with water and where it can get sunlight. The mountains are thick with trees, and there are a few small waterfalls. Well, smaller than what we're used to."

"I wish I could see it," Cimree said longingly. The thought of the waterfalls reminded her that she hadn't finished telling him about the others. "The reason Trinati went back to Clairvaux is to perform a penance. Then she will rejoin you at Tirich Mir."

"She's going to climb the Wilderswill?" Azra said with a chuckle of disbelief.

"You find that amusing?"

"I find it unnecessary," Azra said. "Lilith gave me that choice when I was brought back to Clairvaux. As I understand, I was the only man she ever offered it to. Climb a waterfall without any graftings, bearing a heavy burden. Or die of old age in a cell in Montheron. I chose Montheron."

"Why?" she asked him, feeling both options were terrible.

"Because I knew in my heart that marrying Delara was not a sin. It was never part of the Oldknow's design to withhold intimacy from each other that which we were meant to share."

One of the serpents flicked its tongue at Azra's hand as he touched her chin. But it did not strike him.

"When the new Gallows Tree grows, we will have to figure all that out," Cimree said. "All the ceremonies we've done as angel sworn...what good are they?"

"We follow the good," Azra said, tilting her chin up. He wanted to kiss her. She could feel that desire in him despite his inner reluctance. "And see where that leads us."

She turned her head away. "What's happened to me. I'm struggling to even think about it, Azra. Let alone cope with it. About us. I'm afraid," she confessed.

"You're alive, though."

"This is not how I wanted things to be between us."

"What are you afraid of?"

"I'm afraid of how it will make you feel about me," she said. "I'm already the most loathsome woman in the world. If I could have back that moment when you thought I was beautiful."

He stroked her chin with his thumb and turned her face back toward him. "This is difficult. But I can still see you with my hands. We will figure this out, one way or another," he said. "I will do what I can to help you cure this."

"And if it can't be cured? What if this manifestation of metamorphistry is permanent?"

"It doesn't change how I feel about you. But it will be difficult. We'll face those challenges together."

She knew in her heart that she wanted to be with him. It didn't feel like the amulet's magic was compelling either of them this time. She reached out and squeezed his hand, feeling stronger, more determined to persevere. To endure the loneliness. To protect herself from those who would try to kill her. All with the goal of being reunited.

Yet why did this feel so strangely familiar to her? A memory suppressed?

Without her memories, she could only wonder at the symbol that Chrys had drawn on her palm and what it might say about her past and maybe her future

Epilogue
The Morgarten

Captain Jodocus approached Ecbatana like a falcon, soaring with the clouds to view the city far below. He was flanked by five other angel sworn wearing dark armor, their capes rippling in the wind as they followed the gusting breezes. He could sense the variations of air flow and responded instantly to them, allowing himself to stay airborne for a long time. His shoulder blades tingled from the grafting magic, but he had an affinity for falcons and had been flying for hours. His eyes were sharp as he observed the details of the blighted city below. A falcon's vision, especially at a distance, was uncanny, but he could also focus on the angel sworn at his sides. From what he saw below, he could tell Ecbatana was in the throes of destruction.

Jodocus knew of the varying levels of walls, each a different color, and that the centermost housed the royal palace and the treasury. The coin and treasures of Ecbatana meant nothing to him. They were evidence of decadence and festering sin. No, the treasure he sought was infinitely more valuable. The last seed of the Gallows Tree, stolen by the traitors of Clairvaux. He would see Clairvaux restored to its former glory and honor. And he would destroy the fallen angels who had fled, abandoning the Queen Mother to her grisly fate.

Tilting his head, Jodocus began to dive, and the angel sworn at his flanks followed suit, plunging from the buffering of clouds. His stomach thrilled at the intensity of the descent. He'd always enjoyed the feeling of his lungs full of air, no matter how fast he went. His razor-sharp vision saw the sprawling city, witnessed the carnage. The gévaudan were prowling the streets within the second barrier, drawn by the desire to feast on mortal flesh. They'd already conquered two levels of Ecbatana. But that was nothing compared to the death and destruction within the inner city.

Clashes between rival factions must have been going on all night, leaving the victims to rot in the sun.

Jodocus saw archers appear atop the inner walls to begin shooting at the descending angel sworn. He maneuvered swiftly and plunged down to their ranks, drawing two mirror blades just as he reached the height of the walls. The defenders looked fatigued, but they were no match for the Morgarten, the sworn defenders of the Gallows Tree, who swept through their ranks effortlessly, flying to close the gap and slaying any foolish enough to attack them.

Jodocus gave a quick nod of satisfaction as his victim tumbled off the wall and fell to the street below. Within moments, a gévaudan reached the wounded man and began savaging him.

"To the palace!" he shouted to his company after all the defenders on that portion of the wall had been killed. The falcon he'd bonded with had begun to circle overhead, giving him a perspective of the whole scene from above while he stood beneath.

He lifted into the air and soared over the next section of the city, wondering at the destruction that had happened in so short a time. The member of the Long Patrol who had notified him of Trinati's band in Ecbatana had described a prosperous city that could withstand a siege of monsters for months. She'd described orchards of fruit trees and fertile farmlands carefully protected within the city walls. It made perfect sense to him that the fallen angels that had thwarted him would bring the seed and plant it in Ecbatana and usurp control of the city through their awful tradition of choosing a tyrant queen.

No one had expected the bloodletting to begin this quickly.

Since the palace was in the middle of the city, beyond the gold-encased walls, it was easiest to find, and they arrived in the midst of a round of pillaging, quickly dispatching the marauders weighed down with gold and silver necklaces, gemstones, and ornate dishes and chalices. The six angel sworn made quick work of them. The damage to the palace was severe. The door had been battered down, windows shattered. Jodocus patrolled the entrance, still holding his mirror blades and keeping alert at all times.

"Tinaret, find a servant or someone who might bring useful information," Jodocus ordered. "They might know where the fallen are."

"Yes, sir," Tinaret said, giving a crisp salute before taking flight again. These five were some of the fiercest warriors to survive the destruction of Clairvaux. There were four men and one woman, but they all had pledged fealty to Jodocus after the Queen Mother had elevated him. They were completely loyal to him.

He walked around the entrance hall, gazing in disgust at the foul luxury on display. The others followed, their steps quiet and careful as they walked along.

Beyond the entry, they found two huge doors open and torches burning brightly. The torches were sparking with unnatural heat, which allowed his falcon vision to see even more clearly. The area had a rotten smell and was silent like a crypt. There were no lavish jewels inside or decorations. The chamber looked like it had been rampaged. Stone tables had been overturned. There was an unholy feeling in the place that made Jodocus's skin crawl. The taint of dark magic. He gripped his blades, gazing through the debris for any explanation of what had happened. There were no corpses, but it still felt like a place of death.

"This is a lychgate," said Aetania with a scowl, her beautiful features wrinkling with disgust.

"Had the Queen Mother known of it, she would have ordered us to destroy Ecbatana long ago," Jodocus said. "Do you see the corruption of wealth?"

The others nodded in agreement, casting aspersive looks with their eyes as they continued to examine the scene of tumult. Deeper in, there were cages with the skeletal remains of creatures still inside. The shapes made no sense and looked like no animals that Jodocus had ever heard about. Something like a bear but with a beak instead of a snout. Another like the form of a grimalkin, except longer and with a bony tail.

After some exploration, Jodocus heard a set of footsteps approaching. Tinaret returned with a man seized by the collar. He cowered and trembled with fear as he was brought into the sanctum of evil.

"Kneel before the archangel," Tinaret commanded and shoved the fellow to a kneeling position in front of Jodocus. He cautiously lifted his head, but looked terrified being there. The Queen Mother's last command to Jodocus had been to find the seed of the Gallows Tree. To restore Clairvaux. She had also bestowed him with Trinati's rank. He, a man.

"What is this place?" Jodocus demanded, nodding to the chamber.

"I know not, archangel," said the man. "Only Lord Roque entered here."

Jodocus snorted. "And where is Lord Roque?"

"I learned his body was discovered in the forbidden garden. He's rotting away. None of the dead have been buried since the purge began."

Jodocus gazed at him angrily. "Do you know where the angel sworn are?"

"They have left. They are all gone."

"All?" Jodocus said, growing frustrated at having missed his chance to get revenge on Trinati, Azra, and Cimree. After they had defeated him by the mountain lake, they had hidden their escape from Clairvaux well and had disappeared off the face of the earth until they'd come to Ecbatana. But Jodocus was determined to find them. He'd sent survivors from the Long Patrol to Tirich Mir to await their arrival. But that mountain range was vast and dangerous. There had been no sign of approach so far.

"Well...they did leave a curse."

Jodocus tilted his head. "What kind of curse?"

"There is a fruit in Ecbatana that can turn a man into stone. The angel sworn cursed it. Hundreds have been turned into statues. It happens quickly with just a look. Someone said the angel sworn had a serpent on a pole and whoever gazes at it turns to stone. The mansion that they were given is surrounded by the statues of the dead. No one goes there now. I beg you, my lord, please remove this curse from us!"

His words were utterly incomprehensible to Jodocus. A fruit that turned someone to stone? A serpent on a pole?

"At Lord Felaket's mansion, hundreds were turned into stone instantly," the man proclaimed. "Surely this is a grievous curse. How may we repent and have your wrath turned away from us?"

He gave Jodocus a beseeching look, his hands clasped before him pleadingly.

"Our Queen Mother was beheaded, her body desecrated, and you ask us for mercy?" Jodocus said.

The man began to weep and prostrated himself on the floor.

Jodocus snarled and jerked his head for Tinaret to drag the fellow away. Tinaret raised an eyebrow with a questioning gaze.

Jodocus nodded curtly. All these earthborn deserved death.

It would be a mercy to hasten it.

AUTHOR'S NOTE

In 1981, the film *Clash of the Titans* came out and of all the monsters in the movie, it was the Medusa that petrified me the most (ha!). The hero, Perseus, went on a quest to cut off the head of the monster to use it to stop the Kraken from destroying the beautiful woman he loved who was going to die as a ransom for her kingdom. The only way to protect himself from the Medusa's gaze was for Perseus to glimpse her reflection from his shield before slicing off her head. That was my introduction into the legend of Medusa and it gave me nightmares.

But Medusa's story is so much deeper than that. In the Greek tale, she was a beautiful woman, a victim of sexual assault, and was cursed for it. She was betrayed by everyone, even the goddess she fled to for help. She's a victim. She's misunderstood. But she is terrifying because just looking at her can cause irrevocable harm to friend or foe and she has snakes for hair. Snakes have always been frightening to me. What would it be like to be her?

For this story, I wanted to recast the legend of Medusa and put it in new light, to explore some of the contours and edges of being such an outcast. What happened to Cimree was not a choice she made but she was a victim of the Golem's rage against humanity.

That it was created by an unloving creator, forged out of bone and muscle and metamorphically transformed into something it didn't want to be either, like Frankenstein's monster. So many things we fear are misunderstood.

What defines our character isn't the negative things that happen to us, many of which are beyond our control. It is what we choose to do next, how we learn to cope with affliction and setbacks that forge our character. Will Cimree let the events decide her future, or will she find a way to reverse the magic and be reunited with those she loves and has served, even though she was betrayed by some of them?

Character is formed in crucibles, and Ecbatana is Cimree's crucible. What happens next will be decided by what Cimree chooses to do with her awful situation. A bridge has been crossed. It is time for her to find out who she truly is.

And when you next see someone who repulses you, or who you assume earned their fate through poor choices, maybe you might resist the impulse to judge and wonder whether you understand all the factors or not.

We are all a little misunderstood.

About the Author

Jeff Wheeler is a Wall Street Journal bestselling author of over thirty epic fantasy novels, including the *King-fountain* and *Muirwood* series. His stories captivate readers with strong, moral protagonists, complex characters, and richly detailed worlds. Known for clean, compelling fantasy, Jeff's books explore themes of integrity, loyalty, and growth, with interconnected series that keep fans eagerly turning pages. A husband, father of five,  and active in his faith community, Jeff draws on his life and history to craft uplifting tales. Discover his worlds at jeff-wheeler.com or through his online classes at Writers Block (writersblock.biz).